MARGARET LAURENCE

(1926–1987), was born Jean Margaret Wemyss, of Scots-Irish descendants. She grew up in the small prairie town of Neepawa, Manitoba, Canada, and began to write when young – her first stories were published in her high school paper. At the age of eighteen she left home to study at United College (now Winnipeg University), from which she graduated in the Arts in 1947. In the same year she married John Laurence, a civil engineer, with whom she had a daughter and a son.

Her husband's job took them to England, to Somaliland in 1950, and then in 1952 to Ghana, where they spent five years. *A Tree for Poverty* (1954), a collection of translated Somali poetry and folk tales, and the later travel book, *The Prophet's Camel Bell* (1963), grew out of her East African experiences. Margaret Laurence's first novel, *This Side Jordan*, set in Ghana, was published in 1960 when she and her husband were living in Vancouver.

In 1962 Margaret Laurence moved to England with her two children and a year later her first collection of short stories, *The Tomorrow-Tamer*, set in West Africa, appeared. Whilst living in Penn, Buckinghamshire, Margaret Laurence wrote her famous Manawaka sequence: *The Stone Angel* (1964); *A Jest of God* (1966, filmed as *Rachel, Rachel*, directed by Paul Newman and starring Joanne Woodward); *The Fire-Dwellers* (1969); *A Bird in the House* (inter-connected stories, 1970), and *The Diviners* (1974). It is this fiction, drawing on the town of her youth, for which Margaret Laurence is acclaimed as one of Canada's most powerful modern authors. She received Governor General Awards for *A Jest of God* and *The Diviners* in 1967 and in 1975. She has also published two volumes of essays and four children's books.

In 1972 Margaret Laurence was made a Companion of the Order of Canada. She has also received several honorary degrees, a Molson Award in 1975, and in 1977 she became a Fellow of the Royal Society of Canada. Margaret Laurence returned to that country in 1973 and lived in Lakefield, Ontario until her death at the age of sixty one.

VIRAGO
MODERN
CLASSIC

NUMBER

252

A JEST OF GOD

MARGARET LAURENCE

With a New Afterword by
CORAL ANN HOWELLS

Published by VIRAGO PRESS Limited 1987
41 William IV Street, London WC2N 4DB

First published by McClelland & Stewart, Toronto and Montreal 1966
First published in Great Britain by Macmillan and Company Limited 1966

ACKNOWLEDGEMENTS
I wish to thank the following, who have kindly given permission for the use of
copyright material: Harcourt, Brace & World Inc., for the lines from 'Losers',
from *Smoke and Steel*, by Carl Sandburg, © 1920 by Harcourt, Brace & World Inc.,
renewed 1948 by Carl Sandburg.

M.L.

British Library Cataloguing in Publication Data
Laurence, Margaret
    A jest of God.
    I. Title
    813'.54[F]   PR9199. 3.L33

    ISBN 0-86068-817-8

Printed in Finland
by Werner Söderström Oy, a member of Finnprint

If I should pass the tomb of Jonah
I would stop there and sit for awhile;
Because I was swallowed one time deep in the dark
And came out alive after all.

CARL SANDBURG, *Losers*

ONE

The wind blows low, the wind blows high
The snow comes falling from the sky,
Rachel Cameron says she'll die
For the want of the golden city.
She is handsome, she is pretty,
She is the queen of the golden city —

They are not actually chanting my name, of course. I only hear it that way from where I am watching at the classroom window, because I remember myself skipping rope to that song when I was about the age of the little girls out there now. Twenty-seven years ago, which seems impossible, and myself seven, but the same brown brick building, only a new wing added and the place smartened up. It would certainly have surprised me then to know I'd end up here, in this room, no longer the one who was scared of not pleasing, but the thin giant She behind the desk at the front, the one with the power of picking any coloured chalk out of the box and writing anything at all on the blackboard. It seemed a power worth possessing, then.

Spanish dancers, turn around,
Spanish dancers, get out of this town.

People forget the songs, later on, but the knowledge of them must be passed like a secret language from child to child — how far back? They seem like a different race, a separate species, all those generations of children. As though they must still exist somewhere, even after their bodies have grown grotesque, and they have forgotten the words and

1

tunes, and learned disappointment, and finally died, the last dried shell of them painted and prettified for decent burial by mortal men like Niall Cameron, my father. Stupid thought. Morbid. I mustn't give houseroom in my skull to that sort of thing. It's dangerous to let yourself. I know that.

> *Nebuchadnezzar, King of the Jews,*
> *Sold his wife for a pair of shoes.*

I can imagine that one going back and back, through time and languages. Chanted in Latin, maybe, the same high sing-song voices, smug little Roman girls safe inside some villa in Gaul or Britain, skipping rope on a mosaic courtyard, not knowing the blue-painted dogmen were snarling outside the walls, stealthily learning. There. I am doing it again. This must stop. It isn't good for me. Whenever I find myself thinking in a brooding way, I must simply turn it off and think of something else. God forbid that I should turn into an eccentric. This isn't just imagination. I've seen it happen. Not only teachers, of course, and not only women who haven't married. Widows can become extremely odd as well, but at least they have the excuse of grief.

I don't have to concern myself yet for a while, surely. Thirty-four is still quite young. But now is the time to watch out for it.

The bell rings for end of recess. Quickly, I have to gather my children in. I must stop referring to them as my children, even to myself. It won't do. We all say it, of course. Even Calla says of the Grade Fives, 'Want to see the poster my kids painted today?' But the words are no threat to her. She feels only a rough amused affection and irritation towards any or all of them, equally.

'Come along, Grade Twos. Line up quietly now.'

Am I beginning to talk in that simper tone, the one so many grade school teachers pick up without realizing? At first they only talk to the children like that, but it takes root and soon they can't speak any other way to anyone. Sapphire Travis does it all the time. Rachel, dear, would you be a very

2

very good girl and pour me a weeny cup of tea? Poor Grade Ones. How do they endure it? Children have built-in radar to detect falseness.

'Come along, now. We haven't got all day. James, for goodness' sake, stop dawdling.'

Now I've spoken more sharply than necessary. I have to watch this, too. It's hard to strike a balance. It's so often James I speak to like this, fearing to be too much the other way with him.

Why didn't I put my coat on, to come out? The spring wind is making me shiver. My arms, wrapped around myself for warmth, seem so long and skinny. The days are fine and mild lately, but the wind is still northern and knifing. I'm susceptible to colds, and when I get one it hangs on and on, and really pulls me down.

James is the very last inside, as usual. That boy is the slowest thing on two feet when he's going into the room. Leaving, he always seems about to take off like a sparrow and miraculously fly. Looking at his wiry slightness, his ruffian sorrel hair, I feel an exasperated tenderness. I wonder why I should feel differently towards him? Because he's unique, that's why. I oughtn't to feel that way. They are all unique. What a pious sentiment, one which Willard Siddley would endorse. Certainly they're all unique, but like the animals' equality, some are more unique than others.

Calla Mackie is in the hall as I go in. I shouldn't try to avoid her eyes. She's kind and well-meaning. If only she looked a little more usual, and didn't trot off twice a week to that fantastic Tabernacle. She bears down, through the noisy shoal of youngsters pushing upstairs like fish compelled upstream. Calla is stockily built, not fat at all but solid and broad. She says she ought to have been Ukrainian, and in fact she has that Slavic squareness and strong heavy bones. Her hair is greying and straight, and she cuts it herself with nail scissors. I'll bet she's never even set foot inside a hairdresser's. She combs it back behind her ears but chops it into a fringe like a Shetland pony's over her forehead. She

3

wears long-sleeved smocks for school, not for neatness but so she can wear the same brown tweed skirt and that dull-green bulky-knit sweater of hers, day after day without anyone noticing. Maybe she washes the sweater in the evenings from time to time, and dries it on the radiator in her flat. I wouldn't know. She drenches herself with Lemon Verbena cologne. Her smock today is the fawn chintz that looks like kitchen curtains. Well, poor Calla — it isn't her fault that she has no dress sense. I look quite smart in comparison.

Oh God. I don't mean to be condescending. How can it happen, still, this echo of my mother's voice? My navy wool dress is three years old and much longer than they're being worn now. I haven't had the energy to take up the hem. Now it seems like sackcloth, flapping around my knees. And the ashes, where are they? I dramatize myself. I always did. No one would ever know it from the outside, where I'm too quiet.

'Rachel — oh Rachel — come here a sec, will you?'

'What is it?'

'Wait for me after school,' Calla hisses. 'I've got something for you.'

'Yes. All right.'

She is a generous person. I know that, and shouldn't have to keep reminding myself. But it's embarrassing. I never know what to say. Once she gave me a necklace of hers. It was horrible, made out of polished peach stones. I'd only admired it out of politeness. And then I had to wear it.

Late afternoon, and the children are drawing pictures. Free choice — they can draw anything they like. A number of them cannot think what to draw. I have to make suggestions — their own houses, what they did last weekend.

'Did any of you go out for a walk, beyond town? Did anyone find any pussywillows?'

My own voice sounds false to my ears, a Peter-Rabbitish voice, and I find I am standing beside my desk, holding a new piece of orange chalk so tightly that it snaps in

4

my fingers. But the children do not seem to have noticed. A small chorus of response goes up – from the girls, of course.

'Me! I did, Miss Cameron.'

'My brother and me, we found about a million pussywillows.'

Interesting creatures, very young girls, often so anxious to please that they will tell lies without really knowing they're doing it. I don't suppose more than a few of them were actually out in the country at all. They only think I'd like to hear it. And yet I feel at ease with them in a way I don't with the boys, who have begun to mock automatically even at this age.

Except James Doherty. He is too preoccupied with his own concerns to bother with anything else. He goes his own way as though he endures the outside world but does not really believe in it. His schoolwork is, generally speaking, poor. Yet he knows a staggering amount about how cars work, and electricity, and jet planes. The car part of it I can understand. He's picked it up from his father at the Manawaka Garage. But where has he got the rest from? They aren't a reading family. He's had no encouragement at home. Those parents of his have likely never opened a book. It seems cruel that he should have had to make his appearance there, with them. Grace Doherty is all but moronic. She doesn't know what kind of child James is. All she cares about is that he should get a good report card, not because this would show he was learning something, but only so he wouldn't do worse than her sister-in-law's boy.

'Let's see what you've done, James. May I?'

He hands over the page. Tentatively, because he cares about it. No houses or feeble pussywillows for him. The spaceship is marvellously complex, with many detailed parts – knobs, props, instrument panels, oxygen tanks, hydroponic containers for growing vegetables in mid-space, weird protuberances which have some absolute necessity, stark fins, pear-shaped windows, and small bulbous men

5

muffled in space suits, ascending to the ship on swaying ropes, thickly pencilled, like angels climbing Jacob's ladder.

'That's good, James. What's this bit here?'

And he explains, the words torrenting out to make the thing known.

I tell him – *splendid*. He takes the page back in silence, pleased. But when I move on to the next child, I find myself forced to say *splendid* once more, this time over Francine MacVey's drawing, a lady of appalling unoriginality. The stilted glamour and the pursed lips and curling eyelashes have been copied straight from some ten-cent colouring book of Snow White or a movie doll-queen. How unfair this is to James, to demean praise in this manner. But if I don't – what might happen, if ever he or any of them discovered how I value him? They would torment me, certainly, but this is nothing to the way they would torment him. The old words for it, the child's phrase – it's so cheap, so cold and full of loathing. It frightens me so that I can't even form the words to myself. But James would be cruel, too, if he knew. He'd find some means of being scathing. He'd have to, out of some need to protect himself against me. That's what stings the most.

After school I sit at my desk, waiting for Calla to appear. But when the knock sounds and the door opens, it is Willard Siddley. He's always very nice to me. I can't claim he isn't. There is no real reason why I should dislike him, none at all. It's that pompous manner of his, I think, the way he has of seeming to insist that his slightest word has significant meaning, and if you aren't able to see it, the lack is yours. He is a good principal, though. I don't question that. Everyone says so.

'That's an enigmatic smile, Rachel. Is it the Sphinx or the Mona Lisa?'

His humour. I didn't know I was smiling. If I was, it was only out of nervousness. Which is ridiculous. I've nothing to be afraid of, with him. He has never given a bad report to the School Board on my teaching, as far as I know. I don't know why I should even think he might have. I can feel my face paling to the peculiar putty colour it takes on when I'm thrown a little off balance.

'I didn't know I was smiling.' I have to explain my presence. 'I was just going now. I've been sorting out the mimeographed pages for the—'

'Yes,' Willard says. 'Well, I won't keep you a moment.'

I know I must not stand up now, not until he's gone. I am exceptionally tall for a woman, and Willard is shorter than I. He arranges it whenever possible so that when we are talking either he is seated or I am, and there is no comparison. He hates to be considered a short man. He makes up for what may seem to him his stunted stature by being six hundred times more brisk than anyone needs to be. He calls this efficiency. He reads books on Time-Motion Study and draws charts on how to make your head save your heels.

He strides across to my desk now, places his hands on the edge of it, leans down and looks at me earnestly from behind his glasses. His eyes are pallid, like the blue dead eyes of the frozen whitefish we used to get in the winter when I was a child, and I always choked on that fish, recalling the eyes.

At morning recess today James tripped Gil Maitland and made him go down on his knees in the gravel. I saw. I was standing near by and had my back half turned, so there was no necessity to let on I'd seen. Willard saw, too, did he? That's what he wants now. 'Just a word, Rachel—I'm not an old-fashioned disciplinarian, as I am sure you know, but— must restrain the child against his or her own violence—we must not hesitate, must we, Rachel, when it is in the child's own best—'. I know he'll say it. What he doesn't know is that Gil jumped off the teeter-totter yesterday, purposely, when James was at the top end, way up in the air, and the plank crashed down. I didn't go to James, although I knew he was hurt. I never do with any of them, because I know I mustn't, unless they're crying. He didn't cry, of course. I should have told him off today, though, I guess. Tripping is forbidden. Willard likes using the strap on boys. He claims he only does it as a last resort. But he's always looking for occasions.

'What is it?' An hour seems to have passed since he spoke, but it's only a second. I can't keep this stupid edge of anxiety out of my voice. 'Anything the matter?'

'Oh no,' Willard says, looking surprised. 'Angela and I wondered if you'd come over for dinner tonight, that's all.'

That's all he had to say. An invitation for dinner. Angela, his petulant do-gooding wife, for ever proffering kindness to the single teachers. I don't want to go. I can't, I really can't anyway.

'Oh—thanks—that's awfully nice of you, but I'm afraid I can't. Tonight is Mother's bridge night. I always do the coffee and sandwiches. She gets too fussed if she has to do everything herself.'

Willard nods. There's something reptilian about the look of him. Not snakelike—more a lizard, sleek, dry-skinned, dapper, and his eyes now dartingly quick and sly, glinting at me, thinking he knows all about me. The skin on his hands is speckled, sun-spotted, and small hairs sprout even from his knuckles.

'Well, I'm sorry you can't make it,' he says. 'An old friend of yours is going to be there.'

Then he is off, at the door already, with that scurrying walk of his.

'Who?'

He turns and shakes a finger at me.

'Uh-uh. Too late now. Unless you'll change your mind?'

'I'm sorry. I told you—I can't go.'

He's gone. My own hands, spread out on the desk, are too large. Large and too thin, like empty gloves.

Why did I have to ask him who? Like that. So eagerly. Was that how it sounded? As though I couldn't wait to be told. And he, so malicious, replying like that. Once Calla said to him, 'Don't be mean, Willard', over something he'd said to me, and he replied, 'Oh come on, now, can't you take a joke?'

8

It is only now, concentrating on my hands, the nails nicely manicured and coated with colourless polish, that I realize something else. When Willard Siddley's spotted furry hands were on my desk, I wanted to touch them. To see what the hairs felt like. Yet he repulses me.

I didn't. I won't. I didn't feel that way. I'm only imagining things again.

'Hallo, child.'

Calla. I wish she wouldn't call me *child*. It sounds ridiculous. I've asked her not to, but she doesn't stop. She's carrying, I see now, a potted plant. A hyacinth, bulbously in bud and just about to give birth to the blue-purple blossom.

'Here you are. For your desk. So you'll be convinced spring is upon us.'

'Calla – it's lovely. How kind of you.' It really is, and I'm not thanking her sufficiently. She may guess how awkward I feel about her generosity. 'Thanks ever so much. You shouldn't have.'

'Bosh,' she says, waving a brawny chintz-encased arm. 'I was getting some for the Tabernacle. It's my week to do the flowers. So I thought I might as well get two extra, one for you and one for me. It's rather a nice one, isn't it? I got them at Zimmer's. They had some gorgeous lilies as well, but I have a mean prejudice against those, as you know.'

Calla's mother was exceptionally fond of white lilies, and christened her only daughter after one variety of them. Calla detests her name and no wonder. Nothing less lily-like could possibly be imagined. She's a sunflower, if anything, brash, strong, plain, and yet reaching up in some way, I suppose, even though that Tabernacle of hers seems an odd way for anyone to choose.

'We're having a special service tonight,' she says, almost shyly now, the meagrely hopeful voice she uses for this one purpose. 'Out-of-town speaker, supposed to be worth hearing. I don't suppose you'd care to come along, Rachel?'

I've gone with her once or twice, against my better judgement. They sing the hymns like jazz, and people rise to

9

testify, and I was so mortified I didn't know which way to look. How can they make fools of themselves like that, so publicly?

'Oh, I'm terribly sorry, Calla. I'd like to go, but it's Mother's bridge night.'

'You don't get out enough,' she frowns.

I know it's only that she is concerned, but what business is it of hers?

'It's none of my business,' she says, as though knowing my mind. "But—well, even if you don't believe, it's a way of getting out. For me, it's the rock of my soul, kid, but even if you can't feel that way, it would still—'

Does she imagine I'm that much in need? Anything for an evening out?

'The next special service, I'll go,' I hear myself promising.

'Oh well—don't feel you have to. I didn't mean—'

'No, no, I'd love to, really. Honestly. It's just that this particular evening—'

'Yeh. Okay. Well, we'll see, then.'

At least I have postponed it, and perhaps by that time some reasonable excuse will come along, or I'll be dead.

I wish I hadn't noticed the look of disappointment on her face as she went out. But all the same, she tried bribing me with hyacinths—what a nerve.

At last I can leave. The halls are quiet, and from upstairs I can hear the swishing and clash of the janitor's broom and dustpan. The daylight stays longer these days, and the streets are not quite dusk yet. The maple branches are black and intricate against the white unwarm sky. The leaves will not be out for another month. The cement sidewalks are nearly dry, the last of the melted snow having seeped away. I turn at River Street and walk past the quiet dark brick houses, too big for their remaining occupants, built by somebody's grandfathers who did well long ago out of a brickworks or the first butcher shop. Long ago meaning half a century. Nothing is old here, but it looks old. The timber houses age fast, and even the brick looks worn down after

10

fifty years of blizzard winters and blistering summers. They're put to shame by the new bungalows like a bakery's pastel cakes, identical, fresh, tasteless. This is known as a good part of town. Not like the other side of the tracks, where the shacks are and where the weeds are let grow knee-high and not dutifully mown, and where a few boot-leggers drive new Chevrolets on the strength of home-made red biddy. No – that's as it used to be when I was a kid, and I would go with Stacey sometimes, because she was never afraid. I don't know what it's like now. Half my children live at that end of town. I never go there, and know it only from hearsay, distorted local legend, or the occasional glimpse from a child's words.

How cold the wind is becoming. I should have worn a scarf and my woollen gloves. I've just managed to get rid of that nasty hacking cough. I certainly don't want it back again. If I could put on a little weight, I wouldn't feel the cold so. But I've always been too thin, like Dad. Stacey takes after Mother, and in consequence has a good figure. Or had. I haven't seen her since the last two were born. I haven't seen my sister for seven years. She never comes back here. Why should she? She's lived away for years. She has her own home, and wouldn't be bothered to visit here, not even so Mother might see the children. She's very decisive, is Stacey. She knew right from the start what she wanted most, which was to get as far away from Manawaka as possible. She didn't lose a moment in doing it.

My great mistake was in being born the younger. No. Where I went wrong was in coming back here, once I'd got away. A person has to be ruthless. One has to say *I'm going*, and not be prevailed upon to return.

But how could I? I couldn't finish university after Dad's death. The money wasn't there. None of us ever suspected how little he had, until he died. He'd had a good business, or so we thought. Mother said, 'I hate to say it, but there's no doubt where it all went'. If she hated to say it, why did she? Then it was – 'Only for a year or so, Rachel, until we

11

see'. See what? She couldn't be the one to move—I do see that. She'd be lost any place else. Stacey was already married, and with a child, and Mac selling encyclopaedias at the west coast. She said I must see how impossible it would be for her. Yes, I saw, I see. Seesaw. From pillar to post. What could I have done differently?

I've been teaching in Manawaka for fourteen years.

A faint giggle. I've been walking with my eyes fixed downwards. Who is it?

'Hello, Miss Cameron.'

'Oh—hello, Clare. Hello, Carol.'

I taught them in Grade Two. Now they're about sixteen, I guess. Their hair is incredible. Piled high, finespun, like the high light conical mass of woven sugar threads, the candy floss we used to get at fairs. Theirs is nearly white and is called Silver Blonde. I know that much. It's not mysterious. It's held up by back-combing, and the colour sprayed on, and the whole thing secured with lacquer like a coating of ice over a snowdrift. They look like twins from outer space. No, not twins necessarily. Another race. Venusians. But that's wrong, too. This is their planet. They are the ones who live here now.

I've known them nearly all their lives. But it doesn't seem so. Does thirty-four seem antedeluvian to them? Why did they laugh? There isn't anything to be frightened of, in that laughter. Why should they have meant anything snide by it?

I have my hair done every week at Riché Beauty Salon. It used to be Lou's Beauty Parlour when I got my hair done first, at sixteen. They'd find that amusing, probably. I say to the girl, 'As little curl as possible, if you can'. So it turns out looking exactly as it's always done, nondescript waves, mole brown. What if I said some week, 'Do it like candy floss, a high cone of it, and gold'? Then they would really laugh. With my height. How silly I am to think of it. But what beats me is how the Venusians learn to do all these things for themselves. They don't have their hair done. Who

12

teaches them? I suppose they're young enough to ask around. At that age it's no shame not to know.

Japonica Street. Around our place the spruce trees still stand, as I remember them for ever. No other trees are so darkly sheltering, shutting out prying eyes or the sun in summer, the spearheads of them taller than houses, the low branches heavy, reaching down to the ground like the greenblack feathered strong-boned wings of giant and extinct birds. The house is not large – it often surprises me to realize this. The same way it will surprise my children to return when they're grown and look around the classroom and see how small the desks are. The house used to seem enormous, and I think of it that way yet. Rust brick, nothing to set it off or mark it as different from the other brick houses near by. Nothing except the sign, and the fact that the ground floor doesn't belong to us.

When I was a child the sign was painted on board, pale-grey background, black lettering, and it said *Cameron's Funeral Parlour*. Later, my father, laughing in some way incomprehensible to me then and being chided for it by Mother, announced other times other manners. The new sign was ebony background and gilt lettering, *Cameron Funeral Home*. After he died, and we sold the establishment, the phraseology moved on. The blue neon, kept lighted day and night, now flashes *Japonica Funeral Chapel*. All that remains is for someone to delete the word *funeral*. A nasty word, smacking of mortality. No one in Manawaka ever dies, at least not on this side of the tracks. We are a gathering of immortals. We pass on, through Calla's divine gates of topaz and azure, perhaps, but we do not die. Death is rude, unmannerly, not to be spoken to in the street.

It was in those rooms on the ground floor there, where I was told never to go, that my father lived away his life. All I could think of, then, was the embarrassment of being the daughter of someone with his stock-in-trade. It never occurred to me to wonder about him, and whether he possibly felt at ease with them, the unspeaking ones, and out

13

of place above in our house, things being what they were. I never had a chance to ask him. By the time I knew the question it was too late, and asking it would have cut into him too much.

We were fortunate to be able to stay on here, Mother and I. We sold the place outright, but for much less than it was worth, for the right to stay. Hector Jonas got a bargain. He already had a house. He didn't want the top floor of this one. At least we live rent free in perpetuity, or near enough to suit our purposes. I sometimes wonder what I'll do when Mother dies. Will I stay, or what?

'Hello, dear. Aren't you rather late tonight?'

'Hello, Mother. Not especially. I had some clearing up to do.'

'Well, I've got a nice lamb chop, so I hope you'll eat it. You're not eating enough these days, Rachel.'

'I'm fine.'

'You *say* you're fine, but don't forget I know you pretty well, dear.'

'Yes, I know.'

'You're too conscientious, Rachel, that's your trouble. Other people don't allow their work to get on their nerves.'

'It's not. I'm fine. A little tired tonight, perhaps, but that's normal.'

'You fret about them too much, whether they're doing well or not. But mercy, you didn't bestow their brains on them, did you? It's not up to you. Small thanks you'll get for it, if you ask me anything.'

She stands beside the stove. Her heart is very tricky and could vanquish her at any moment. Yet her ankles are still slender and she takes pride in wearing only fine-denier nylons and never sensible shoes. Her hair is done every week, saucily stiff grey sausage curls, and the frames of her glasses are delphinium blue and elfin. Where does this cuteness come from, when she's the one who must plump up the chesterfield cushions each night before retiring and empty

14

every ashtray and make the house look as though no frail and mortal creature ever set foot in it?

'What are you having tonight?'

'Asparagus rolls, I thought,' she says earnestly, 'and that celery and ham mixture. I've got it made. All you have to do is spread them. Can you do the asparagus rolls or shall I do those first?'

'I can do them. It's all right.'

'Well, we could do them and put them in the fridge. It might be easier.'

'If you like. We'll do them after dinner, then.'

'I don't mind, dear – whatever you like,' she says, believing she means it.

How strange it is that I do not even know how old she is. She's never told me, and I'm not supposed to ask. In the world she inhabits, age is still as unmentionable as death. Am I as far away as that, from the children who aren't mine? She's in her seventies, I can guess with reasonable accuracy, as she bore me late, but the exact positioning is her wealth, a kept secret. And it matters. It means something. Does she think someone cares whether she's sixty or ninety?

I could have gone to Willard's for dinner. I could have gone with Calla. I wish I had. Now that it comes to it, I do not know why I didn't, one or the other.

It's her only outlet, her only entertainment. I can't begrudge her. Anyone decent would be only too glad.

As I am, really, at heart. I'll feel better, more fortified, when I've had dinner. I don't begrudge it to her, this one evening of bridge with the only three long long friends. How could I? No one decent would.

Thank God, thank God. They are finally gone. The last cup is washed and put away. The living-room is tidied enough to suit her. It might be the midsummer gathering of a coven, the amount of fuss we go to, lace tablecloth, the Spode china, the silver tray for sandwiches, the little dishes

15

of salted nuts to nibble at. Well, it's only at our place once a month. I can't complain, really. And it *is* nice for her. She enjoys it. Her face grows animated and her voice almost gay—'Verla, you're not going into no-trump—you wouldn't dare! Oh girls isn't she the meanest thing you ever saw?' She doesn't have much to interest her these days. She never reads a book and can't bear music. Her life is very restricted now. It always was, though. It's never been any different. Just this house and her dwindling circle of friends. She and Dad had given up conversing long ago, by the time I was born. She used to tell him not to lean back in the upholstered chairs, in case his hair oil rubbed off. Then she put those crocheted doilies on all the chair backs. And finally on the chair arms as well, as though she felt his hands could never be clean, considering what he handled in his work. Maybe she didn't feel that way at all. Maybe it only seemed so to me.

This bedroom is the same I've always had. I should change the furniture. How girlish it is, how old-fashioned. The white spindly-legged dressing-table, the round mirror with white rose-carved frame, the white-painted metal bed with its white-painted metal bow decorating the head like a starched forgotten hair-ribbon. Surely I could afford new furniture. It's my salary, after all, my salary we live on. She'd say it was a waste, to throw out perfectly good furniture. I suppose it would be, too, if you think of it like that.

I always brush my hair a hundred strokes. I can't succeed in avoiding my eyes in the mirror. The narrow angular face stares at me, the grey eyes too wide for it.

I don't look old. I don't look more than thirty. Or do I see my face falsely? How do I know how it looks to anyone else? About six months ago, one of the salesmen who was calling on Hector Jonas, downstairs, asked me out and like an idiot I went. We went to the Regal Café for dinner, and I thought every minute somehow I knew would see me and know he sold embalming fluid. Of course someone has to sell it. But when he told me I had good bones, it was too much. As though he were one of the ancient Egyptians who interred the pharaohs and knew too intimately the secrets of the core and marrow. Do I have good bones? I can't tell. I'm no judge.

Go to bed, Rachel. And hope to sleep.

The voices of the girls, the old ladies, still echo, the prattling, the tiny stabs of laughter making them clutch their bosoms for fear of their hearts. They feel duty bound to address a few remarks to me, remarks which have fallen into a comfortable stability. 'How's school, Rachel?' Fine, thank you. 'I guess they must keep you pretty busy, all those youngsters.' Yes, they certainly do. 'Well, I think it's marvellous, the way you manage – I always think that anyone who's a teacher is marvellous to take on a job like that.' Oh, I enjoy it. 'Well, that's marvellous – don't you think so, May?' And Mother nods and says yes it certainly is marvellous and Rachel is a born teacher.

My God. How can I stand –

Stop. Stop it, Rachel. Steady. Get a grip on yourself, now. Relax. Sleep. Try.

Doctor Raven would give a few sleeping pills to me. Why on earth don't I? They frighten me. What if one became addicted? Does it run in the family? Nonsense, not drugs. It wasn't drugs with him. 'Your father's not feeling well today.' Her martyred voice. That sort of thing is not physical, for heaven's sake, not passed on. Yet I can see myself at school, years from now, never fully awake, in a constant dozing and drowsing, sitting at my desk, my head bobbing slowly up and down, my mouth gradually falling open without my knowing it, and people seeing and whispering until finally –

Oh no. Am I doing it again, this waking nightmare? How weird am I already? Trying to stave off something that has already grown inside me and spread its roots through my blood?

Now, then. Enough of this. The main thing is to be

17

sensible, to stop thinking and to go to sleep. Right away. Concentrate. I need the sleep badly. It's essential.

I can't. Tonight is hell on wheels again. Trite. *Hell on wheels*. But almost accurate. The night feels like a gigantic ferris wheel turning in blackness, very slowly, turning once for each hour, interminably slow. And I am glued to it, or wired, like paper, like a photograph, insubstantial, unable to anchor myself, unable to stop this slow nocturnal circling.

This pain inside my skull – what is it? It isn't like an ordinary headache which goes through like a metal skewer from temple to temple. Not like sinus, either, the assault beginning above my eyes and moving down into the bones of my face. This pain is not so much pain as a pulsing, regular and rhythmical, like the low thudding of a drum.

It's nothing. How could it be a tumour? It's nothing. Perhaps I have a soft spot in my head. This joke doesn't work. I can't hold on to the slang sense of it, and its other meaning seems sinister. Fontanelle.

Something meaningless, something neutral – I must focus on that. But what? Now I can't think. I can't stop thinking. If the pain is anything, then I'll see Doctor Raven, of course. Naturally. It wouldn't hurt to go in for a check-up soon, anyway. It might be a very good idea. I can't afford to let myself get run down.

I can't sleep.

– A forest. Tonight it is a forest. Sometimes it is a beach. It has to be right away from everywhere. Otherwise she may be seen. The trees are green walls, high and shielding, boughs of pine and tamarack, branches sweeping to earth, forming a thousand rooms among the fallen leaves. She is in the green-walled room, the boughs opening just enough to let the sun in, the moss hairy and soft on the earth. She cannot see his face clearly. His features are blurred as though his were a face seen through water. She sees only his body distinctly, his shoulders and arms deeply tanned, his belly flat and hard. He is wearing only tight-fitting jeans, and his swelling sex shows. She touches him there, and he

18

trembles, absorbing her fingers' pressure. Then they are lying along one another, their skins slippery. His hands, his mouth are on the wet warm skin of her inner thighs. Now —

I didn't. I didn't. It was only to be able to sleep. The shadow prince. Am I unbalanced? Or only laughable? That's worse, much worse.

I feel myself sinking at last into the smooth silence where no lights or voices are. When the voices and lights begin again, in there where I am lying, they are not bright or loud.

— Stairs rising from nowhere, and the wallpaper the loose-petalled unknown flowers. The stairs descending to the place where I am not allowed. The giant bottles and jars stand there, bubbled green glass. The silent people are there, lipsticked and rouged, powdered whitely like clowns. How funny they look, each lying dressed in best, and their open eyes are glass eyes, cat's eye marbles, round glass beads, blue and milky, unwinking. He is behind the door I cannot open. And his voice — his voice — so I know he is lying there among them, lying in state, king over them. He can't fool me. He says run away Rachel run away run away. I am running across thick grass and small purple violets — weeds — dandelions. The spruce trees bend, bend down, hemming in and protecting. My mother is singing in a falsetto voice, the stylish tremolo, the ladies' choir voice.

Bless this house dear Lord we pray, keep it safe by night and day.

TWO

Brushing away the curtains with my hand and leaning a moment out my window, I can feel the fineness of the day. Even the spruces look light, the needled boughs having lost their darkness in the sun and now looking evergreen as they are meant to, and not everblack as they seem when the sky is overcast. The sky today is the colour of the turquoise in the bracelet my father gave me as a child.

I must hurry or I'll be late. That's one thing I can say for myself. I've never been late for school in all this time, never once. When I first began teaching, Mother used to call me every morning, but now I waken before she does.

My underwear is all getting that shabby too-much-washed look. I must get some more. I always think what does it matter – who sees but me? But that's a wrong attitude. It's not even the thought of being run over and taken to hospital and pried into, everything underneath seen and sized up. It's self-respect, really. When Stacey was here the last time she came into my bedroom while I was dressing. She never knocked or said could she come in. Maybe in her house everyone is so casual they never bother. She saw me putting on the same things I'd worn the day before, the same everything. She said, 'Don't you change every day?' And then, as though she believed she intended it only to explain or pardon me, 'Well, I suppose it doesn't matter quite so much if you're not living with anyone.' But it was only because I hadn't got my laundry done over the week-end, and I hadn't got it done on account of her, for she'd just arrived then. Usually I changed. It hardly ever happened that I didn't. I told her so. My voice was not upset in the slightest. 'Don't be ridiculous,' I said.

I didn't, though. I didn't say a word. I don't know why I didn't. Stupid. Stupid. How could I not have?

What is more stupid is to think of it now. As if it mattered. I've been very careful ever since then, though. A person could let themselves go, without noticing. It could happen.

Hurry, hurry, Rachel, or you'll be late for school. All right. All right. I'm hurrying.

Mother has a letter in her hands and is unfolding it.

'One thing about Stacey,' she says, 'she is always very good about writing. I don't think she's ever missed a week, has she? It can't be easy, with the four children to look after, and that big house.'

'No, I suppose not.'

Considering that Stacey does nothing else for Mother, writing once a week doesn't seem such an exorbitant effort. When Stacey was here that time, seven years ago, I asked her at the end of the one week if she wouldn't consider staying a month. The children would be all right with Mac's sister, and it would mean a lot to Mother. Stacey wouldn't, though. 'I guess it must sound crazy to you, Rachel, but another three weeks and I'd be up the walls – I don't mean because of anything here and that – it's just missing Mac – not only around and to talk to – I mean, in bed.' What made her so certain it would sound crazy to me?

Mother is reading Stacey's letter aloud. She always does, as though not entrusting it to my hands and eyes. Sometimes I think she occasionally leaves parts out. Stacey can be extremely outspoken, and if it was a reference to me, Mother wouldn't let me see.

Oh Lord – I've no evidence, none, of any pitying or slamming phrase.

'... less than a month till summer holidays – horrors! Although I guess Rachel will be glad. Her free season starts when mine finishes. But I have to admit the kids are pretty good generally these days – the boys already making plans for putting up tent in back yard and sleeping there — mighty woodsmen and all that — perfectly safe, Mother, so don't panic — '

Stacey always rattles on in this way. It is nice for Mother to get news of the grandchildren, of course. Stacey flutters around those children such a lot. Every time one of them has a cold or a sore throat, we hear about it. She'd learn not to fuss if she had thirty to cope with every weekday. Four on her hands for only two months, and in summer, doesn't seem such a terrible prospect to me. But she worries all the time about them. She's not doing them any favour, hovering over them like that, especially the boys.

Is it true, what she said that time, and I can't understand? When I said why not stay longer, and she said that about Mac, then she told me she couldn't be away from the children any longer, either. 'I know they're quite okay, and safe, but I don't feel sure unless I'm there, and even then I never feel sure — I don't think I can explain — it's just something you feel about your own kids, and you can't help it.'

She didn't think I could see that, or know at all. She's so positive she understands everything. She doesn't give anyone else any credit for having the slightest degree of —

Damn. I've slopped my coffee on to my saucer and it's burned my hand.

'Well, I'm surprised she'd let the boys sleep out in the yard. She's so everlastingly particular with them.'

'I wouldn't have said that,' Mother fences, offended. 'She takes decent care of them. That's hardly a fault. But I wouldn't have said she was too particular.'

League of matriarchs. Mothers of the world, unite. You have nothing to lose but your children. Then they wonder why people want to leave home. Stacey's will do just as she did, quite likely, and she'll never know why.

Willard is waiting for me in my classroom. He's standing there with his back to me. Although he's short, he looms against the light from the window. His back is hunched,

like a picture of a vulture in a geography book, and then I
see it is only because he is stooping to look at something on
my desk. What is he looking for? What has he found? Have
I done something? He straightens and wheels and faces
me.

'Morning, Rachel,' he says, pleasantly enough. 'I was just
having a look at your attendance sheet.'

'Oh—' I can feel my face becoming bleached, for absolutely no reason. 'Why?'

'James Doherty's been away quite a lot recently, I
see.'

'He's had tonsillitis.' Why should Willard pry? He has no
right to open my desk.

'He was away most of this week, I see.'

'Yes. It was the same trouble. Sore throat and fever. I
phoned his mother.'

Willard frowns. 'You did?'

He makes it sound such a curious thing to have done, and
now I see that perhaps it was. I needn't have phoned his
mother. It isn't usual.

'He'd been having so many bouts of tonsillitis, I just
wondered—and I thought maybe I should—so I just, I
mean, gave her a ring—'

Worse. I've made it worse. I can see myself stumbling
and floundering through the words, like wading through
deep snow.

'Did he bring a note when he came back yesterday?'
Willard asks.

'Oh yes. Of course. Here, I've got it somewhere. It must
be somewhere in my desk. I generally keep them for a
month, you see, in case—'

'It's all right,' Willard is saying, quite gently. 'I'll take
your word for it.'

He sighs and takes his glasses off to clean them, breathing
on them noisily and then polishing with his handkerchief.

'I'm reluctant to bring this up, Rachel,' he says ponder-
ously, 'and you may certainly rest assured that I am not in

any way blaming *you* for it. But I'm afraid you may have to have a word with the boy's mother. Angela paints, as you know – '

I can't see the connection. Willard's wife marches regularly down into the valley beyond town, carrying a portable easel, looking most peculiar, and returning with little sketches labelled *Banks of the Wachakwa*.

'. . . and this is the third time,' Willard is saying, 'that she's encountered the Doherty boy. Not encountered him, exactly, but seen him in the distance, running into the bushes. On school days. Unmistakably him. You could spot that red hair a mile away.'

Does James hate school that much? He loves to draw pictures. I always thought that even though he found arithmetic difficult, he enjoyed some subjects. I always thought he responded when I spoke to him about his drawings. I thought he liked me, at least some.

'His mother,' Willard says, 'is partly to blame, for giving him notes to excuse his absence. I think you'd be well advised to have a talk with her, before we notify the truant officer. It's possible that a little straight speaking, coming from the school, might be sufficient.'

I'm angry enough at Grace Doherty to be able to speak my mind. What does she think she's doing? How can a child's mother be so irresponsible, as though it didn't amount to anything, as though he didn't amount to anything? I could say it to her this instant. But it won't be until tomorrow or next week, and that I dread.

Willard *is* a good principal. All at once I'm grateful to him for not having gone directly to the truant officer, who has been old so long that he'd no longer comprehend how a boy might be drawn to the valley at this time of year, after the shut-in winter, without its necessarily meaning a thing. But Grace – how could she? She ought to know better. The ignorance of some people is too much. She doesn't deserve to have him.

'In the meantime,' Willard says, turning to go, 'I think

you'd better send the young man in question into my office. Around ten o'clock will do nicely.'

'You're not going to—you won't strap him?'

'I don't see,' Willard blandly says, 'that I have any alternative.'

He is smiling as thinly as a skull. His eyes seem covered with a film of respectable responsibility, grave concern, the sadness of duty's necessity, all to conceal the shame-burning of pleasure.

'It won't do him any good.' This is true. I don't feel certain of much, but I feel certain of this.

'We don't *know* that, Rachel, do we?' Willard says. 'I would venture to put forth the opinion that under the circumstances it is decidedly worth a try. We must not let our emotions get the better of us, must we?'

What of his emotions, Willard's, the ones he would not admit to having? Yet now I can't argue. I don't know whether I only feel the way I do because I care about James, and wouldn't willingly see him hurt. Is there a better reason for not wanting him hurt? Now I no longer know whether I have the right to feel as I do. How could I be wrong about this, when I feel it so? Or can a person be mistaken about everything? Willard's a good principal. I said so to myself not a moment ago.

'I'll send him in, then.' There's a dullness in my voice. Willard has won. Maybe he is even right. He has two of his own. Could I be expected to know what is best?

'Good girl,' Willard says.

But when I've sent James in, and he has returned, his face like bone, his eyes staring my betrayal at me, then I want only to go to Willard and tell him to listen, just to listen. *I am not neutral—I am not detached—I know it. But neither are you, and you do not know it.*

I won't go, though. The day seems to have ended, and yet I still sit at my desk, thinking quite calmly how much I would like to leave this school. How is it I can still be so afraid of losing my job?

'Hello, child.'

Calla is standing in the doorway looking like a wind-dishevelled owl, a great horned owl, her fringed hair like grey-brown feathers every which way, her eyes ringed with the round brown frames of the glasses she wears only rarely so that they never stop seeming unusual on her. She looks so comically earnest that I feel badly, and wonder why I haven't asked her over to our place more often. I've gone to her place often enough, and she always makes an occasion of it, and toasts sandwiches and buys a bakery cake. I should care what Mother thinks of her. What does it matter? If only Calla wouldn't insist on talking about the Tabernacle in Mother's hearing. Mother thinks the whole thing is weird in the extreme, and as for anyone speaking in a clarion voice about their beliefs – it seems indecent to her, almost in the same class as what she calls foul language. Then I get embarrassed for Calla, and ashamed of being embarrassed, and would give anything to shut her up or else to stop minding.

'Remember saying you'd like to come along with me to the next special service, Rachel?'

'Oh yes. That's right. I did.' I feel the weight of the granite inside. No escape now. I brought this on myself.

'I didn't want to mention this before, not until we were more sure of it – sure it would last, you know, and was the genuine article and not just a nine-day wonder or something –'

'Mention what?'

'Well, a few – some of us – not many, you know, so far, but some –' Calla's usually firm voice fumbles, 'some have been given, it seems, the gift of tongues.'

What shows in my face? I dare not think. Whatever it is, it makes her forge explanations instantly, strongbows of argument, as if she believes I'm bound to be conquered by them.

'It was a perfectly accepted thing in the early Church. Nobody thought there was anything strange in it then. We hold ourselves too tightly these days, that's the trouble. Afraid to let the Spirit speak through us. Saint Paul cautions, of course. Not to let it take the place of ordinary prayer which can be understood by everyone. We've been careful about that. But he accepts it, Saint Paul, I mean. He says *I thank my God I speak with tongues more than ye all.* And what about *the tongues of men and of angels?* What else does the tongues of angels mean, if not glossalalia?'

'What?'

She can't mean a word of it. But she does. I don't know which way to look, and yet I can't take my eyes off her face. She doesn't look fanatical. She looks sturdily cheerful and now something else – determined to make me see.

'Glossalalia,' she says. 'That is the correct word for it. But we mostly say *the gift of tongues* or *ecstatic utterances* because – well, those words describe it better, see?'

'People speak – aloud – and don't know what they're saying? And nobody else knows, either?'

'Sometimes another one can interpret,' Calla says, talking quickly but in a subdued voice quite unlike her usual. 'Listen, child, I know it must sound unbelievable. I thought so, too, at first. But now I know – well, I just know. I've seen it happen. Even if no one understands, the undeniable thing is the peace the person who's been gifted comes back with.'

'Have you – ?'

She looks for a moment stricken, her square, strong face saddened as though by some deprivation.

'No, it hasn't been given to me. Not yet, anyhow.'

All I can think about is what if it's given to her tonight? If I have to endure to be there, and see her rising, hypnotized, and hear her known voice speaking gibberish, I think I will faint. How to get out of it? I can't bear watching people make fools of themselves. I don't know why, but it threatens me. It swamps me, and I can't look, the way as children we used to cover our eyes with our hands at the dreaded parts in horror movies.

Calla is looking thoughtfully at me.

'Perhaps you'll not want to come along, now. I had to tell you, though. It wouldn't have been right not to. If you don't want to come, Rachel, it's quite okay. Don't worry about it. I wouldn't want that.'

'Oh, I'm not worried in the slightest.' The lie rises to my mouth before I can prevent it, and then I have to go on. 'I'll come along, Calla. Of course I will. I said I would.'

There is some obscure comfort in this. At least I'm not breaking my word.

'Are you sure?'

'Oh yes. Certainly.'

Why am I trapped into this falseness? I don't want to hurt her feelings. I don't want to argue. I just don't feel up to it.

But I don't want to go. I cannot bring myself to go.

Calla smiles so thankingly that I feel I ought to say *No, don't,* or to warn her. When she has gone, I'm left with this helplessness. I can't go. I can't not go.

I'm to meet Calla at the Tabernacle. I told Mother we were going to a movie. If I had said Calla's place, she might have phoned.

I'm not sorry it's raining this evening. It means that hardly anyone is out. That's stupid – even if I did meet someone I know, how could they tell where I'm going? What about at the door of the Tabernacle, though? That's what bothered me most the last time. If anyone sees, it is certain to be one of Mother's bridge cronies, and the information will be relayed back at sonic speed, and there will be the kind of scene I dread, with Mother speaking more in sorrow than anger, as she's always claimed she was doing.

Japonica Street is deserted. The sidewalks are slippery and darkly shining like new tar with the rain, and the leaves on the maples are being pulled and torn like newspaper in the wind. The lawns have that damp deep loam smell that comes with the rain in spring.

This raincoat is the only new thing I've bought this season. I'm glad I got white. It looks quite good, and I thought that on a black night such as this it would be almost luminous, more easily seen by a driver if I'm crossing a badly lighted street.

Reaching River Street and passing the locked and empty stores, I can see myself reflected dimly, like the negative of a photograph, in the wide glass of display windows. The white coat stands out, but not as handsomely as I'd hoped. To my passing eyes it looks now like some ancient robe around me, and the hood, hiding my hair, makes my face narrow and staring. As in the distorting mirrors at a fair, I'm made to look even taller than I am. I have to pass myself again and again, and see a thin streak of a person, like the stroke of a white chalk on a blackboard.

At the foot of River Street, past the shopping part and down the slow curve of the hill, the old olive-green house stands, high and angular, encrusted with glassed-in porches, pillars with no purpose, wrought-iron balconies never likely to have been used except in the height of summer, a small turret or two for good measure, and the blue and red glass circle of a rose-window at the very top. It was built by some waistcoated gent who made good, and then made tangible his concept of paradise in this house. Whatever family once owned it, they've moved now, shrugged it thankfully off their shoulders, I expect. The sign extends the full width of the house, and is well lighted. The crimson words are plain to see.

Tabernacle of the Risen and Reborn

People are going in, knots and clusters of them. I haven't seen a soul I know, thank God. But I can't go in. I won't. Now I want to turn and run. But Calla is beside me.

'You're looking very smart tonight, Rachel, in spite of the rain.'

'Oh – thanks. I'm glad you think so.'

'Well, c'mon,' she says encouragingly, taking my arm, 'let's get inside. I feel like a drowned rat. What a filthy night, eh? Never mind, we'll soon be in the warm. This way, kiddo.'

The room is larger than I remember it, almost as large as though the place had been a proper church. The chairs are in semi-circular rows, the same straight, thickly varnished chairs one used to find in every school auditorium, but replaced there now with lighter ones which can be stacked up, and the old ones probably sold to establishments such as this. The painted walls are heavy with their greenish blue, not the clear blue of open places but dense and murky, the way the sea must be, fathoms under. Two large pictures are hanging, both Jesus, bearded and bleeding, his heart exposed and bristling with thorns like a scarlet pincushion. There is no altar, but at the front a kind of pulpit stands, bulky and new, pale wood blossoming in bunches of grapes and small sharp birds with beaks uplifted. The top of the pulpit is draped with white velvet, like a scarf, tasselled with limp silver threads, and on the velvet rests a book. The Book, of course, not jacketed severely in black but covered with some faintly glittering cloth or substance impersonating gold, and probably if the room were dark it would glow — or give off sparks.

'Let's sit near the back.'

'Oh, okay, if you like.' Calla is disappointed, but willing to make any concessions because she's actually got me here. We push our way past feet, past coats containing people whose faces can't be seen because their heads are bowed. Then we're sitting in the middle of the row, and although I would have preferred the end, I can't move now.

I can't move, that's the awful thing. I'm hemmed in, caught. On one side of me sits Calla, bunched up in her gaberdine trenchcoat, and on the other side an unknown man, middle-aged, or so I'd guess from his balding head. He is leaning forward, head down, his large-knuckled hands clenched on his knees. He is a farmer, I think, for the back of his neck is that brick red that gets ingrained from years of sun and never fades, not even in the winter.

I must focus my mind on something, and not think of this

meeting hall and everything around me. I must go away, pretend it isn't. When I first came back to Manawaka, Lennox Cates used to ask me out, and I went, but when he started asking me out twice a week, I stopped seeing him before it went any further. We didn't have enough in common, I thought, meaning I couldn't visualize myself as the wife of a farmer, a man who'd never even finished High School. He married not long afterwards. I've taught three of his children. All nice-looking kids, fair-haired like Lennox, and all bright. Well.

The two ceiling bulbs are bare, and can't be more than forty watts. The light seems distant and hazy, and the air colder than it can really be, and foetid with the smell of feet and damp coats. It's like some crypt, dead air and staleness, deadness, silence. The scuffing of incoming shoes has stopped. They are all assembled now. Perhaps they are praying.

How can Calla sit there, head inclined? How can she come here every week? She is slangy and strident; she laughs a lot, and in her flat she sings with hoarse-voiced enjoyment the kind of songs the teenagers sing. She can paint scenery for a play or form a choir out of kids who can't even carry a tune – she'd take on anything. But she's here. Don't I know her at all?

Will there be ecstatic utterances and will Calla suddenly rise and keen like the Grecian women wild on the hills, or wail in a wolf's voice, or speak as hissingly as a cell of serpents?

Stop. I must stop. This is only anticipating that worst which never happens, at least not in the way one imagines. Nothing will happen. Yet my hands are clasped together more tightly than those of the quiet man beside me. What is he thinking? I wouldn't want to know.

A man has risen. A stubby man, almost stunted, an open candid face, nothing menacing, nothing so absurd that it can't be borne. He goes to the pulpit. He welcomes one and all, he says, one and all, spreading brown-sleeved arms and

31

smiling trustingly. Now I'm ashamed to be here, as though I'd gate-crashed, come in under false pretences.

Singing. We have to stand, and I must try to make myself narrower so I won't brush against anyone. A piano crashes the tune. Guitars and one trombone are in support. The voices are weak at first, wavering like a radio not quite adjusted, and I'm shaking with the effort not to giggle, although God knows it's not amusing me. The voices strengthen, grow muscular, until the room is swollen with the sound of a hymn macabre as the messengers of the apocalypse, the gaunt horsemen, the cloaked skeletons I dreamed of once when I was quite young, and wakened, and she said 'Don't be foolish – don't be foolish, Rachel – there's nothing there.' The hymn-sound is too loud – it washes into my head, sea waves of it.

> *Day of wrath! O day of mourning!*
> *See fulfilled the prophet's warning!*
> *Heaven and earth in ashes burning!*

I hate this. I would like to go home. Sit down. The others are sitting down. Just don't be noticeable. Oh God – do I know anyone? Suddenly I'm scanning the rows, searching. Seek and ye shall find. Mrs Pusey, ancient arch-enemy of my mother, tongue like a cat-o'-nine-tails, and Alvin Jarrett, who works at the bakery, and old Miss Murdoch from the bank. How in hell can I get out of this bloody place without being seen?

Rachel. Calm. At once. This isn't like you.

The lay preacher is praying, and I can't hear the words, somehow, only his husky voice, his voice like a husky dog's, a low growling. Beside me, the hulked form of the farmer sits crouched over. They all seem to be crouching, all of them, all around me, crouching and waiting. They are (of course I know it) praying. It's not a zoo, not Doctor Moreau's island where the beastmen prowled and waited, able to speak but without comprehension.

Then the lay preacher's voice forms into words in my

hearing and I realize what he's talking about. The prayer is over, and he's addressing the congregation.

'Soon, very shortly, my brethren, I am going to read to you from The Book of Life, The Counsel of Heaven, the true words written by Him on High, He the sole Author. All things shall be made clear, and the doubts of the doubters shall be laid low. We have doubted, yes. We have been infirm, yes. We have failed to trust the gifts given freely and fully by the Spirit. Did not Saint Paul chide the Corinthians for the same weakness? And it is through his letter to these people, these Corinthians, that marvellous first epistle, that thrilling document of the holy word of God, that all our doubts shall pass away and we shall enter the peace of His spiritual fullness, for in the words of Saint Paul, that great and mild apostle, *God is not the author of confusion but of peace, as in all the churches of the saints.*'

His voice is creamy as mayonnaise. He makes Paul sound like a fool. What—Paul, mild? When he says *thr-ill-lling* it sounds like a Technicolor movie, one of those religious epics.

'The church of the apostles, the church of Peter, the church of Paul, the church of Philip who converted Simon the sorcerer, this very church, the church of the ancients, our brothers in faith, this church did indeed practise and enjoy to the fullest extent every gift of the Spirit. This church did in all knowledge know there was a place, and a holy place, for all the gifts of the Spirit, each and every one of the gifts of the Spirit. *Now there are diversities of gifts, but the same Spirit. For to one is given by the Spirit the word of wisdom—to another the word of knowledge—to another the gifts of healing—to another prophecy—to another divers kinds of tongues—*'

My hands are slippery with perspiration. Around me, the people stir—uneasily? Calla's face is withdrawn, absorbed, not her outgoing look, something fixed and glazed, and I cannot look at her any more. Will she? Imagine having to see someone you know, someone you are known to be friends with, rise in a trance and say—what? What would she say? I cannot bring myself to think.

The preacher has grown in stature. He actually seems taller. The pulpit has another step, maybe, and he has mounted it. Can that be it? He is all fervour now, and yet his voice is not loud. His arms are stretched, as though he knew there were something above and if he strained he might reach it—or else pull it down to his level. His voice no longer growls—it reaches out like arms of strength, to captivate. I must leave. I cannot stand this. But I cannot move. I see myself having to say 'Excuse me—pardon me', scraping and bumping past the other people in this row, feeling them glare at my discourtesy, having to push past this boulder of a man next to me, past his solid pillars of legs and the huge unmoving hands clenched there. I can't.

'Saint Paul advises moderation—of this we are well aware. And that the gift of tongues should not replace the more usual forms of worship—of this we are well aware. But if we speak of ecstatic utterances, my friends, we must ask— ecstatic for whom? In the early Church, the listeners were ecstatic. Yes, the listeners as well as those gifted by the Spirit. Thus can we all participate—yes, participate—in the joy felt and known by any one of our brothers or sisters as they experience that deep and private enjoyment, that sublime edification, the infilling of the Spirit—'

I feel so apprehensive now that I can hardly sit here in a pretence of quiet. The muscles of my face have wired my jawbone so tightly that when I move it, it makes a slight clicking sound. Has anyone heard? No, of course not. Their minds are on the preacher and—the hymn. The hymn? I can't stand. I seem to be taken to my feet, born ludicrously aloft, by the sheer force and weight of the rising people on either side of me.

> *In full and glad surrender,*
> *I give myself to Thee,*
> *Thine utterly and only*
> *And evermore to be.*

Can we at least sit down again, at last? Thank God. But someone will utter now. I know it. How can anyone bear to make a public spectacle of themselves? How could anyone display so openly? I will not look. I will not listen. People should keep themselves to themselves — that's the only decent way. Beside me, Calla sighs, and I can feel my every muscle becoming rigid, as though I hoped to restrain her by power of will.

A man's voice. Suddenly, into the muffled foot-shuffling and the half silence, a man's voice enters, low at first, then louder. I don't know where he is. I can't see him. He hasn't risen. He is sitting somewhere in the blue-green depths of this room, and he is speaking. His voice is clear, distinct, measured, like the slow careful playing of some simple tune. He speaks the words like a child learning, imitating. Slowly, stumblingly, then gaining momentum, the pace and volume increasing until the entire room, the entire skull, is filled with the loudness of this terrifyingly calm voice. For an instant I am caught up in that voice.

I see him. He is standing now. He is not old. His face is severe, delicate, and his eyes are closed, like a blind seer, a younger Tiresias come to tell the king the words that no one could listen to and live. The words. Chillingly, I realize.

Galamani halafaka tabinota caragoya lal lal ufranti —

Oh my God. They can sit, rapt, wrapped around and smothered willingly by these syllables, the chanting of some mad enchanter, himself enchanted? It's silly to be afraid. But I am. I can't help it. And how can anyone look and face anyone else, in the face of this sinister foolery? I can't look. I can only sit, as drawn in as possible, my eyes willing themselves to see only the dark-brown oiled floorboards.

He has stopped. I can't stand for a hymn. I'll stay sitting. But that would be too obvious. The decision is taken out of my hands as once again I'm lifted by the unasked-for pressure of elbows.

Rejoice! Rejoice! Emmanuel
Shall come to thee, O Israel!

35

All I can visualize are the dimly remembered faithful of Corinth, each crying aloud his own words, no one hearing anyone else, no one able to know what anyone else was saying, unable even to know what they themselves were saying. Are these people mad or am I? I hate this hymn.

Celebrate confusion. Let us celebrate confusion. God is not the author of confusion but of peace. What a laugh. Let the Dionysian women rend themselves on the night hills and consume the god.

I want to go home. I want to go away and never come back. I want—

Are we seated? There is a kind of hiatus, a holding of breath in the lungs, a waiting. The quiet man beside me moans, and I'm shocked by the sound's openness, the admitted quality of it. Has his pulse been quickened or made infinitely slow? Impossible to tell. But I can see the vein in one of his wrists. Throbbing.

Calla is holding herself very still. I can feel the tension of her arm through our two coats. If she speaks, I will never be able to face her again. I can feel along my nerves and arteries the squirming and squeamishness of that shame, and having to walk out of the Tabernacle with her afterwards, through a gauntlet of eyes.

Silence. I can't stay. I can't stand it. I really can't. Beside me, the man moans gently, moans and stirs, and moans—

That voice!

Chattering, crying, ululating, the forbidden transformed cryptically to nonsense, dragged from the crypt, stolen and shouted, the shuddering of it, the fear, the breaking, the release, the grieving—

Not Calla's voice. Mine. Oh my God. Mine. The voice of Rachel.

'Hush, Rachel. Hush, hush—it's all right, child.'

She is crooning the words softly over me. We are in her flat. The chesterfield is covered with an old car rug, green and black plaid, and it is on this that I am lying. I remember only vaguely our getting here, walking through the streets and the wind, the rain pelting against me and I hardly noticing it at all. As for the rest, I remember everything, every detail, and will never be able to forget, however hard I try. It will come back again and again, and I will have to endure it, over and over.

The crying has stopped now. Calla hands me a handkerchief and I blow my nose.

'How long did it go on?'

'You mean—crying? You started in the Tabernacle, and I took you out right away, and—'

'No. I didn't mean that. I meant—the other.'

'Oh. Only a minute. Less, probably.'

'You don't have to be kind. How long?'

'I've told you,' Calla says. 'But if you won't believe me, what can I do?'

'Was it—was I—was it very loud?"'

'No,' Calla says. 'It wasn't loud at all.'

I have no way of knowing whether she is telling me the truth or not. She is looking at me closely and questioningly, as though trying to decide whether to say something.

'Look—it's okay,' she says at last. 'I know it wasn't—well, you know—a religious experience, for you.'

I feel absolutely cold and detached from everything. My voice sounds flat and expressionless, nearly a monotone.

'I guess it's a good thing you realize that, anyway.'

'I'm not,' she says with unexpected bitterness, 'entirely lacking in all forms of understanding.'

'I didn't say you were.'

'No, but you think I'm a crank for going there. Maybe I am. I wanted you to go so you'd see it wasn't faked. And now look what's happened, what I've done. Oh, Rachel, I'm sorry—honestly I am. I should never—'

'*You're* sorry?' I can't understand this. 'I was the one who—'

I can't go on. I won't think of it. Calla is looking at me with a pity I can't tolerate.

'If only you didn't feel that way about it,' she says.

'Do you know what I detest more than anything else? Hysteria. It's so — slack. I've never done anything like that before. I'm so ashamed.'

'Child, don't. Don't be so hard on yourself.'

'I can't be hard enough, evidently. What will I do next, Calla? I'm — oh, Calla, I'm so damn frightened.'

She is kneeling beside the chesterfield, and the grey fringe of her hair is almost brushing against my face. She puts an arm around my shoulders and I realize from the rasping of her breath that she is actually crying. What has she got to cry about?

'Rachel, honey,' she says, 'it practically kills me to see you like this.'

Then, as though unpremeditated, she kisses my face and swiftly afterwards my mouth.

My drawing away is sharp, violent. I feel violated, unclean, as though I would strike her dead if I had the means. She pulls away then, too, and looks at me with a kind of bewilderment, a pleading apology, not saying a word. How ludicrous she looks, kneeling there, her wide face, her hands clasped anxiously. My anger feels more than justified, and in some way this is a tremendous relief.

It takes me less than a minute to get to the front hall and put on my coat and hood.

'Rachel — listen. Please. It was just that — '

I can't listen. I won't slam the door. I must shut it very quietly. Once I am outside, I can begin running.

THREE

'Hurry up, dear, or we'll be late.'

Her voice comes meadowlarking in through my bedroom door with such a lightness that I marvel at it, and she seems all at once marvellous, not letting on all that often about the frailty of her heart, although she had a slight attack two nights ago and the skin around her mouth was violet.

'Coming. I'll be right there.'

Going to church is a social occasion for her. She hasn't so many. It's mean of me not to want to go.

I always do go, though. When I came back to teach in Manawaka, I told Mother the first Sunday that I didn't think I'd go. She said 'Why not?' I didn't say God hadn't died recently, within the last few years, but a long time ago, longer than I could remember, for I could not actually recall a time when He was alive. No use to say that. I only told her I didn't agree with everything. She said 'I don't think it would be very nice, not to go. I don't think it would look very good.' But I didn't go. I held out three weeks. She didn't reproach me, not openly. She only relayed comments. 'Reverend MacElfrish asked after you, dear. He said he hoped you were well. I suppose he thought you probably weren't, as he hasn't seen you.' I thought what was the point in upsetting her, so I went. And have done, ever since.

She hasn't mentioned the Tabernacle. That was more than a week ago, and if anyone were going to tell her about it, they'd have done so by now, surely. I was in an agony for days, wondering if she would find out. I still can hardly believe she won't.

'Rachel – aren't you ready yet?'

'Yes, I'm just coming now.'

'Oh – are you going to wear that orange scarf, dear? Isn't it a little bright, with your green coat?'

'Do you think so?'

'Well, perhaps not. I would have thought your pink one would've gone better, that's all. But never mind. You wear whichever one you want.'

I won't change. I don't like that pink scarf. But now I won't feel right about the orange one, either. If ever I said to her, 'this is what you do', she'd be hurt and astounded and would deny it. She believes absolutely that she never speaks ill of anyone or harmfully to a soul. Once when I was quite young, she said to me, 'Whatever people may say of it, your father is a kind man – you must always believe that, Rachel.' Until that moment it had never occurred to me that he might not be thought a kind man. No wonder he never fought back. Her weapons are invisible, and she would never admit even to carrying them, much less putting them to use.

How can I think this way about her, when only a moment ago I was worrying about her heart?

Japonica Street is filled with morning light, and Mother in her new flowered-silk coat walks along like a butterfly released from winter. Really, she is amazing for her age. Am I walking stiffly? I always wonder if my height makes me appear to be striding. Mother takes quick, short steps, the kind I find impossible. She and Stacey look all right walking down the street together, for they're much the same height. With her, I always feel like some lean greyhound being led out for a walk.

I can hear the church chimes. They used to have a solitary bell there, summoning the faithful in plain clarity, but recently they have acquired a carillon which tinkles *The Church's One Foundation*.

Here we are. Mother flicks through the Hymnary to look up the hymns in advance. I wonder what she believes, if anything. She's never said. It was not a subject for discussion. She loves coming to church because she sees everyone, and in spring the new hats are like a forest of tulips. But as for faith – I suppose she takes it for granted that she believes. Yet if the Reverend MacElfrish should suddenly lose his mind and speak of God with anguish or joy, or out of some need should pray with fierce humility as though God had to be there, Mother would be shocked to the core. Luckily, it will never happen.

Mr MacElfrish's voice is as smooth and mellifluous as always, and he is careful not to say anything which might be upsetting. His sermon deals with Gratitude. He says we are fortunate to be living here, in plenty, and we ought not to take our blessings for granted. Who is likely to quibble with that?

The wood in this church is beautifully finished. Nothing ornate – heaven forbid. The congregation has good taste. Simple furnishings, but the grain of the wood shows deeply brown-gold, and at the front, where the high altar would be if this had been a church which paid court to high altars, a stained-glass window shows a pretty and clean-cut Jesus expiring gently and with absolutely no inconvenience, no gore, no pain, just this nice and slightly effeminate insurance salesman who, somewhat incongruously, happens to be clad in a toga, holding his arms languidly up to something which might in other circumstances have been a cross.

Oh Rachel. Carp, carp. Is that all you know how to do? The Tabernacle has too much gaudiness and zeal, and this has too little.

My father would never go to church. She used to say, 'It isn't very nice, Niall, for a man in your position not to go.' Perhaps she thought his absence would imply that when he dressed the dead and combed their hair, he did it in the conviction that they'd found by now all there was – oblivion. Undoubtedly he did think so. Immortality would have appalled him, perhaps as much as it does me.

'Why on earth do they let him?' Mother hisses softly.

41

'What?'

'Tom Gillanders – he's going to sing a solo. Honestly. I ask you.'

'Well, he's been in the choir such a long time. Mr Mac-Elfrish doesn't like to say no, I guess.'

Inwardly, though, I'm as much on edge as Mother. Tom Gillanders used to have a good voice, but that was years ago. He must be eighty now. He rises in the choir loft and stands alone, his black choir gown making him look like an emaciated crow.

> *Jerusalem the golden,*
> *with milk and honey blest –*

His voice is like the grating of sandpaper on rough wood. Sometimes it trembles and he loses the tune entirely. How can he do it? Doesn't he know how he sounds and how it makes him look?

Did I, in the Tabernacle? Did I know? I knew, and still I couldn't help it. Maybe the old man knows, too, and still cannot help it. If I believed, I would have to detest God for the brutal joker He would be if He existed.

> *I know not, O I know not*
> *What joys await us there –*

He's wandered away from the accompaniment, and the organist is fumbling madly to find him again. Beside me, Mother squirms. I can't blame her. Surely one might reasonably expect not to have to be embarrassed in *this* church, at least.

When I was a child, some people called Dukes had a mongoloid son. I remember him as a huge creature, but possibly because I was small. He must have been about sixteen then, his face puffy and his eyes, seeing but blind, almost buried within that unhealthy-looking flesh. They used to bring him to church sometimes, and those Sundays were a torment as pure as anything I've known since. He would talk aloud, in a high slurred voice, all through the service, but still they'd stay, on and on, and wouldn't leave unless he started saying swear words. Or even worse. *I got to pee, Mama.* And everyone would sit with burning faces, pretending they hadn't heard.

Well, thank God, the old man has finished, and at last the benediction is pronounced and we are allowed to go.

'They shouldn't let him,' Mother says, as we walk. 'It's a disgrace. Don't you think so, yourself, Rachel?'

'Yes. Yes, I certainly do.'

And yet with some part of myself I am inexplicably angry at this agreement.

Willard did not come to my classroom today, as he usually does when he has something to say. Instead he sent a note, saying would I please go to his office. I feel I'm being summoned like a naughty child. What right has he? What have I done?

Willard is sitting behind his desk. He has his glasses off and is rubbing his eyes as though they were sore or sleepy. This gives him, momentarily, a look of such vulnerability that I feel almost affectionate towards him, and want to draw back swiftly so he won't know and be troubled by the intrusion of my seeing him this way. He guards and cherishes his dignity so much. And now I remember his telling me once that he had to start wearing glasses when he first went to college, and he detested them. That's the only personal thing he has ever told me about himself. For some reason it touched me, and I could imagine him, straight from the small town where he grew up, and made gauche as well by his shortness, just as I was by my height, and then having spectacles to add to his misery.

He puts his glasses back on, and the heavy navy-blue frames define and strengthen his face. Now I remember the point of his telling me that about himself. He said he decided the only thing to do was to emphasize the glasses rather than trying to hide them, so he got the thickest and darkest frames he could find. Thus a natural disadvantage can

43

always be turned to gain, he said. And I wondered uneasily what he was hinting I ought to do.

'Oh, Rachel. Come in. I'll be with you in a moment.'

He does not ask me to sit down, so I have to remain standing while he fusses officiously with papers on his desk, not really doing anything, just applying a few paper-clips. Kept purposely waiting like this, I may soon blurt out something unpardonable, only to unbind the tension.

Once again, his hands on the desk seem to be drawing my eyes. With them he touches his wife, and holds the strap to strike a child, and—

My own stare repulses me, and yet I'm reassured by it. However unacceptable it may be, to want to brush my fingertips across the furred knuckles of someone I don't even like, at least they're a man's hands.

Has he noticed my looking? That I could not endure. Quick, look at something else. The calendar on his wall says *Bank Of Montreal* in gold on a royal-blue background and is not so frivolous as to display any picture.

'Now then,' Willard says, glancing up. 'Have you seen that boy's mother yet, Rachel?'

'Oh. You mean—James Doherty's mother?'

'Yes,' he says, with a slight air of impatience. 'That's the one. The boy who comes to school only when he feels like it.'

'He hasn't missed a day, recently.'

'Have you seen her, though?'

'Well, not yet. I thought—'

And now I see, startled, that I have been putting it off. The days seem to have gone by so quickly. I can't explain this negligence, because there is no explanation.

'It would be advisable to see her without delay, Rachel. Summer holidays are coming up, and after two months running wild, he is not likely to be improved. It would be just as well to make the situation eminently clear to the boy's mother right now. Whatever our shortcomings here, I would not want it said that we were a slack school, would you?'

'No – of course not. I'm sorry I haven't seen her, Willard. Honestly. I've been meaning to, and – '

I can hear my own voice, eagerly abject. Probably I would get down on my knees if this weren't frowned upon. I hate all this. I hate speaking in this way. But I go on doing it.

'Well, never mind.' He cuts me short, as though bored, which he probably is. 'You'll see to it, then?'

'Yes. Certainly. I'll send a note home with James tomorrow.'

'I would have thought,' Willard says, 'that a phone call might be somewhat more reliable. More likely to reach its destination, as it were.'

I want to say – *that's not fair – you've no right to imply that about James – he would never do a thing like that.* But why should Willard believe me? And when it comes to it, am I certain James wouldn't? Looking now at Willard's face, I'm certain only of what he says, as though his eyes have the reptilian gift. It is said that a person cannot be hypnotized against their will, but that can't be true.

'I'll phone, then.'

I want only to get away. I would agree to anything. What does it matter?

'Fine. That's settled, then,' Willard says, and I see I'm dismissed, permitted to go, let out of school.

Calla is in the Teachers' Room, making tea. I had a feeling she would be. She must have seen my cardigan hanging there, and known I hadn't gone yet.

'Hi,' she says. 'Like a cup of the brew that cheers but does not inebriate?'

Another of her favourite sayings. She has dozens. They get on my nerves. But I suppose they always provide her with something to say.

'Oh – thanks. I mustn't be long, though. I have to pick up some meat before the butcher's closes.'

'Sure,' she says, quite gently, hardly a trace of irony. 'Okay.'

45

Only now do I see how obvious I've been, saying something like that, without thinking, merely out of nervousness, a warning. An unnecessary one — is that what she is trying to tell me? That I needn't worry? That she won't attempt? But what in God's name do I think she's likely to attempt, anyway? I know very well I don't need to be afraid. She's the same Calla I've known for years. I've told myself this, over and over. And yet some portion of myself wants to avoid her for evermore. She knows it — she must know — and when I think she realizes, I feel ashamed at my unenlightenment. I'm a reasonably intelligent person. I'm not a fool. I've done a certain amount of reading. But it doesn't make much difference. I hold myself very carefully when she's near, like a clay figurine, easily broken, unmendable. We've talked with each other in an excessively cheerful way ever since that evening. I suppose this is as good a way as any, to camouflage the awkwardness we both feel and cannot admit or ever speak about.

'Been seeing the boss, Rachel?'

She pushes the tea cup towards me, across the table. She used to put the sugar and cream in my tea, for me, but she does not do that now. Another thing — she does not say *child* any more. Only *Rachel*. As though formality or great care had been forced upon her. I've wanted her to stop saying *child* or *kid* for a long time, yet now I feel unreasonably bereft.

No, I don't. That's senseless.

'What?' What did she ask me? 'Oh — yes. I don't see why he's making such an issue of James. Remember — I told you? You'd think the reputation of the whole school was at stake.'

'He likes playing games with people, that's all. If you once said to him, "Now listen here, Willard, quit making a mountain out of a molehill — "'

'You could do it. But not me.'

'Why not?'

'I — ' I have to search for an adequate reason. 'I can't bear scenes. They make me ill.'

But this is too serious, and I want to change to something undangerous.

'Did you see Sapphire Travis's shoes, Calla?'

'Sure. You could see them a block away. She painted them herself.'

'Really?'

'Yeh,' Calla says. 'Some gloop she bought, a do-it-yourself shoe-painting kit. But why that screeching pink, I ask myself.'

'It's a little bright, I agree.'

'It's explosive. All her kids were staring like mad. With admiration, she thought. Well, this is uncharitable and lousy-minded of me. What harm does it do, after all? Brighten the corner where you are, and so on. Maybe I'll get around to doing my old brogues a pale lilac.'

'Polka-dotted with silver.'

'Sure. Just the job.' And she chuckles throatily. She would probably do it, too, and find it more amusing than anyone. I envy this quality, but it appals me as well. She is gathering up the tea cups, whistling *She's Only a Bird in a Gilded Cage.*

'Did I tell you I got a canary?' she says.

'No. Did you?'

'Yeh. Moronic little thing, actually. Not even a cheep out of it. I don't think it's scared of me. My guess is it is just simply anti-social and unmusical. I've tried singing all kinds of things. But no response. It's not fond of hymns, and pop music makes it jittery, so what can I do?'

'What a shame. Maybe it'll change, though.'

'The other possibility,' Calla says, 'is that it isn't a canary at all. It is a bleached sparrow which has been fobbed off on me.'

She's trying so valiantly, as she has done whenever she thought I was depressed, and so I do laugh, not to disappoint her. Then it occurs to me that she never speaks of the Tabernacle any more. I want to ask her how it is there, these days, just to show I can speak of it. I want to ask her in a perfectly

47

ordinary voice, if she's yet received the gift of tongues. I ought at least to enquire politely.

But as soon as I think of that place at all, I'm back there in that indefensible moment, trapped in my own alien voice, and the eyes all around have swollen to giants' eyes. How will I ever be able to forget?

'I must go now.'

Before I've even quite realized it, I've snatched my cardigan off the hook and I'm halfway down the wide grey cement stairs outside. Calla will think it's peculiar, that I should rush off like this. But I can't go back. The knowledge of having to go back tomorrow morning is difficult enough.

Grace Doherty is plump and neat. She wears a white straw hat with veiling, and a light-blue spring suit, new, and high-heeled shoes. Why has she found it necessary to get dressed up like this? An interview with the teacher? But the teacher is Rachel Cameron, whom she's known all her life. Is it possible she doesn't think of it like this, and is edgy herself, wondering what I will have to say about James? I can't believe it. She was always self-assured, a girl who never bothered about schoolwork and managed to convey the impression that those who did were laughable or else had nothing better to do.

James is waiting for her in the hall. It seems a little cruel to keep him there, after all the others have gone, waiting and wondering what we're saying in here. But I couldn't talk to her in his presence.

I find I can't call her Grace. But to say Mrs Doherty would be silly. I won't be able to address her directly at all.

'These absences of James—' my voice sounds distant, cold, a robot's mechanical voice or someone reading from a printed form, 'they've been causing some concern to us.'

'Why?' she asks, as though innocently.

Why? Listen to the woman. She wouldn't care, I suppose, whether he ever got a scrap of education or not. He could

48

grow up illiterate – it would make no difference to her. If ever he decides he doesn't want to follow his father in the garage business, she'll stare at him with total blankness. If he's in a silver ship that one day lands on the moon, she'll write him off sorrowfully as a boy who didn't turn out well. Unless he gets in the papers or on TV for it. Then she would know it was all right to be approving. How shall I handle this?

'I'll have to tell you frankly. On two occasions, when he was supposed to be sick, he was seen in the valley. I'm sure you didn't know. Perhaps you were out, and – '

I have to allow her to save face, I suppose, although that is not my inclination. I don't want to look at her, but when I do, I see that her mild placid eyes are in a fever.

'Of course I knew!' she cries. 'What do you take me for, Rachel?'

I'm so startled I don't know what to say. I must be gaping at her foolishly.

'Who saw him?' she asks fiercely. 'If I may be so bold as to enquire.'

'I don't know that I ought to – '

'Well, in that case,' she says scathingly, 'it must've been Mrs Siddley. She spends half her time wandering around down there with her little camp stool and that jazzy easel of hers. I'd like to see the inside of *her* house. I bet it's a pigsty. You know as well as I do, Rachel, that she – '

She breaks off, glances at me, and then looks frightened.

'I didn't mean to say that.' Her voice sounds subdued and discouraged, but then she speaks defiantly again. 'If she'd only looked a little closer those two afternoons, she'd have seen I was with James.'

My first reaction is that she is lying, to pardon him. But when I scrutinize her face, it seems to me she isn't lying after all.

'But – why? If he was well, why wasn't he at school?'

'He'd had this bad tonsillitis,' Grace says. 'The weather was so warm and fine, on those two days, and he was much better, but still not quite himself. I thought it would do him more good than school, just those few times, to go out around the river, that's all.'

Her look is defensive now, and yet insistent, trying to explain.

'He's only seven, Rachel, and he's a clever kid. I mean, I think he's quite clever. And yet if he's sent to school too soon after being sick, and he isn't feeling up to much, it only makes him cranky. I don't see how he can learn anything then. I hate him to miss days like that, but then I wonder if it wouldn't be worse to set him against school? I don't want that. I want him to go on, as far as he –'

I cannot hear her any longer. I cannot listen as she elaborates. How could I not have known it of her, the way she feels, her determination and her hesitance? The way she cares about **him**.

'Listen, it's all right, Grace. Now that I know what happened, it's quite all right. I wouldn't even have brought it up, if I'd known.'

The door creaks open a crack, and James's blue eye peers in.

'Okay, honey, you can come in now,' she says. 'We're just going.'

He comes in and stands beside her, and she brushes his russet hair away from his forehead, as she's been doing for years, no doubt. She has the right to touch him, at least sometimes. She puts an arm around his shoulders, and he squirms away, frowning. She smiles, not unpleased that he wants to be his own and on his own.

'Well, that's all okay, then, Rachel?'

Her voice is filled with capability. She gains strength from his presence. This is what happens. I've seen it with my sister. They think they are making a shelter for their children, but actually it is the children who are making a shelter for them. They don't know.

As she goes out with him, I wonder if James has told her he got the strap. He couldn't have. She would have mentioned it. Why didn't he tell? Didn't he know how un-fair it was? Or did he know only too well?

I'm tired, tired, tired. And this wretched headache won't go. I promised Mother we would go to a movie tonight, but I don't feel up to it. I think I'll postpone it. I'll take two aspirins and go straight to bed.

Some days it seems more difficult to be patient. There are times when they could riot, or shriek with twenty-six voices simultaneously, and I wouldn't be upset. Other times, the slightest thing will be enough to set me off. I must try to be more equable. It's the only way — it's only right. But some days the slightest snick of a door latch, the slightest sign of scrabbling, will set my teeth on edge. This morning is one such day. I don't know what's the matter. Just that they seem to make so much noise.

Just — noise. The scraping of their feet on the floor. The juggling of books from inside the desk to outside — such an easy procedure — how can it be so complicated for them? The trading of crayons back and forth, someone having a more exotic colour than someone else. The whispering that grows to a hissed largeness until finally in justice I cannot ignore it but have to deal somehow with it, nicely and reasonably, not doing as probably any distracted parent would be bound to do, shouting *Shut up!* Just shut up. Please.

'Peter, have you finished your arithmetic?'

Stoic silence. No reply.

'James — are you finished?'

Without warning, he puts his elbows protectively over the page. No speech. No explanation. Only this indrawing of his arms over the paper.

'Let me see.'

As soon as I've said it, I know it was mistaken, the last thing I ought to have laid claim to. But now I can't turn back.

'Let me see how far you've got.'

51

This is all wrong, and I know it. He doesn't intend to let me see, and I'm intruding and ought to approach him in another way, cool, unheated.

But his uncombed and untidied sorrel hair, and his self-protected face which seems to warn everyone away — there is something I cannot bear here.

There. I've pushed aside his arms, not with my hands but with the ruler I'm holding. At first he offers no resistance. His elbows go slack, allowing themselves to be shoved across the desk surface. Then he changes his mind and his finger ends curl around the page, determined I should not see.

What's there? What has he done instead of simple subtraction? A caricature? An unendurable portrait? He looks at me with a sly gopher-like idiocy, all innocent nothingness — *see, I'm too dumb to have anything here worth looking at.* The cunning nonentity of his face. Is this necessary? Does he feel this is necessary with me?

He does not give a damn. He hates me. I am the enemy. God damn, what is this child hiding?

He won't give in. All right. I'll have to wrench it from him. What right has he? If he despises me, I must go on anyway. What is being hidden from me?

I must not tear his page, though. As I put my hand on it, his hand clamps down, firm, absolute. What is he doing? Why does he fight me so? Then he looks at me. His eyes are extremely blue, not the translucent blue of water or sky, but the assertive and untransparent blue of copper sulphate, opaque, not to be seen through. I do not know at all what is going on in those eyes.

'Have you finished your subtraction questions, James?'

No voice. I cannot get any response. He holds everything very still within himself. He will not let me see. He does not intend that I should ever see.

Crack!

What is it? What's happened?

The ruler. From his nose, the thin blood river traces its

course down to his mouth. I can't have. I can't have done it. Slowly, because a reason for all things must be found, I take the unresisting page between my fingers and force myself to look at it.

No pictures. No obscene caricatures. Only—two sums completed, out of ten, and those two done incorrectly. That's all.

He has what we used to call a nosebleed. It won't stop. His blood won't stop.

'James, put your head back. It will stop then.'

I cannot say I'm sorry. Not in front of them all, twenty-six beings, all eyes. If I do say this, how shall I appear tomorrow? Cut down, diminished, undermined, very little left. If I do not say it, though, there's enough gossip for a month or more, to friends and fathers and lovingly listening mothers— *you know what Miss Cameron went and did?* Did she? And to James, space venturer, first man on the moon?

He is not crying. Maybe I knew I could rely on that. He has dug out from some obscure and unnoticed pocket a tardy handkerchief, never seen before. With it, he is mopping away the scarlet from his face, not dramatically but very simply and practically, as though this were the only thing to be considered at the moment, to wipe the stained confusion away.

If I could put my hands upon him, lightly, and comfort him. If I could say something. It is not for me to say or do anything. How can one retrieve anything at all? Is it always past the appointed hour?

James—I'm sorry. But I haven't spoken the words aloud.

James puts his handkerchief away. His nose has stopped bleeding. The others are looking at me. Everyone within our gates will hear before nightfall. The only thing I can do now is to bring it off as though I meant it to occur, as though I were at least half justified. If I capitulate, they will fall upon me like falcons.

'All right, James. Get on with it. See if you can get through the next few.'

I hear my voice, controlled. I don't know what I could ever say to him, to make up for what I've done. I don't think I could ever say anything which might make him forget.

The day does end, of course. Am I walking home unusually slowly? I feel as though I were. Summer holidays will begin in another two weeks. This year's children will be gone then, and gradually will turn into barely recognized faces, no connection left, only *hello* sometimes on the street. There will be new ones, and I will have to learn their names and faces, their quirks and their responses.

I am trying to recall when I last hit a child. I cannot remember. It was not all that long ago – a year, perhaps. Yet now I cannot remember, cannot put a face and name to it, or a reason. In a year or two, will I have locked today away in some junkbox, never to be found among all the other scraps and trifles?

When did I, the last time, and who was it, and why? I must be able to remember. Why can't I?

Now don't start thinking your memory is failing, Rachel. That isn't so. I can't be expected to remember everything.

Two weeks. Not very long to make a peace. Not half long enough. Probably that is all he will remember of me, that one instant, the thin wooden stick across his face. 'I had a teacher once who hit me so hard my nose bled, no kidding.' And listeners – friends or lovers or his own children – will express astonishment that such acts were allowed in those barbaric olden days.

I must stop at the Regal Café and get some cigarettes. I don't smoke much any more. It is foolhardy to take chances with one's health, after all. But I do enjoy a cigarette after meals, and sometimes if I have a bad night, I may get up and smoke a couple – never in bed, no matter how wakeful I am. People have set fire to themselves that way.

The café is crowded with slick leather-jacketed youngsters. Behind the counter Lee Toy stands, his centuries-old face not showing at all what he may think of these kids. He has been here ever since I was a child, and he seemed old then. Now he is dried and brittle and brown like the shell of a lichee nut, and he has two younger men in partnership, nephews, perhaps. They could even be sons, and I wouldn't know. He has spent most of his life here, but in a kind of secrecy, living alone in the rooms above the café. My father told me once that Lee Toy's wife was still in China, still alive and living on the money he sent, but unable to come here, first because of our laws and then because of theirs. Maybe she is there yet, the woman he has not seen for more than forty years.

Beside the Coca-Cola poster on the wall there hangs a painting, long and narrow like an unrolled scroll, done on grey silk – a mountain, and on the slope a solitary and splendidly plumaged tiger.

I have to walk through the tight knot of teenagers. They don't make way or part ranks. They remain clustered around the jukebox, boys with their arms around their girls, and the girls, also, each with their arms around some boy. Have I taught any of them, years ago? I don't want to look directly at them to see who is recognizable and who is not.

They take up all the space. A person can hardly squeeze inside the door. They're everywhere. I wish I hadn't come in. I don't like having to shove past them, having to endure the confident dismissal of their eyes.

At last I've got my cigarettes. As I'm reaching out for the change, I find myself glancing sideways and looking into the face of a girl. Lipstick a whitish pink like salve, softly shining skin with virtually no powder, and then everything lavished on the eyes – bluegreen like the sea, underneath, and greenblue lids above, with the lashes thickly black. She is staring at me. What do those plain eyes in their jewelled setting see? I don't want to know. It doesn't concern me, what she thinks. Why should it? What does it matter? Who does she think she is?

'Hello, Miss Cameron.'

'Oh – hello.' I don't know her. Whoever she once was – that's long gone. Some child I was drawn to, perhaps and may have shown it, and she remembers and can't forgive it, for she detests now and would like to kill for ever the little girl who believed it was really something if the teacher was pleased with the work she'd done.

I must get out of here.

Japonica Street. The days are longer now, and the light lasts into the evening, but Hector Jonas has turned on the neon sign. *Japonica Funeral Chapel*. It winks and beckons, and as I walk up the petunia-edged path, I see all at once how laughable it is, to live here, how funny lots of people must think it, how amusing, how hilarious.

Oh stop. It's a house. It's decent. Mother wouldn't feel at home anywhere else. You'd think she would want to leave but she doesn't. She always let on to my father that she didn't enjoy living here. She used to say 'Your father's so attached to this place', and then sigh delicately. But if he had been able to move anywhere, I don't suppose she would have gone.

He really was attached to it, though. He had come here and settled in as soon as he got home from the First War. He must have been very young then. He never talked about that time in France, and when the Armistice Day parades were held, he never would go. Mother used to say, 'Everyone goes, Niall – it looks so peculiar, for you not to.' He would agree to nearly anything, for quiet, but not to that. He would stay downstairs that day, with the silent company if there happened to be anyone in residence waiting burial, or else alone, and he wouldn't come upstairs all that night, either, being unable to move sufficiently, I guess. What could have happened to him, all those years ago, to make him that way? When the Second War came, the Cameron Highlanders marched through the streets of Manawaka on their way off, because so many of the town boys were in that regiment. I was a child, and excited at it, because they bore our name. I came back and pounded on the door of his establishment, the only time I ever remember doing that. 'Dad – come and see – they've got pipers, and they're playing "The March of the Cameron Men".' He stood in the doorway, his face showing no feeling at all. 'Yes, I expect they are, Rachel. It has a fine sound, the lies the pipes tell. You run away, now, there's a good girl.' That's all.

'You're late this evening, dear,' Mother says.

'I'm sorry.'

'What's the matter, Rachel? Aren't you feeling well?'

'I'm all right. A bit of a headache, that's all. How are you?'

'Oh, just fine, really. I had that miserable pain again this afternoon, but I lay down on the chesterfield for an hour, and it's almost gone now.'

'You shouldn't be up. You go and lie down again now. I'll see to dinner.'

'No, truly, I'm fine now, dear. A little tired, but that's nothing serious. I'll take it easy, though. I know I must, although it's not easy for me, having always been so active. I just hope you're not coming down with 'flu. I don't like these headaches you've been getting. Have you got a temperature?'

'No, I don't think so.'

'Let me feel your forehead. You're a bit warm, I'd say.'

'I'm all right, Mother, for goodness' sake. You go and lie down now. Please.'

'Well, I will then, dear, if you're quite sure you're all right. You haven't got an upset stomach, have you?'

'No, no. My stomach is perfectly all right. It's just a bit of a headache. I'll take a two-twenty-two.'

'Yes, you be sure to do that, dear. You don't take enough care of yourself, Rachel. It doesn't do to take chances with your health. If you do, you'll pay for it when you're older.'

When I'm older. She speaks as though I were about twelve. What a strangely pendulum life I have, fluctuating in age between extremes, hardly knowing myself whether I am too young or too old.

57

At dinner she eats well. She seems all right. What is the matter with me? Do I doubt her pain? At times I do, and then again at other times it causes a panic in me, and I wonder what I'd do here, by myself.

'You know the Stewart girl, Rachel?'

'Cassie? The one who works at Barnes' Hardware?'

'That's the one. I only heard today. You know she's been away?'

'I hadn't noticed.'

'Well, she has been. It's dreadful for her mother, a nice woman, nothing to write home about, but quite a nice woman, Mrs Stewart, I've always thought. The girl isn't married and no one even in prospect, so I gather.'

This circumlocution is necessary for Mother.

'You mean she's had a child?'

Mother spoons the last drop of vanilla ice cream slowly into her mouth, letting it melt and dribble down her throat before she replies.

'Twins,' she says sepulchrally. 'What a heartbreak for her mother. Imagine. *Twins.*'

I have to resist some powerful undercurrent of laughter. Twins. Twice as reprehensible as one.

'Is she going to keep them?'

'That's the awful thing,' Mother says. 'Apparently she refuses to have them put up for adoption. I can't fathom the thoughtlessness of some girls. She might consider her mother, and how it'll be for her. It was Mrs Barnes that told me. I said to her, I thank my lucky stars I never had a moment's worry with either of my daughters.'

Had. Past tense.

Mother took her sleeping pill soon after dinner. By nine, she was sleeping like a baby. I've finished the dishes and done some laundry, and I'm ready for bed myself.

Each day dies with sleep. I wish it did. My headache has gone, but I'm restless. The slow whirling begins again, the night's wheel that turns and turns, pointlessly. When I close

58

my eyes, I see scratches of gold against the black, and they form into jagged lines, teeth, a knife's edge, the sharp hard hackles of dinosaurs.

I must sleep.

The blood ran down from his nostrils to his mouth's edge. He wiped it away as though it were only to be expected. What can I ever say that might make him forget?

I have to get to sleep. I must. The one who grows out of shadows won't venture near tonight. Even that solace isn't deserved.

— When Egypt's queen received Antony, that book said, she used to fall upon him even before he had taken off his armour. Think of that — even before he'd taken off his armour. They used to have banquets with dozens there. Hundreds. Egyptian girls and Roman soldiers. Oasis melons, dusty grapes brought in the long ships from somewhere. Goblets shaped like cats, cats with listening ears, engraven in gold, not serpents or bulls, not Israel or Greece, only golden cats, cruelly knowledgeable as Egypt. They drank their wine from golden cats with seeing eyes. And when they'd drunk enough, they would copulate as openly as dogs, a sweet hot tangle of the smooth legs around the hard hairy thighs. The noise and sweat — the sound of their breath — the slaves looking on, having to stand itchingly immobile while they watched the warm squirming of those —

The night is a jet-black lake. A person could sink down and even disappear without a trace.

FOUR

Holidays are enticing only for the first week or so. After that, it is no longer such a novelty to rise late and have little to do. I don't really know what to do with myself these days. I invent duties and expeditions. I see the children from my last class, on the streets, and they are so busy running somewhere that they hardly notice me.

Already July smells of dust and dryness, and I hope we aren't going to have one of those yellowing summers, with no rain, and the green seeping away from the grass and leaves.

River Street is almost empty this morning, only a few bicycles buzzing slowly like bluebottle flies, and the occasional kingfisher flash of a car driven by some impatient housewife bored with shopping. Outside the Parthenon Café, Miklos is sponging his windows dawdlingly, spinning the job out to last the morning while his wife waits stoically on the customers inside. The Flamingo Dancehall is shut tight and locked, blinds drawn, but tonight it will be all mauve and green shifting lights, and blare, and couples. In the summer there are dances every night here now. It used to be only once a week, Saturdays, when I was about seventeen. Sometimes I'd go with three or four other girls, scarcely wanting to, for the peril undertaken, the risk of no one asking a person to dance. But I dreaded not going even more – having to make up an excuse which anyone could see through. What a relief when one actually was asked to dance, no matter by whom. Except if it was Cluny Macpherson from the B.A. Garage, and then I used to want to get out of it, but couldn't, being unable to say I'd promised the dance as it was obvious I hadn't. He used to like to dance with me because he liked being a clown. I've often wondered how anyone could enjoy that. He was exceptionally short and broad, like a bulldog, and I was my full height then, and must have looked like some skinny poplar sapling. Naturally I'd falter or lose a step and he would croon to the band tune in his carrying voice so no one would miss the joke — *Don't watch your fee-eet, don't watch your feet.* Maybe he even thought he was doing me a kindness, teaching me to dance. He must have been thirty-five then. He's in his fifties now. Probably he still goes to the dances at the Flamingo. What do the cool-eyed youngsters there now say to him? Has his foolery worn a little thin, even to himself, or does he still go on, unaware, or else compelled to be a card, a character, until he drops? What would he say if unexpectedly I turned up there one night? Perhaps we'd twist (is that still current?) for old times' sake, two caricatures, dog out-reached to tree, the others' laughter howling louder than the music.

I honestly do not know why I feel the daft sting of imagined embarrassments. The ones that occur are more than plenty, God knows. I must not let myself think like this. I don't know why I do. Unless to visualize something infinitely worse than anything that could possibly happen, so that whatever happens may seem not so bad in comparison.

On the steps of the Queen Victoria Hotel a few old men sit, absorbing the sunlight through their grey buttoned-up sweaters and loose grey unpressed trousers, talking in thin voices. Perhaps if my father were alive, he'd be there with them. He'd be about that age by now, I guess. I hate to think of him like that, crinkled face not properly shaven, an adam's apple moving up and down in a scrawny throat. I'm not sorry he didn't live, if that is the measure of it.

Mother is as bright and flighty as she ever was, though. More so, really, since he's not here — not that she'd ever see

61

or acknowledge that. No one could say mortality had very noticeably laid claws on her, not yet. Except when she's ill, of course. The breathing is so erratic. And that worrying purple that tinges her mouth like potassium permanganate. I think I ought to tell Doctor Raven those new pills aren't doing her as much good as we'd hoped. I must remember to do that today, and also without letting her know. No use in upsetting her. That will be something for me to do this afternoon. Straight after lunch I'll pop into Doctor Raven's office. He'll say —

'Hello, Rachel.'

Has someone spoken to me? A man's voice, familiar. Who is it?

'It *is* Rachel, isn't it?' he says, stopping, smiling enquiringly.

He is about the same height as myself. Not thickly built, really, but with the solidity of heavy bones. Straight hair, black. Eyes rather Slavic, slightly slanted, seemingly only friendly now, but I remember the mockery in them from years ago.

'Nick Kazlik. You haven't been back in Manawaka for a long time.'

'No, that's right, I haven't.'

'What are you doing now?'

'Teaching,' he says, 'in a High School.'

'In the city?'

'Yes,' he says, with a quirk of a smile.

I oughtn't to have said *the city*. As though I believed it were the only one anywhere. Why didn't I say Winnipeg?

'What're you doing back here?' I have to rush to fill the empty space with words, and then I realize there is only one thing he could be doing here.

'I came back to be with my parents for the summer. They're getting on.'

'Yes, of course. I — well, of course.'

'What are you doing here, Rachel?'

'I — oh, I live here.'

62

What a moronic thing to say. As though that explained my presence.

'Oh? You're married, then?'

'No. No – I'm living with my – I keep house for my mother since my father – he's dead, you know. And I teach, of course.'

Of course. As though he would be bound to know. Why should Teresa Kazlik write to him of me? I never had anything to do with him. He's a year older than I am, I think. And anyway, I just didn't. Mother used to say 'Don't play with those Galician youngsters'. How odd that seems now. They weren't Galicians – they were Ukrainian, but that didn't trouble my mother. She said Galician or Bohunk. So did I, I suppose. She needn't have worried. They were raw-boned kids whose scorn was almost tangible. They would never have wanted to play with us. I knew that Nick went to university, but I never knew him there, either.

'I mean – ' but I'm fumbling this amendment, 'I'm a teacher – also.'

'Are you? Whereabouts?'

'Grade Two.' I find I'm laughing – tittering, maybe – yes, for Christ's sake, that. 'I wouldn't want to cope with High School.'

'Trample their egos firmly,' Nick says. 'It's the only way.'

'Oh – I wouldn't have thought so – '

He laughs. 'No?'

Why didn't I see he didn't mean it, before? I don't know why I take people's words at their surface value. Mine can't be taken so. But I do. And then they think – *What naïveté – who could believe it?* Is he thinking that?

'Been here long, Rachel?' he asks.

There is something almost gentle in his voice, and suddenly I long to say *Yes, for ever*, but also to deny everything and to say *Only a year – before that, I was in Samarkand and Tokyo.*

'A while. My father died – '

'Yes. You said.'

Yes, I did say, didn't I? So why again? What can he be thinking? Never mind. Whatever he thinks, it's not even approaching the truth. Who does he think he is? High School or not. Nestor Kazlik's son. The milkman's son.

It can't be myself thinking like that. I don't believe that way at all. It's as though I've thought in Mother's voice. Nick graduated from university. I didn't.

'I'm sorry,' Nick is saying, still speaking about my father, whom momentarily I had forgotten.

'Well – it was some time ago.' So no condolence is required, and I've pushed away his well-intended words? I must say something. 'Anyway, that's when I came back. I didn't finish college.'

'I didn't know that.'

'No, of course. I mean, of course you wouldn't know.'

'What is there to do here in the summer?' Nick asks.

'I don't – well, not a great deal, I guess.'

'Would you come to a movie on Friday night, Rachel?'

'Oh. Well – I guess – well, thanks. I – yes, I'd like to.'

'Good. Fine. Eight?'

'Yes. That's – fine.'

'See you, then. Oh, wait, Rachel. I don't know where you live.'

'In the same – you remember? My father had the – '

'Yes. I remember.'

'The man who took over the business didn't want the upstairs flat, so we – my mother and I – we've kept it on.'

'I see.'

'You can't miss it,' I am shrilly saying. 'There's a neon sign.'

He laughs, but I cannot tell whether it is done in puzzlement or what. Then he walks on, saying 'So long', and I must walk on quickly as well, not remain standing here.

At home, Mother has the table set and is waiting for the lamb chops for lunch.

'I'm sorry. I didn't mean to be so long.'

'It's quite all right, dear. I did begin to wonder a little, that's all, what could possibly have kept you so long, or if you'd had some kind of accident—'

'Oh Mother. For heaven's sake. It's only half past twelve. I was talking to someone. Nick Kazlik, actually. He's back for the summer.'

'Who dear? I don't believe I know him.'

'Nick Kazlik. You know.'

'Oh—you mean old Nestor's son?'

'Yes. He's a High School teacher. In the city.'

'Really? How did he manage that?'

'I couldn't say. Some miracle, I suppose. Divine intervention, maybe.'

'Really, Rachel,' she says, exceedingly perturbed, 'There's no need for you to speak to me like that. If you please.'

'I'm sorry. I'm sorry.'

I'm not sorry. And yet my anger is childish. It's not her fault. Half the town is Scots descent and the other half is Ukrainian. Oil, as they say, and water. Both came for the same reasons, because they had nothing where they were before. That was a long way away and a long time ago. The Ukrainians knew how to be the better grain farmers, but the Scots knew how to be almightier than anyone but God. She was brought up that way, and my father too, and I, but by the time it reached me, the backbone had been splintered considerably. She doesn't know that, though, and never will. Probably I wouldn't even want her to know.

How shall I tell her I've agreed to go out with him? This is what I keep on wondering through our evening, the TV clanging and bellowing, and Mother belching softly on the sofa and gnawing peppermints for indigestion.

I wonder why he asked me out. I suppose he didn't have anything better to do, and thought he might as well.

Why in God's name did I say that about the neon sign?

The first time I ever went to a movie with a boy, I was fifteen. The adult price wasn't charged until sixteen. The boy was sixteen. I stood beside him on the winter street,

65

outside the ticket window, shivering, obsessed with one thought – how would I ever walk past the ticket girl and face the usherette if he bought a child's ticket for me? He didn't, of course, so I had upset myself needlessly.

'Where are you going, Rachel? Are you going somewhere?'

'Yes.' I should have told her before, I know. 'I'm going to a movie.'

'Oh. What's on? Maybe I'll come along.'

'I mean I'm going – with someone.'

'Oh. I see. Well, you might have said, Rachel. You really might have told me, dear.'

'I'm sorry, Mother. I just – '

'You know how glad I am, dear, when you go out. You might have mentioned it to me, that's all. It's not too much to ask, surely. After all, I do like to know where you are. I would have thought you could have said, Rachel.'

'I'm sorry.'

'Well, it's quite all right, dear. I'm only saying if you had let me know, it would've been better, that's all. I could have invited one of the girls in, maybe. Well, never mind. I shall be quite fine here by myself. I'll just slip into my housecoat, and make some coffee, and have a nice quiet evening. I'll be just dandy. Don't you worry about me a speck. I'll be perfectly all right. If you'd just reach down my pills for me from the medicine cabinet. As long as they're where I can get them handily, in case anything happens. I'm sure I'll be fine. You go ahead and enjoy yourself, Rachel.'

I can never handle this kind of thing properly. What's behind it can never be brought out. She'd only deny, and be stricken and wounded. Maybe she really doesn't know what she's saying. She half convinces me, all the same, because it is true that something might happen when I'm away, and then what? All my fault. It worries me, anyway, even apart from whose fault.

'Maybe I shouldn't go.' Do I mean this?

'No, no. You go ahead, dear. It isn't so often that you –

and I'll be perfectly fine. After all, you're young. I must expect to be a bit lonely sometimes.'

'I'm sorry.' We could pace this treadmill indefinitely.

'You never said who it was, dear. It doesn't matter in the least, but it does hurt me just a little when you don't even—'

'Nick Kazlik.'

'Who? I don't believe I—'

'I told you the other day that I met him on the street. Nick Kazlik.'

Mother, flitting around the living-room, having suddenly decided that the pictures all need straightening, pauses with one small white mauve-veined hand on the autumn-coloured print of The Strawberry Girl.

'You mean the milkman's son?'

The milkman's son. The undertaker's daughter. But she wouldn't laugh. I must be very calm and careful. Anything else is useless.

'The same.'

An infant sigh bubbles from her lips.

'Well, of course—I mean, it's your business, dear. You go ahead and have a nice time.'

If only once she'd say what she means, and we could have it out. But she won't. Maybe it would be worse if she did. I don't know.

Doorbell. Quick—I must get her pills for her, first. They are on the top shelf of the medicine cabinet so that no one will take them by mistake. She can't reach that high.

'Here—they're on top of the TV. Is there anything else you need?'

'No, no.' She has moved on to the straightening of a simpering puce-mouthed Madonna. 'I told you, dear—I'll be quite all right. I may just get started on the laundry.'

'Mother—you're not to! You know you mustn't lift things, or strain too much. I'll do it tomorrow morning.'

Doorbell again.

'Well, Rachel dear, I only thought I might as well get going on it, as I haven't anything much to do.'

'*Please.*'

She glances at me with the innocent guile I've seen so often on the faces of my children.

'I'll see how I feel, dear. I only thought I might as well be doing something useful.'

'Promise me not to. Please.'

'We'll see. There are those blankets we've been meaning to wash all spring – '

'Mother!'

Why does she do this now? Why not half an hour ago, when I would have had the time to cajole. That's why she didn't, then, of course.

'All right. All right. Wash them if you like. I can't stop you, can I?'

Going down the stairs, rapidly, my heels clattering, I can see again the astonished disbelief on her face. I can't believe, myself, that I could have said what I did. What an awful thing to say. I don't care. I don't give a damn. I'll care later. Not right now.

'Hi.'

Nick is leaning against the door frame, looking up at the neon sign, to which Hector Jonas has recently added a refinement. It now goes off and on, automatically, like the delphinium blinking of eyes.

'Hello. I'm sorry to have kept you waiting.'

'That's okay. You're looking very nice.'

'Oh. Thank you.' My black linen, sleeveless, with the gold pin on the shoulder. But now I wonder if it isn't too dressy. Only a movie, after all. Maybe I should have worn my blue and white cotton. Too late now. Will he think it looks as though I don't know what to wear? Or that I'm giving some kind of importance to this evening? That's not so. It isn't so at all. If I speak quite coolly, he'll realize it.

'I see what you mean about the sign,' Nick says as we get into his car.

'I hate living here.' This is the last thing in the world I ever intended to say. He'll say *Why don't you move, then?*

Or think what a peculiar outburst when we hardly know each other.

'I don't blame you,' he says offhandedly. 'Damn this car. Something's the matter with the ignition.'

Finally it starts.

'I've got to trade this old wreck in,' he says, 'before it gets any worse. It's depreciating God-knows how many dollars every hour – every second, probably.'

'It doesn't seem like an old wreck to me. But I don't know anything about cars.'

'Neither do I. That's why I always get rooked on them. Never buy another secondhand car, I tell myself. But I go on doing it. I'm more like my old man than I think, I guess.'

I don't see his father at all any more. The milk is delivered by someone else, a hired man, these days. But when I was a child – I'd forgotten until this moment – Stacey and I used to cadge rides on Nestor Kazlik's sleigh in the winter, a big wagon-sleigh drawn by two horses, and all the milk bottles were carefully covered with a tarpaulin so they wouldn't freeze and burst. We would grab hold of the back and be pulled along dizzyingly, as though skiing or flying, until our arms nearly broke and we dropped off on to the hard rutted snow of the road. He used to be a big man, a great bear of a man, with a moustache thick as an untrimmed hedge.

'How do you mean?'

'He still won't have a car. He says he has the milk truck and that's plenty. Anything more would be an indecent expenditure. It took about ten years of persuasion before he would even get the truck instead of a wagon. He still can't believe that he isn't on the verge of penury and hasn't been for quite a few years. You talk cars to him and he starts muttering proverbs or something – you know? Extolling thrift. You got to learn to be careful, he tells me, or you won't have enough money to pay for your own funeral. I don't care about my own funeral, I tell him. What a disgrace, he says, a *teacher* and they can throw him in a field

69

and let the crows eat his eyes for all he cares – what kind of man is this?'

'He doesn't mean it, though.'

'He means it,' Nick shrugs, 'and also doesn't mean it. He never feels any need to be consistent. He took my mom to Banff last summer on a holiday, and that's what they went in, this little van-type truck with *Kazlik's Dairy Manawaka Manitoba* painted on the side. He made Jago get out the old wagon to deliver the milk, so he could take the truck. My mom wanted to go by bus, but he wouldn't hear of it. He actually took her to the Banff Springs Hotel. My God, what a crazy man he is. My mother wrote me about it. He's not in the market even for a secondhand car, but all at once he decides he's a prince. The *best*, he tells her. For once, *the* best. My mom is horrified, but she can't bear to tell him, because he's enjoying himself so much. So they go bowling in, with *Kazlik's Dairy* truck, among all the herd of Cadillacs and Lincolns. My mom creeps around amid the fashion plates like some kind of stout silent tortoise, you know? Massive retirement into the shell. But not him. Hell, no. The first night, he disappears. Before dinner. At ten he still hasn't turned up. There is nothing to eat in the room, not even a chocolate bar. My mother is sitting there in the middle of the Banff Springs Hotel, starving to death. Imagine it. Finally he comes blasting in with about ten new acquaintances. They are all wealthy oil men from Alberta, but never mind – now they have learned all about how to start a dairy farm, right from the word go. Should the oil business ever fail, you understand. I don't know what the hell the point of this story is, Rachel, or how I got started on it.'

He's easy to listen to. Easy as well, it almost seems, to reply to. If only it could be that way.

'Cars. It started with cars. I think he sounds wonderful, your father.'

Nick gives me a quick sideways glance.

'Yeh. I get quite a kick out of him, myself.'

He is suddenly withdrawn. What did I say wrong? He

thinks it sounded false, or even worse – gushing. Is that it? Or what?

'Here we are,' he says.

The Roxy Theatre has never been a theatre, as far as I know, except for the occasional minstrel show years ago, put on for the Red Cross or some deserving cause. The movies used to change once a week. Now they change twice.

'It'll be crumby as hell, probably,' Nick says, looking suspiciously at the multi-tinted posters.

He's quite right, as it turns out. The film is indifferent, improbable. I can't seem to concentrate on it. I don't know what it's about. I can hear him breathing, beside me, and he's sprawled a little in the seat, close by.

If he puts his arm around me, will I move closer or away? He won't, of course. The High School kids do that. He's thirty-five, not fifteen. He is past such gauche and public performances. What are you worried about, Rachel? I'm not worried. I'm perfectly all right. Well, relax, then. I am relaxed. Oh? Shut up. Just shut up.

He does not shift himself in the movie seat to be even six inches closer. Well, why should he? Who would want to? We have discussed this a long time ago, you and I, Rachel. Haven't you seen it yet?

'Would you like some coffee?' Nick asks, when the picture is over.

I would, but somehow I don't want to walk into the Regal Café or the Parthenon. Like putting on an act which everyone would know for what it was, a charade.

'Oh, thanks, but I think I'd better get straight home. Mother has a kind of uncertain heart. I'm always a little concerned in case – '

'Are you?' Nick says. 'Okay, then.'

When we get to Japonica Street and the blue neon, he stops the car.

'Thanks, Rachel.'

'Thank *you*.'

He laughs. 'How polite you are. Are you always?'

71

'Well –'

But before I can say anything – not knowing anyway what could be said – he reaches over and puts his hands on my shoulders. He kisses gently and exploringly. I am – as though undecided. But it's unreal, anyway. If it isn't happening, one might as well do what one wants. His tongue is rough-textured and wet and has its own life inside my mouth. It is he who draws away, after a while, not me.

'Well,' he says.

Is he surprised, or what? I resent his surprise, if it is that. I'd like to let him know that I can want, too. I'm thirty-four. That's not old. I haven't fossilized. Why do people assume it's so different for men? Is he laughing?

When he kisses me again, I hold myself against him and feel the bones of his shoulders and his ribs, through his clothes. The skin on his face doesn't smell of anything extraneous, nothing like shaving lotion or soap, only of himself. And when I put my face against his, and breathe him in – oh my God. Now I really do want him. Now I would do anything –

Yet he's put his hand on my breasts and I have actually pushed him away. He doesn't resist. He accepts it. Why wouldn't he? He didn't want to touch me all that much.

'I've – got to go in, now.' I suppose it must be my voice, although God only knows what it is saying. 'I mean – Mother will be wondering where I am, you see, and – '

'That wouldn't do, would it?' he says.

He traces with his hand a line down my face, from my temple and across my cheekbone and down to my mouth. He is smiling in the darkness. I can't see his smile but I know it is there, from his voice. It hurts as much as if he'd slapped me. More.

'See you, Rachel,' he says.

'Yes – I hope – I hope so,' I am inexcusably saying.

Everything is automatic, walking up the sidewalk, hearing the car zoom away, opening the door and walking up the stairs. It is not the moment to think of anything. Only – is

Mother in bed yet? Is she asleep? Is she awake, and has she noticed the car parked out there? How long a time has it been?

'Rachel?'

'Yes? Are you still awake?'

'Well, dear, I was beginning to drift off, but I don't ever settle down too well until you're in. Was it a good movie?'

'Very nice, thanks.'

'Would you like a cup of coffee, dear?'

'No, thanks. I think I'll go straight to bed. Are you all right?'

'Oh, yes. A little over-tired, maybe, but that's nothing out of the ordinary. I'll be off to sleep in a while, probably, with any luck.'

She didn't do the laundry, of course. I saw that as soon as I turned on the kitchen light.

'Did you have to take one of your heart pills?'

'No, I didn't think it was really necessary. It's hard for me to judge, sometimes. But I thought if I lay down, it might be all right. I made myself some cocoa.'

'Did you take a sleeping pill?'

'Well, no. I thought –'

She never sleeps without one. She can't. Unaided sleep hasn't been possible for her within my living memory.

'I'll bring you one now.'

'Maybe that would be best. Thank you, dear.'

Scarlet and blue capsule, and a glass of water. She is lying propped up on three pillows. She has washed off her powder and what little lipstick she uses, but she's brushed her hair, I see, coaxed it into grey lace around her head, so that although wan she looks her best. Very touching. Oh – can I possibly be this mean? She might really have been ill when I was out, and might have died, and then I would have been forever in the wrong, not so much for going out but for feeling this way, for letting myself.

'Did you have a nice time dear, really?'

'Quite nice, thank you. Sure you're all right now?'

73

'Quite sure. Goodnight, dear.'
'Goodnight.'

Finally I'm in my own room and can be by myself at last. It is not at all likely that I will see him again. If I think this now, it will make it easier for me, later, when it happens that way.

FIVE

The phone. If only I can reach it before Mother does. In the hall mirror I can see this giraffe woman, this lank scamperer. Slow down, Rachel. Yet I know now the phone is within my easy grasp, and I could pounce for it if I had to. I can't be thinking this way. It isn't like me.

Mother is in the living-room, dusting in small feathery strokes as though the duster were a chiffon handkerchief and she were waving it from some castle window. She is pretending not to be listening. I swear I'm going to get an extension cord put on this damn phone so I can take it into my bedroom. I won't, though. How could I ever explain it in any way she could accept?

'Hello – '

'Hello. Rachel?'

'Oh. Calla. Hello.'

'Are you all right, Rachel?'

'Of course I'm all right. Why shouldn't I be?'

'Oh, I don't know. You sounded kind of – well, I guess it was just in my mind that you might not be well or something, as I haven't seen you since holidays started.'

'No, I've been quite all right. Just – you know – busy.'

'Well, I've been wanting to phone you, but I sort of thought that you might be busy – '

She expects me to say something. I won't. Why does she have to phone me? Why can't she leave me alone? Maybe I shouldn't be rude to her. But if she keeps on phoning me in this way, she's asking for it, isn't she?

'Well, I *was* busy. That's what I said.'

I didn't intend to sound quite so snappish. But it's her lookout. She's asking for trouble. What does she think I am, anyway? Suddenly I'm terribly angry at her, so angry that I can hardly keep from putting the phone down, slamming the receiver.

'I was just wondering,' Calla says, 'if you'd like to go to a movie tonight. Or any time this week. Or next week.'

There is a hesitance in her voice, something that has been there ever since that night. She never used to sound this way, but now she has to. Now she feels compelled to beg my pardon over and over again. I hate this. I ought to feel — what? Pity? No. Liberal-minded people feel compassion — it's nicer. But all I feel is nothing. Only the desire for her to go away, and for myself not to have to be bothered, not to have to deal with this. Strangely, the anger is gone.

'I'd like to go, Calla, but I don't think I can for a while. I'm — I'm going to take an extension course in English, and I'll be pretty well tied up with that for the rest of the month.'

'You shouldn't work all the time, Rachel.'

'I want to get it done. That's the only way I can work. I want to concentrate on it. I must.'

I can hear my voice rising as I speak, growing edgy and shrill, defending my right to work as though it were in her power to keep me from it. And for a non-existent course. I didn't want to tell lies. She forced me.

'All right,' Calla says, with extreme quiet. 'Okay. I get the point.'

Oh God. She does, too. She doesn't believe there's a course, not for a second. She knows I would have had to register for a correspondence course, with the university, long before now, and that I would have mentioned it months ago.

'Listen, Calla — I'll phone you, eh? In a little while. When I'm — when I've got things straightened out.'

'Yeh. Sure, Rachel. Okay.' Her voice sounds drab, unresisting.

'When do you go to your brother's?' I must take some interest; I must at least be polite.

'I'm not going there this summer. Two of his kids have chickenpox, and I've never had it.'

'Won't you be going away at all, then?'

'No. I'm kind of—oh, I don't know—tired, I guess. I thought I'd just do nothing much. Anyway, I promised to help re-paint the woodwork at the Tabernacle.'

The first she's mentioned the place since that night. I have to say something. I must. Only to let her see it doesn't matter to me—I've forgotten it—it was nothing, nothing of any importance. But my hands have tightened and I can feel the phone receiver slimy with sweat.

'Oh. That's nice. How is the Tabernacle these days?' Idiotic. As though I were asking after her aunt's health.

'Pretty good, thanks.'

'I always meant to ask you—' Horribly, I can hear my squeaking giggle, 'if you ever—you know—spoke in tongues—'

'No. That hasn't happened. The gift hasn't been given to me.'

Her voice is grave and sad, just as though something really had been withheld from her, something real, some kind of grace. Senselessly, this frightens me. Can't I get away now? Haven't we talked long enough?

'Well—I'll give you a ring, Calla.'

What a stupid way of saying you'll phone anyone. There's an ambiguity about the phrase that seems both silly and sinister. I won't say that again.

'Fine. Don't work too hard, Rachel.'

'No, I won't. Good-bye.'

Did she mean that last remark as a crack? It doesn't matter. But now I see I'm stuck with the lie, and will have to invent complicated explanations to cover it.

> *Oh what a tangled web we weave*
> *When first we practise to deceive*

Mother's voice, lilting and ladylike, telling me that as a child. I can't remember what my sin was, only the burden of listening to the jingle, knowing she would never smack me and get it over with, because she never did – that wasn't her way. She used to tell me over and over how my misdemeanours wounded her. They also hurt Jesus, as I recollect. Well, poor Jesus. No doubt He weathered it better than I did.

Why couldn't it have been Nick who phoned?

That's nonsense. I didn't expect him to. He won't. Why should he?

I don't know whether I want to see him or whether I only want to correct the impression he must have of me.

'Rachel – '

'Yes?'

'I wasn't listening,' Mother says, 'but I couldn't help hearing you mention some course or other. You never told me about it.'

'It's not definitely settled yet. I was only considering it.'

'Well, of course it's your own business, dear. I mean, you don't have to tell me what you're doing. It's just that it seems a little odd, never to mention it.'

'I'm sorry, Mother. It's just that it wasn't definite.'

'Of course, dear, I quite understand. It's perfectly all right. It isn't as though I expect you to tell me everything you do. I mean, after all, it is your life, isn't it? It's just that it seemed rather a peculiar thing to keep quiet about. I mean, it isn't as though there were any reason to conceal it.'

'Please, Mother. Let's not have a scene about it. Please.'

'Scene? Of course not. I'm not annoyed, Rachel – you mustn't think that. I couldn't be annoyed over a thing like that. A little hurt, perhaps. But there. It's probably foolish to feel that way. You have a perfect right to keep anything secret if you want to – '

'It wasn't a secret. It was – oh, never mind. I'm sorry. I just never thought, I guess. I'm sorry.'

'Never mind, dear. Everyone's thoughtless at times, I guess. I can't expect—'

This is our conversation. This is the way we talk, the way we go on.

It's been a week now since I went out with him. A week ago today. I don't know why I even bother to think about it at all. It isn't as though I ever expected him to ask me out again. He's probably taking out some teenager now. Someone pretty, and obliging. And poised. A girl who is able to do everything easily.

Once in spring I was walking in the fields on the hillside just beyond the cemetery. There was snow, still, in the small hollows where the sun had not reached, snow latticed with the earth specks that never show until the drifts begin to melt. At the edge of the cold black-veined whiteness, in among the stalks of last year's grass now brittle and brown like the ancient bones of birds, the crocuses were growing, the flowers' faint mauve protected by the green-grey hairs of the outer petals. I crouched to pick some, scraping away the dead grasses and the soiled snow. Then I looked up and saw, at the foot of the hill, in a poplar bluff, only a few yards away, the boy and girl. They'd be sixteen, perhaps. I knew them both, although their names were gone. They'd been children of mine, once. The girl had opened her coat and put it around him, and they were private and close together in their shelter. I was the intruder. They didn't move apart or look away. They regarded me with unstartled eyes. And then I wondered how I must look to them, squatting here as though I'd had kidney trouble and had to go on this open hillside. Or else as though I were looking at them on purpose, a peeping Thomasina. In a torment of embarrassment, I called out, 'I just came here to look for crocuses.' It was the boy who replied, 'Yeh,' he said. 'Us, too.' Then they could not hold back their laughter any longer, and while they laughed I could see despite the tent of her coat that he had spread his legs and was holding her between them.

I got away somehow, marvelling at the webbed ironies. They hadn't intended cruelty. They likely would only have said, afterwards, 'Did you see the look on her face? Aw, never mind—she's just jealous', never actually suspecting it might be so, interpreting it really as my disapproval. And I recall myself walking back up the hill road into Manawaka that day, wondering if people would see something in my face or if they would merely say, 'There's Miss Cameron— she's always going on walks by herself.' I could see myself like that, on every side road and dirt track for miles around, over the years. *I wandered lonely as a cloud*—like some anachronistic survival of Romantic pantheism, collecting wildflowers, probably, to press between the pages of the *Encyclopaedia Britannica*. I wish I could forget that day, and those kids, but I can't. Such moments are the ones that live forever.

I don't know what to do with myself. In winter I always say how much I need the sun, yet here it is July, and I'm free, and the sun is high and is blazoning warmth everywhere, and I haven't set foot outside the house all day.

'Where are you going, Rachel?'

Mother is sitting at the living-room window, her favourite post of vigilance these days. She watches Japonica Street like a captain on the bridge of a ship, watching the ocean and hoping for some diversion. She almost yearns for funerals. They create a miniature parade on the street, and she can overhear the voices from the Funeral Chapel below. Well, she's got little enough to entertain her. I ought to take her for a walk. I took her out yesterday and she was so slow. It's not her fault. I must not be impatient. It's not fair; it's not right. I must be more patient. Also, more cheerful. I'm not cheerful enough with her.

'I thought I'd just walk downtown and get some ice cream for supper. Would you like to come along?'

'I don't think so, dear. I'm played out today. I don't know what it can be. That long walk yesterday, maybe. I think it's exhausted me.'

'Oh – I shouldn't have taken you so far.'

'Well, never mind, dear. You were enjoying it – I didn't want to suggest turning back.'

Oh God. Again. I can feel myself beginning to grow dizzy, as though a leather thong had lassoed my temples.

'I'm sorry. I should have noticed. You rest now, then. Is there anything you want, before I go?'

'Oh no. I'm perfectly all right, dear. I've got my magazine. And I'll make myself a cup of tea, later on.'

'I'll be back by then.'

River Street, and there is Willard. He isn't strolling, like everyone else, in the lethargic afternoon. His short form hurtles along the sidewalk. No concessions must be made to the sun – that would be the rot setting in, he thinks. Will he stop or will he catapult past, without seeing me?

He stops and smirks, and for a second I can glimpse his bustling as only sadly absurd. But what about the day he strapped James, and my own stumbling into that betrayal? I have to be wary.

'How are you, Rachel? You're looking well. Holidays agree with you, eh?'

What does he mean by that? I mustn't be so suspicious.

'I'm fine, thanks.'

'I hear you met our mutual friend, after all.'

'What?'

'Prairie drums,' he says. 'News carries, doesn't it? That's what they used to call smoke signals, if my memory of history serves me correctly – prairie drums. No, actually, Angela happened to see you in his car last week.'

'Oh.'

So it was Nick who was at Willard's the evening I refused to go. I might have met him a month earlier. But it wouldn't have been any good. I'm always off-balance at Willard's house, with Angela pouring perfumed graciousness all round.

Angela, naturally, would just happen to see. She is the

81

reverse of those three wise monkeys that used to be a paper-weight on my father's desk. Angela hears all, sees all, and tells the whole works. I must not think this way. I've always hated that about Manawaka, but I've grown the same, bounded by trivialities.

'He's a bit of a joker, I thought,' Willard is saying. 'Mind you, I'm not suggesting he isn't a perfectly nice fellow. But he strikes me as not being very serious. Wouldn't you agree?'

'I don't know him all that well.'

'Never mind, maybe that'll be remedied, eh?'

As I walk on, I don't seem to be seeing the street. I can smell the dust that is blown along the sidewalk by the incessant summer wind. I can hear the store awnings fluttering and flapping like the exhausted wings of pelicans. And I can feel, still, the innuendo in Willard's voice.

Home. As I'm walking up the steps, the phone rings. Mother answers it.

'Who? No, I'm sorry. She's out.'

'I'm here!'

'Oh. Wait a moment. She's just come in.'

The receiver is in my hands. Hello.

'Hello—Rachel? Hi. I was wondering if you're going to be busy tonight?'

'No. No, I'm not.'

'Can I see you, then?'

'Yes. Yes, I guess so. Yes, that would be nice.'

Afterwards, I have to go into my bedroom and close the door. A perfectly ordinary occurrence. I'm not worked up in the slightest. I'm quite glad he phoned, that's all. It's not of any real importance.

It's not only my hands that are shaking. My nerves pull me like a papier mâché doll jerked by a drunken puppet-master. How the boy and girl in the valley would laugh. I won't do this. I won't. There's no sense in it, no reason.

I can be poised, good company, gay. Men don't like women to be too serious. Is that true, and who told it to me first? My sister, likely. She used to go to every Saturday evening dance from the time she was sixteen. It never bothered her. Or if it did, she never said. She used to tell me what they had said to her, how they had said please please please. I used to wonder if it were all true or if she had embroidered. I guess I never really doubted it was true for her. I wonder how she managed to draw that response from them, invariably instead of occasionally.

Could a person be Calla's way, without knowing it, only it might be obvious to a man, say, or at least sensed, and then he wouldn't – no that's impossible. It's mad. I must not.

What will I wear?

'The movie doesn't seem very promising,' Nick says, half apologetically. 'Would you just as soon go for a drive?'

He's wearing a dark-green sports shirt and grey flannels, no tie or jacket. The evening is saturated with heat, and still almost as light as noon. He drives along the highway, out of town, and then on to a side road that dawdles through bluffs of poplar with their always-whispering leaves that are touched into sound by even the slightest wind, and choke-cherry bushes with the clusters of berries still hard and green, and matted screens of wild rose bushes with nearly all their petals fallen, only the yellow dying centre remaining.

'This road leads to the Wachakwa.'

'Yeh, I know,' Nick says. 'I haven't been down around the river in years. I thought I'd like to have a look at it again. My brother and I used to come here a lot when we were kids.'

'I'd forgotten you had a brother. Didn't he – ?'

'Yes.' Nick's interrupting voice.

He doesn't want me to talk about it. I should have realized and said nothing. He thinks I'm tactless. Stefan Kazlik died, but I don't remember how. That was years ago. They couldn't have been more than eighteen. *They* –

'Oh. I remember now. You were twins.'

'That's right,' he says grudgingly. 'But not identical.'

'What difference does that make?'

'Oh, I don't know. I used to be glad we weren't the same, that's all. How would you like there to be someone exactly the same as yourself?'

I've never thought about it. Would it make a person feel more real or less so? Would there be some constant communication, with no doubt about knowing each other's meanings, as though your selves were invisibly joined?

'I don't know whether I'd like it or not. You'd never feel alone, at any rate.'

'That's what I wouldn't care for,' Nick says. 'Even with Steve and myself, people used to group us together, although we were quite different. He never seemed to mind. He just laughed it off. But I hated it.'

'Why?'

'I don't know. I just did. I wanted to be completely on my own. And then it happened that way.'

What is he thinking? His voice is hard, cold, flat, nothing in it to give himself away. Did he reproach himself, when it happened, for having once wanted to be the only one? Was he surprised at how bereft he found himself? Or was he relieved, inadmissibly, and has never since been able to forget that relief or forgive himself for it? I can't tell. I can't tell at all what he's thinking. I never can, not with anyone. Always this futile guessing game.

He stops the car.

'Here's the place. Let's go down by the river for a minute, eh?'

The barbed-wire fence is slack, and Nick holds the two top strands wide apart, with foot and hand, while I slide through, trying not to snag the blue folds of my dress on the metal thorns. I never wear high-heeled shoes because of my height, and this is fortunate. The pasture is hillocked, filled with stumbling-places, gopher holes, stones. The rough sparse grass is not high except in tufts here and there. Beside the river, though, it is different. The grass is thick and much

84

greener. The willows grow beside the Wachakwa, and their languid branches bend and almost touch the amber water swifting over the pebbles.

Am I naïve to have come here so readily? Or am I naïve to imagine he might be thinking of anything except a half-acknowledged pilgrimage to a remembered place?

He is so apart. He walks purposefully, but as though he were alone. Probably he is. Why ask me to come here, then? Because it would look stupid to walk here by himself? But he wouldn't think that. He's not that sort of person. I don't know what sort of person he is. He doesn't reveal much. He only appears to talk openly. Underneath, everything is guarded. What do I expect? Why do I want to go so quickly, to get to know what he really feels? I don't speak openly to him. But I could. I might. My God, you've only seen the man twice, Rachel. Show some sense.

Yet I've touched him, touched his face and his mouth. That is all I know of him, his face, the bones of his shoulders. That's not knowing very much.

He stands beside the river. I don't know what to say, what remark to make. I'm sure I don't know why I came here. He didn't want me to come. Anyone else would have done as well, just for the company. Is it like that? I feel I must be taller than he, and this is excruciating, until I force myself to look at him and see it isn't so. As I knew it wasn't, really.

Nothing is clear now. Something must be the matter with my way of viewing things. I have no middle view. Either I fix on a detail and see it as though it were magnified — a leaf with all its veins perceived, the fine hairs on the back of a man's hands — or else the world recedes and becomes blurred, artificial, indefinite, an abstract painting of a world. The darkening sky is hugely blue, gashed with rose, blood, flame pouring from the volcano or wound or flower of the lowering sun. The wavering green, the sea of grass, piercingly bright. Black tree trunks, contorted, arching over the river.

Only Nick's face is clear. Prominent cheekbones, slightly

slanted eyes, his black straight hair. Before, it seemed a known face because I knew the feeling of it, the male smell of his skin, the faint roughness along his jaw. Now it seems a hidden Caucasian face, one of the hawkish and long-ago riders of the Steppes.

I'm dramatizing. To make all this seem mysterious or significant, instead of what it is, which is embarrassing, myself standing gawkily here with no words, no charms of either kind, neither any depth nor any lightness.

He sits down on the grass, and because I don't know what else to do, I sit down beside him, arranging my cotton dress with a primness I despise and yet can't avoid. Then I see he hasn't noticed anything. His mind is on something else. He laughs, a dismissing laugh, shrugging.

'Pointless to come here,' he says. 'I don't know why I wanted to see it, this particular place. There's nothing for me here now. I knew it, of course, but that never stops anyone. These treks back – they make me sick, to tell you the truth. I always swore I'd never do it.'

'Why not? What's the harm? Isn't it natural to want to see some place you've been fond of?'

'I don't have a clue what's natural and what's unnatural,' he says cheerfully. 'I wasn't fond of it. It was neutral territory, that's all, and if any of the other kids ever came around, Steve and I used to scare them off. We had slingshots, and we were both pretty good, Steve especially. We never had a twenty-two. That used to burn me up. The old man wouldn't let us have one. He always had this belief that all weapons were illegal, really, and he visualized one of us being toted off to jail for life for the possession of arms. Know what I mean? He knew this wasn't so, but he could never believe it. I don't know what he thought we'd do with a twenty-two – start a revolution, maybe.'

'What did you mean – a neutral place?'

'Oh, just that it wasn't the town,' Nick says offhandedly, 'and it wasn't the farm, and it wasn't used for anything, in those days, not even for pasture. Apart from the few kids

86

who made the mistake of encroaching, I never saw anybody here except sometimes hoboes, and we didn't mind them. They didn't have much place anywhere, either.'

All this sounds so strange to me that I can hardly believe it. But when I turn to him, and look, he looks away.

'Rachel,' he says, as though trying out my name to see how it will sound. 'Rachel Cameron. You must think I'm nuts. We'll change the subject. I got off on this track the last time I saw you, too. I certainly didn't mean to. Hardly a soul I used to know is left here now—you know? They've moved, and different people have come, and—anyway, that's no excuse for shooting off my mouth to you. At one time I would've dropped dead rather than talk like this. At least I've changed some, thank Christ. Mellowed, as I like to think, although this may be some vast conceit.'

Neutral territory—that was what he needed then. Some place that was neither one side nor the other.

'Nick—I never knew you'd felt like that, in those days. I always thought—'

'Go on. What did you think? This interests me.'

'I envied you, I guess. I don't mean you, especially. People like you.'

'People like me?' He is grinning now, and I sense that he means to hurt. 'There isn't anybody like me, darling. What you're trying to say is you envied Ukrainians. What I would like to know is why.'

'Because—I don't know—in comparison with the kids at my—'

'At your end of town. It's okay. You can say it. It's not blasphemy.'

'Yes. All right. Well, you—I mean, they—always seemed more resistant, I guess, and more free.'

He laughs, and for the first time touches me, putting a hand on my shoulder and sliding it lightly down my arm.

'More free? That's a funny thing to say. How did you think we spent our time? Laying girls and doing gay Slavic dances?'

'I didn't mean that.'

'How, then?'

'I don't know how to express it. Not so boxed-in, maybe. More outspoken. More able to speak out. More allowed to – both by your family and by yourself. Something like that. Perhaps I only imagined it. You always think things are easier somewhere else. I used to get rides in winter on your dad's sleigh, and I remember the great bellowing voice he had, and how emotional he used to get – cursing at the horses, or else almost crooning to them. In my family, you didn't get emotional. It was frowned upon.'

Nick lies back in the grass. But his hand still rests on my arm.

'That's the most talking you've done so far, Rachel. Did you know that?'

'No. I didn't –'

'I'm a tactless bugger, to mention it. I'm sorry. Well, I see what you mean, and in a way you're right, I suppose, although at one time I wouldn't have seen it. Argument never seemed much of an advantage to me then. My uncle lived at Galloping Mountain, and whenever he came down here, which luckily wasn't more than two or three times a year, he and my dad would nearly kill each other. My uncle – my mom's brother – was never actually a Communist, but he was pretty far left, you know, and the chief tenet of his belief was that it was a good thing for the Ukraine to be part of the U.S.S.R. My dad held the opposite view. He still believes the Ukraine should be a separate country. Incredible, eh? But that is his opinion, and he'll never change it, not ever. The two of them didn't just argue – they engaged in vehement verbal battle, storming away at each other like a couple of mastodons. Steve never minded – he was a lot more easygoing than I was. But it used to irk me like anything, because it was so pointless. Once I remember telling my dad I couldn't care less what the Ukraine did – it didn't mean a damn thing to me. That was true. But I shouldn't have said it. Actually I wish now that I hadn't.'

88

'Was he angry?'

'Yes. But that didn't matter. He was angry at me half his time, anyway. No—it was just that it hit him. It was something he couldn't accept, in the same way he couldn't ever accept the fact that I never learned to speak Ukrainian. My mom was born in this country, and she spoke English to us. My dad tried for quite a while, but finally he gave up and spoke English, too, and this put him at a great disadvantage with us, although he never admitted it, maybe not even to himself. By him, not even the Queen speaks better English than he does. He has this gargantuan faith in himself, and I don't know even yet if it's real or just some kind of barricade. I hope to God I never find out, either.'

'It's too bad, though, that you never learned his language.'

'Well, it had its points,' Nick says. 'My grandmother came over when Dad came, and she lived with us until she died. She was a female warrior-type and sour as a crab-apple. But whatever her disapproval was, it passed right over our heads. How many kids are lucky enough not to be able to exchange a word with their dear old grandmothers?'

He has this streak of flippant bitterness that I can't reply to. I don't know how to interpret it.

'We've talked enough for now,' he says. 'Don't you think so, Rachel?'

We are kissing as though we really were lovers, as though there were no pretence in it. As though he really wanted me. He lies along me, and through our separate clothes I can feel the weight of his body, and his sex. Oh my God. I want him.

'Let's get rid of some of these clothes, darling,' he says.

I'm not good about physical pain. I never was. And how it would shame me, to have him know it hurt, at my age, with only one possible reason for it. I can't. Maybe it wouldn't hurt. The membrane went years ago—I made sure of that, thinking I won't have my wedding night ruined. What a joke. It would hurt, all the same. It would be bound to. I can't let him know that about me. *A woman's most precious*

89

possession. My mother's archaic simper voice, cautioning my sixteen-years' self, and the way she said it made me want to laugh or throw up. But I was neither one way nor another, not buying her view but unable to act on my own. It would have been better for me if I'd wanted to keep myself withheld, or else could have rid myself easily of that unwanted burden with the first boy who asked. The first boy who asked wasn't very insistent, though. I wish he had been. I wasn't more or less afraid then. Just the same. Only then I had more time.

'What's the matter, darling?' Nick's voice, puzzled. 'You want it, too. You know you do.'

His eyes are smiling in a bewildered way. He can't fathom my hesitance. I'm not a child, after all, not a young girl. What in hell is the matter with me? I can't take off my clothes in a field. What if someone saw?

'I can't—here.'

'I told you—no one ever comes to this place.'

'That was years ago.'

'Oh darling,' he says, quite gently, but smiling some reproach, 'it's as private as the grave. What more do you want?'

> *The grave's a fine and private place*
> *But none, I think, do there embrace.*

That's why he said that, maybe. My mother said, 'One thing about your father, he was never one to make many demands upon me, that's one thing you could say for him.' And I thought how terrible for him, the years and years.

'Not everything, Nick. Not my slip.'

'All right, darling. Have it your way.'

In the mind, in that deep theatre, no one ever had to stumble through the awkward acts of undressing. The clothes vanished by themselves. I don't want to watch him, although God knows he does it neatly, slithering out of his grey flannels like a snake shrugging off its last year's skin. No, not a snake, of course.

90

Naked, he's warm and cool. The smoothness of his skin, and the light roughness of the hair along his thighs and between his legs. His sex, unfamiliar and giant and real. Now nothing matters and I am not afraid of anything and nothing is around us, only the dark blue of the night, and I will never again be afraid of anything and he does want me after all.

'Put it in, darling.'

His low voice, speaking some words, and then I realize that if I wanted to change my mind now, I couldn't. It has to be done. But—I hadn't thought or considered or remembered until this instant—

'Nick—you haven't—you know, taken any—'

His mouth searches my face, my eyes.

'Haven't you, Rachel?'

'No. No. I thought—'

I thought the man always would. Not so? Or not any more? Any seventeen-year-old would have known that. I don't know what I'm doing here. I don't want—

'Did you think I went around like a Boy Scout, darling,' he says, 'always prepared?'

I can't bear his anger, if that's what it is. Not now. Not like this. And yet it angers me, too.

'Did you think *I* did?'

'Sh, Sh, darling. It's all right. Don't worry. I won't go off in you.'

A brief searing hurt, and then his sex is in mine and I can feel him piercing warmly, unhurtfully. And—oh, Nick, I can't help this shuddering that is not desire, that's something I don't understand. I don't want to be this way. It's only my muscles, my skin, my nerves severed from myself, nothing to do with what I want to be. Forgive me. Forgive me. Then—

'Oh hell, darling,' he says. 'I meant to get out before that happened, but I—'

I don't care. I don't care about anything, except this peace, this pride, holding him.

'Never mind.'

'Well, you were so worried, before. You'll—take care, when you get home?'

'Yes.'

But I wish he wouldn't talk about it. I'm hardly aware of what he's saying.

'You didn't make it, did you, Rachel? You were pretty tense, darling.'

The peace is gone. I turn my head away from him.

'Yes, I know. I'm sorry.'

'It doesn't matter. It's never much good the first time.'

'Was it so obvious, then?'

'Was what so obvious, Rachel?'

'That it was the first time, for me?'

Now he is the one who turns away.

'Don't say that, Rachel. You don't have to. It's not necessary. Let it be, just as it is. Don't worry—I don't think you're a tramp.'

I can't see what he means. Then I realize. When he said *the first time*, he meant the first time two people were with each other. He doesn't know I never was, before, with anyone. The relief of this realization is so great that for a moment I can think of nothing else. Then the other thing strikes me. He believes I was lying to him, out of some false concern for—what? *My reputation—I've lost my reputation.* Who said that? Some nitwit in Shakespeare. Nick doesn't know—he doesn't know how I've wanted to lose that reputation, to divest myself of it as though it were an oxen yoke, to burn it to ashes and scatter them to the wind. I want to laugh, to rage at him for thinking me a liar, to— Hush. Hush, Rachel. This won't do. Not now. Not here.

The world spinningly returns, the soft scraping of branches against one another in the darkness. Then I see there is no darkness, really, all around us. It's a full moon. Anyone could see.

'Hey, what's the matter, darling?'

But I've shoved him from me with all my strength. Getting into my clothes again takes an hour, an aeon.

'What's the hurry?' he says. He is still lying there in the grass, grinning lazily.

'I've got to go home now, Nick.'

'Oh, do you? All right, then.'

As we drive back, the night seems unbearably warm, the air glutinous and sugary with the heat and the smell of grass and weeds that still clings around us. He drives with one arm around me, and I want to draw closer to him to have him hold me so reassuringly that nothing can ever go wrong again. But I must not move closer to him. He's driving. It would be dangerous. What if we were in an accident, and I were found with my hair all disarranged and my lipstick gone and my dress creased and crumpled?

'Here we are,' Nick says. 'I'll phone you, eh?'

'Yes.' Without thinking, I've put my arms around him, held my face to his, asking to be kissed.

'Oh – Rachel, listen.'

'What is it?'

'You'll – fix yourself, next time, won't you? It's better that way.'

'Yes.' But I can't look at him, can't speak of it like this. Not yet. Give me a little time. I'll get used to it, to this practicality, these necessities, this coldness. Why should this hurt? What do I expect? To have him say he loves me? That he'll never say. He doesn't like people telling lies.

'Are you all right, Rachel?'

'Of course. Why do you ask?'

'I don't know. You look a little strained.'

'No, I'm all right. Good night, Nick.'

'Good night, darling. I'll see you.'

Mother is awake. Of course. Anything else would have been too much to hope for. The instant she hears me on the stairs she flicks on her light. What if she comes out into the

93

hall and sees me like this, dishevelled? I will not be quizzed. I won't be. I'll refuse.

'That you, Rachel?'

'Yes.'

Who does she think it is – the Angel of Death? But maybe that's precisely what she did think. Maybe she has been lying there for hours, listening for uncertainties in her heart's beating. Or worrying about me. She cares about me. I matter to her.

'I'll be there in a minute, Mother. Would you like some cocoa?'

'That would be nice, dear. And I think I could manage a little slice of toast, while you're on your feet.'

Into the bathroom, quickly, to re-do my makeup and hair. There. Now I look neat, usual. And yet, when I'm in her room and handing her the tray, I avoid the querulous fragility of her face, the over-brightness of her eyes rimmed with the shadows of sickness or disappointment. I cannot look at her. She wouldn't know at all; no explanation could ever get through to her. There are three worlds and I'm in the middle one, and this seems now to be a weak area between millstones.

At last she's settled and I can go to bed. I haven't begun to think yet. I've been saving that for when I am alone.

I wish I could tell my sister.

Right now, I'm fantastically happy. He did want me. And I wasn't afraid. I think that when he is with me, I don't feel any fear. Or hardly any. Soon I won't feel any at all.

He thought I lied to him.

I couldn't tell him I hadn't. At least it's better than having him know the absurdity of the truth. But I wish he didn't think I had lied. How could I have been so dense, when he said, 'It's never much good the first time'? I should have seen what he meant. If I had, then the matter of telling lies wouldn't have arisen. Damn. Damn. Why didn't I see? It was quite obvious.

He said, 'You were pretty tense, darling.' Yes. More than

I knew, even? I don't know how one is supposed to be. I don't know what other women are like. Of course he would be comparing. *Tense.* All my actions jagged, jerky, spasmodic, convulsive? I didn't do well. I must have been – no, I won't think of it. I can't. I can't think of anything else. But he said 'Next time – '. God, please. Even if only once more. So I can make up for it. So I can cancel out the clumsiness. Please.

I don't know why a person pleads with God. If I believed, the last kind of a Creator I could imagine would be a human-type Being who could be reached by tears or bribed with words. *Say please, Rachel, it's the magic word.* Mother.

Please, God, let him phone.

And the way I rushed off like that. *What's the hurry?* He was amused. No wonder. Crash! And I'd pushed him away and flashed into my clothes as though there were an unseen audience ready to hoot and caw with a shocking derision. Someone might really have come along, though. Just because the place wasn't much frequented when Nick was a kid, that doesn't mean it's the same now. Someone might very easily have come along. I couldn't have borne that. *What's the hurry?* Oh Christ, I might at least not have done it the way I did. I can see myself now, the frenetic haste, like a person in some early film, everything speeded-up comically.

I must not think. And now I remember. He said, 'You'll take care of yourself when you get home, won't you?' I can't. I haven't got anything. Has Mother? Somewhere, undoubtedly, some antique contraption. A red tube like a catheter, a bag like a rubber udder. The coldness of my nausea is like a stone in my guts. No. I won't get worked up over details. I can't afford that, not any more. Would Mother have kept it? That's the only important question at the moment. She never throws anything away. But where would it be? I can't rummage around now, that's plain. I can't think straight.

What if it happens? When am I due? Not for another two weeks. That's the worst time, too, the most likely, right in the middle of the month. What if? That's crazy. It's stupid to worry. It hardly ever happens the first time. What would I do, though? What would become of me? Maybe—

No, he wouldn't. Anyway, who would want anyone on those terms? A life is too long for reproach. That would be worse than any alternative.

You'll fix yourself? How can I? Listen, Nick—you don't understand. How can I get what is necessary? Doctor Raven has known me since I was a child. I can't see myself going to him. It's out of the question. Or going to the Manawaka Pharmacy, where everybody knows me. How can I? He doesn't understand. He doesn't know. I'll have to tell him. He'll have to. It's up to him. What if he won't? He will, of course. But what if he won't? Then I'll just not see him again.

Yes I will, though.

SIX

'Did you see that awful rubbishy thing that's on at the Roxy this week, May?'

'No. No, I didn't. Rachel and I did intend to go, we fully intended, but Rachel's been rather tired lately, poor child. She's always just that little bit run-down for a full month after school quits. She needs to rest up. It's the only thing. What was the movie, Verla?'

'*Teenage Tigress.* Well, really, I ask you. Just junk, of course. All these awful creatures with those sloppy hair-does and not an ounce of decency or sense among the whole lot of them. I could hardly sit through it.'

'Whose deal? Oh, mine? They're not making any good movies any more, that's the whole trouble.'

'I used to like Claudette Colbert.'

'So did I. She was sweet. So natural. And such pretty hair. Let's see. I think – I think just maybe – yes, I'm going to say one spade.'

'I used to like Ruby Keeler.'

'She was years ago, Holly. Years and years ago.'

'Well, it wasn't that long ago, I don't believe. I'm no older than you are, Verla. It doesn't seem that long ago to me.'

'Florence, what are you bidding?'

'With this mean old hand, I don't know what to do.'

'Well, make up your mind, dear. Nothing venture, nothing gain. Try some of these, Holly. They're not the ordinary Bridge Mixture. These have got chocolate-covered raisins, as well. I think it's a nice addition, myself.'

'Oh, thanks, May. Just a few, then. Maureen tells me I shouldn't eat candies.'

'Mercy, why not? You've hardly gained at all, not to speak of.'

'Well, she says—'

'I'm going to pass, May. Honestly, with this hand—'

'The one next week at the Roxy is *The Doomed Women*. I can't imagine what *it* can be about. I don't suppose it'll be worth seeing. Harold says if I want to go, I can go alone. He's reading the life of Albert Schweitzer. It's very long.'

'I'll go with you, Verla, if you like.'

'Oh, are you sure, Holly? I just hate going alone. I don't feel right about it.'

The voices. Shrill, sedate, not clownish to their ears but only to mine, and of such unadmitted sadness I can scarcely listen and yet cannot stop listening.

There. That's the last of the sandwiches cut fine and bite-size. So Rachel's a bit run-down, is she? She needs to rest, eh? As if I were getting the opportunity to do anything much else. It's been a week, nearly.

So much for my practicality and my stealth, persuading Mother over to Mrs Gunn's where the garden is pleasant to sit in (this pretext flowering so naturally that I wouldn't have found it difficult, myself, to be convinced). Then running back to ransack her dresser like a she-Goth out for loot. Small blue glass bottles, once *Evening in Paris* but long since dried; a stack of heavy clotted-lace doilies she crocheted for the arms of chairs and never used, having a million others; new nylon nightgowns, pink pastel, still folded in the tissue paper, given to her by my sister each Christmas, but believed too delicate to wear—morbidly, she saves them for hospital and the last illness, so she'll die demurely; a sachet of rose petals encased in stiff mauve voile and tied with a royal purple ribbon, the petals now ruined to the appearance of bran flakes; a chocolate box filled with sepia photographs of herself, a ringleted child with enormous long-lashed eyes and prettily pursed mouth,

98

and one picture of Niall Cameron, awkwardly proud and unbelievably young in his new uniform as Private in the Artillery in 1915.

Under all the souvenirs, another one, the thing I was looking for. I took it back to my bedroom and hid it, not examining it, hardly able to pick it up for the loathing I felt. I sat on my bed and smoked and thought *This isn't the way to do it — something is all wrong here.* I won't ever be able to touch that contrivance. Anyway, it probably doesn't work, not any more. It's rotten with age, more than likely.

Let's say I tell Mother I have to go to the city for a few days. What for? I could be buying books. There are plenty of drugstores, and not a soul to know a person. Could I ask, or would I get my words confused, come out with something I never meant to say?

None of this should be, not this way. How can I be steadier? To be nonchalant would be the best thing in the world, if I knew how. It's all right for Stacey. She'd laugh, probably. Everything is all right for her, easy and open. She doesn't appreciate what she's got. She doesn't even know she's got it. She thinks she's hard done by, for the work caused by four kids and a man who admits her existence. She doesn't have the faintest notion. She left here young. She gave the last daughter my name. I suppose she thought she was doing me a favour. Jennifer Rachel. But they call her Jen.

'How about the sandwiches, Rachel? Are they ready?'

'Yes. You don't want them yet, do you? It's only eight.'

'No, I just thought I'd see how you were coming along, dear, that's all.'

'Fine. Everything is ready.'

'Oh, that's lovely, dear.'

The phone. I can't intercept her. She's too quick.

'Rachel — it's for you.'

Her voice rises in questionment. Damn. I am shaking and cannot seem to stop. Mother, her mock-diamond earrings flickering in the hall light, hands me the receiver and a blank look.

'Hello.'

'Hi. Sorry I didn't phone you earlier, Rachel. I meant to, but this place has been like a circus today. Are you busy?'

'When? Now?'

'Yes.'

In the living-room the voices mercifully begin again.

'No – I'm not busy.'

'Can I pick you up in – let's say a quarter of an hour?'

'Yes. That would be fine.'

He laughs. 'I like that polite voice of yours. I'm glad it's deceptive, though.'

'Is it?'

'Well, that's my impression. I could be wrong.'

'Although you so rarely are?'

'That's it, darling. You've got it. Well – see you.'

I have to summon Mother. She comes out looking anxious.

'What is it, Rachel? Is anything the matter?'

'No. No, of course not. It's just – well, I'm going out for a little while. With Nick.'

If she had not answered the phone, I think I would have told her Calla was ill and I had to go over there. It isn't that I want to lie to her. But she invites it, even demands it. Whoever said the truth shall make you free never knew this kind of house. Now she's upset.

'Is it that same person, Rachel?'

'Yes.'

'But it's too late to go to the movie, dear.'

If I laughed, she would be hurt, really hurt.

'We'll go to the Regal and have coffee. I like talking to him.'

'Well, dear, you do what you think best. I'd never suggest you shouldn't go. Only, on a bridge night – well, never mind. We'll just have to stop playing while I do the serving, that's all.'

'I'm sorry. Honestly. It's just that –'

100

'Oh, I quite understand, dear. You go right ahead. I know it doesn't happen very often. It's just that you're always here, on a bridge night, that's all, and it's such a help to me.'

I won't go, then—I find the words are there already in my throat, and yet I force them back. This newfound ruthlessness exhilarates me. I won't turn back. If I do, I'm done for. Yet I can't look at her, either, or see the sallowness of her face.

'Well—' her voice is like a thread of gum, stretched thin from someone's mouth until it may break and dangle, 'I guess Verla won't mind giving me a hand with the cups and things—'

'I'm sorry. I mean, to leave you like this. But I won't be late.'

'No,' she says, circling my wrist with her white sapphire-ringed hand, 'don't be, dear, will you?'

The Kazliks' place is about three miles out of town, along the gravel highway where the telephone wires hum like the harps of the wind. The house is set back from the road, indistinguishable from a thousand frame farmhouses planted among the poplars. The barn, though, is splendid and enormous, as newly white as an egg. At the front of the house someone, Nick's mother probably, has planted orange and yellow calendula, and blue larkspur and zinnias stiff and dowdy as paper flowers.

'I've never been here before.'

'No, I don't suppose you would have been.'

'How long are your parents away for?'

'Oh, just a few days, likely. My mother would like to stay a week, at least, at her brother's place at Galloping Mountain, but the old man will never stay away that long. He doesn't trust me. Jago is here, but nevertheless my dad expects to get back and find the business in ruins. Of course, he's quite right in a way. I don't know the first thing about cows, except what I remember from when I was a kid, and that was as little as possible.'

'Didn't you ever like the place, Nick?'

'I guess before I started school I did. Not after that. Historical irony – it took my father fifteen years to build up that herd of his, and I used to wish every goddam cow would drop dead.'

'What did you wish he'd been?'

'Oh – doctor, lawyer, merchant chief. Even a railwayman.'

'Or undertaker?'

'No,' Nick says with a smile, 'not that. Did it bug you?'

'Yes, I suppose so. Don't misunderstand, though. I loved my father.'

'Never mind. It's a common complaint. Come on, darling, let's go in.'

As we enter the front room, he laughs.

'Seems funny, doesn't it? Waiting until the family is out. Like reverting to adolescence.'

The room has an almost untouched look, the neatness of a living-room in a house where people congregate always in the kitchen. The furniture is old and ornate, pieces gathered with loving frugality, perhaps, throughout a quarter-century of auction sales. A walnut sideboard with a high bevelled mirror, a china cabinet plumed and scrolled woodenly and filled with objects hardly discernible behind the ruby glass. A plum-coloured chesterfield made for some giant race, curved hugely into the bow of the bay window. Then, in the midst of these known shapes, a gilt-bordered ikon, and an embroidered tablecloth with some mythical tree nestled in by a fantasy of birds, and on the wall a framed photograph of long-dead relatives in the old country, the heavily moustached men sitting with hands on knees, wearing their serge suits and rigid smiles, the women aproned elaborately and wearing on their heads black-fringed *babushkas* patterned with poppies or roses.

'Like a drink, Rachel?'

'Yes, all right.'

Now, in his own house, he seems for the first time reticent, or at a loss for words. Or else he thinks – words afterwards. How can I tell?

But when we are in his room, I can't tell him what has been on my mind, what's worrying me. It's his concern, too. I know that. But will he know it? I have to speak of it. I promised myself I would. It's essential. But I can't bring up the subject at all. It crosses my mind that I don't know him well enough. That's ridiculous, of course.

'What's the matter, Rachel?'

'Nothing. Nothing's the matter. I feel better, actually, here in this place.'

'How – better?'

'Safer.'

He laughs. 'Because of its four walls and a roof?'

'You think that's foolish, don't you?'

'Yeh, maybe. But women don't.'

Women. I'm not the only one, then, who feels that way. Nick goes to the windows and opens the curtains.

'My mother always closes them,' he says, 'to keep out the sun. It gives me claustrophobia, having a place shut up like this.'

Then he puts his arms around me.

'Come on, darling, come and lie down beside me.'

There seems to be a kind of tenderness in his voice. After a while I won't feel apprehensive any more. I can even take off my clothes without feeling very unfamiliar about it. See – I have changed.

His hands are careful and gentle and slow at first.

'You have nice small breasts, darling. You're very slender all over, aren't you?'

'I'm too thin.' Then I'm sorry I said that.

'No. I like it.'

'Do you?'

'Yes. I like you here, and here. Very delicate shoulders, too, you have. And beautiful thighs, and the skin there is – feel how soft your own skin is, Rachel, when I stroke you there?'

Am I like that? I never knew.

'You touch me, too,' he says. 'There. Put your hands there. That's good. More.'

Then I want my hands to know everything about him, the way the hair grows in his armpits, the curve of his bones at the hips, the tight muscles of his belly, the arching of his sex.

'Now, Rachel?'

'Yes. Now.' If only I can relax. Relax, Rachel.

'Relax, Rachel.'

'I'm sorry.'

'No – it's all right. Just relax, darling.'

'I'm sorry – Nick – '

'It's all right.'

But it isn't. Without wanting to, I'm holding myself away. But it hasn't hurt after all. Now there is only the swiftness of him, the heaviness of him on me, and at the final moment he does not cry out like before, but his face is so intense I can hardly look upon it, for the open tenderness I feel, seeing him so. Then it is over, and after a while he lifts his head and looks at me. With my fingers I go over the sharp outlines of his face, and touch his eyes and the unruly blackness of his hair.

'Nick – '

'Hello. Was that – I mean, did you, Rachel?'

'Yes.' This is not true, but it is true in every way that is important to me now.

Thought has to return, but it hasn't the power to threaten me, not yet. *What if?* I should be concerned. And yet the knowledge that he will somehow inhabit me, be present in me, for a few days more – this, crazily, gives me warmth, against all reason. After that, though, I'll know definitely I'm once more alone in myself. I cannot really believe I could have a child, that it would be possible. Yet Stacey told me once she never believed it for the whole nine months, with the first one, and only knew it was really true when the child was there to be seen.

Nick lights cigarettes for us both and lies beside me with his head on my breasts, and we are lazy and do not have to get up yet, and through the window I can see the grey light of the evening.

'I could at least make some coffee for you,' he says at last. 'I'm a hell of a host.'

Host. It seems an unusual word, under the circumstances.

We dress and go back down to the living-room, and when the coffee is ready we sit together within the mammoth half-moon chesterfield.

Now I can't think of anything to say. He talks so easily, when he wants, yet he does not seem bothered by silences. I'm the opposite.

'There's no samovar.'

'What?'

'They have an ikon, your parents, but no samovar.'

As I'm speaking, I can feel how uncalled-for a comment it is. Not everyone who came from that part of the world would arrive complete with samovar, for heaven's sake. Now I would give anything not to have spoken.

'What a disappointment,' Nick says. He is laughing, but only just. 'Well, to tell you the truth, my grandma started out with a samovar, but she never got it as far as this.'

'Why not?' How relieved I am, that he is doing the talking now. I'm interested, and yet it is the sound of his voice I like best, just to sit here beside him, in this security and hear his voice, whatever it happens to be saying.

'She traded it to somebody on the boat, and no one knows what she got for it. She used to claim it went for medicine for my dad, but he says he was the only one of all the steerage passengers who wasn't sick. Personally, I think it probably went for vodka to make the trip endurable. Naturally, she wouldn't say. But nobody would've blamed her.'

'They must have been terrible, the immigrant ships.'

'They were. My dad still talks about it sometimes. He can't help it. It was the great traumatic experience, the new life beginning in a reeking hold with everybody retching all

105

over everybody else, and cockroaches the size of bats, if he is to be believed. I used to get annoyed at him for talking so much about it. I was a relatively clueless kid in some ways. You can imagine, though – having to sit attentively while you heard the details for the millionth time. Well, maybe you can't imagine. I guess immigrant ships would be a little bit out of your line.'

For some reason this angers me, although it's quite true. With my father, it was the Great War, but he didn't speak of it.

'My grandfather came over on an immigrant ship, as a boy. Perhaps he used to tell my father. Or maybe he didn't – I don't suppose that would have been his way. None of it filtered down to me. So then I forget, and feel apologetic towards people like your family, that they went through all that. But so did mine – only it was longer ago, and the memory's gone now.'

'How odd you are, Rachel. Why should you feel apologetic?'

'I don't know.' And yet it was he who made me feel like that, saying it would be out of my line, as though things had been easy for the people I came from, easy back into pre-history and forward for ever. What does he know about it?

'It was a funny thing about that trip, you know,' he is saying. 'I guess all the ships were the same. Lots of the people who'd come over on the same boat kept in touch with one another for years and years afterwards. When I went to Winnipeg to college, my grandma said I had to look up a family that she and my dad had come over with. She used to hear from the Podiuks every Easter and Christmas, and my dad saw them occasionally when he went to the city, but she never went so she never saw them. Such good people, she says. My dad is translating all this for me, sternly, so I'll get the full picture. Fine people, she says, the best. All she knows of them is holding Mrs Podiuk's head, or Mrs Podiuk holding hers, while the old tub wallowed, but never mind – the voyage makes them kin for ever. Of course, quite right

106

—so it did, but I didn't see that then. They'll welcome the boy, she tells my dad—he'll be like their own son to them. This prospect didn't exactly fill me with delight. I didn't know the Podiuks from Adam, and I didn't want to. But the first week in Winnipeg, off I went—seventeen, you know, and with this strangely faulty sense of direction—I was always getting on the wrong streetcar and ending up at the opposite side of the city from where I'd intended to go. I finally found the place, a little brown stucco house on Selkirk Avenue, and here were all these thousands of young kids mobbing around the front door. Somehow the sight of them stopped me and I just stood there staring until they got really suspicious and started yelling "Whaddya want, mister?" What I wanted was to get the hell out. It seemed crazy to be looking someone up just because your grandmother had come over on the same boat. I asked them where Mr and Mrs Podiuk were, and they said—all together, you know, like a Greek chorus, this gruesome chanting—*Dead, dead, dead.* I didn't wait to see if the next generation of Podiuks was in residence. I just beat it. All I could think was how relieved I was. I was actually relieved they were dead, so I didn't have to see them. You know?'

He's easy to laugh with. Then I see that his eyes have changed, and even though he's still laughing, he's watching me.

'I talk too much,' he says. 'You should interrupt me. Do you like teaching, Rachel?'

He has asked only out of politeness. I wish he hadn't. I'd rather listen to him talking. There isn't much to say about myself, nothing that can be spoken. And yet, now when he puts his head down on my lap and props his long legs over the chesterfield's rim, I feel as though I might talk to him and he would know what I meant.

'I like it—yes, but there's something about it I can't get used to.'

'How do you mean?'

'Maybe it doesn't affect you. Your classes are older, and

when they move on, they soon move right away and you don't see them any more. But mine are only seven, and I see them around for years after they've left me, but I don't have anything to do with them. There's nothing lasting. They move on, and that's that. It's such a brief thing. I know them only for a year, and then I see them changing but I don't know them any more.'

His face looks momentarily troubled. I shouldn't have said all that. What will he think?

'You get pretty attached to them, I guess, Rachel?'

'Oh – well, I realize one isn't supposed to, and of course I don't with all of them, but there are some you can't help liking better than others, and then you feel – I don't know – it seems kind of futile.'

I saw James on the street a few days ago. I was thinking of Nick at the time, so I could almost not mind when James zoomed past without seeing me. Why should he see me? By the time he has finished grade school he'll have had eight teachers. He can hardly be expected to take much notice of that number, for evermore.

Nick frowns, looking at me now.

'It isn't a very good situation for you, Rachel.' Then, unexpectedly, he jumps to his feet. 'I think there's a little rye left – have some?'

'All right. I – I didn't really mean anything much by what I said about the kids, Nick. You must've thought it sounded peculiar.'

'No,' he says. 'I didn't think it sounded peculiar at all. Quite the opposite, in fact.'

But he wants to change the subject. He brings our drinks, and then goes rambling around looking for cigarettes.

'Jago always keeps an extra packet stashed away somewhere.'

'Where is he tonight, Jago?' The thought has just hit me, and all at once I expect to see him walk in right now. What would it matter if he did? And yet, because I've been to bed with Nick, it seems to me I'd show it. I'd betray everything in my face or by some slipped and askew phrase. But what would Jago care? It's none of his business. Yet if there were something in his face, some suggestion of the situation being furtive, I couldn't bear that. There's nothing furtive about it. I don't care who knows. I do, though. That's the trouble. If it's concealed and surreptitious, it's I who make it so.

'He's at the movies,' Nick says, glancing at me, and then I see I must have spoken with much more alarm than I meant to. 'You worry too much – you know that?'

'I know. It's very silly. But I can't seem to help it.'

'It's not exactly silly. But it's a waste of energy. Look who's talking.'

'You're not a worrier.'

'I don't strike you that way, eh?'

'No. No, you don't.'

'Well, I never thought I was, either, until I came back here this summer. I don't worry about anything that anything can be done about, you understand. Only about things I can't possibly change. That is really a waste of effort. I hadn't been back here for quite some time, as you know. I used to get them to come to Winnipeg once or twice a year. They always thought it was good of me. Good, hell. I didn't want to come back here, that was all. They used to hate those visits, although both of them put on this mighty act of having a wonderful time. My dad used to pace around the apartment and nearly die with boredom. I used to take them to movies. Once I made the awful mistake of taking them to a Russian film – that one about the young soldier trying to get home on leave, and everything goes wrong. I guess it was the Ukraine, millions of miles of nothing but wheat fields. My mother sat there bawling her eyes out, and my dad kept making loud comments about how the Reds had ruined his heart's earth. It was just great.'

'You were embarrassed?'

Nick isn't looking at me, and again I have the feeling that he's talking to himself, and yet, obscurely, he reaches out and moves his hand along my arm.

'Yeh. I was. That's what bugs me, to tell you the truth.'

He is silent. When he speaks again, his voice is low and unemphatic, and with an edge of self-mockery, as though he is warning me not to respond too seriously, and yet he cannot help saying the words aloud.

'*I have forsaken my house — I have left mine heritage — mine heritage is unto me as a lion in the forest — it crieth out against me — therefore have I hated it.*'

Then he draws away and shrugs.

'Jeremiah,' he says. 'A great guy with the gloomy phrase. Did you ever know my sister Julie?'

'She was a few years younger than I. I never knew her very well. I used to see her around town. She's married now, isn't she?'

'Yeh. For the second time. She lives in Montreal. They've got two quite nice kids, one from her first marriage. She thinks I'm a dead loss because I don't come here more often. She can't, she says — look how far away she lives, and how could she leave Dennis and the kids? All quite true.'

'My sister Stacey gives the same reason for not coming home.'

'Really? Well, how can you contradict it? What I was going to say was once when we were kids, my dad got a brainwave about painting the house. Why white, he said. Blue would be more cheerful. He used to get those free paint charts from the hardware store, and study them like he was preparing a thesis. He had the colour all picked out. It was called Robin's Egg Blue, and it was a very violent turquoise. My sister nearly threw a fit. Nobody, but nobody, had houses that colour, she said. Where in the whole of Manawaka could you see houses that were anything except white or light brown? She raised one hell of a row. According to her, the Kazlik abode was going to be the laughing-stock of the entire province. Finally my dad got fed up and didn't paint the house at all, not even white. About five years later, coloured houses came in, and every second person was dolling up their residence with Lime-Green or

110

Salmon-Pink or some such godawful shade. So Julie said very nicely why not paint the house blue, Dad? But he said no, he didn't think so, not now. I haven't thought of that in years. Do you remember what my dad used to be called, around town, Rachel?'

'No. What?'

Nick hesitates, as though he regrets having mentioned it. Then he laughs and says it quickly and lightly.

'Nestor the Jester.'

'But it wasn't meant badly—'

'He didn't mind the name. He used to play up to it. He adored it when he could get a laugh. He always thought people were laughing with him, never at him. At least, that's how he seemed to me then. Now I don't know.'

I am afraid to reply in case I say the wrong thing.

He gets up and begins roaming around again.

'I'll bet Jago's got a mickey of rye hidden behind the stove or some unlikely place.'

But he can't find any, and it's getting late.

'I have to go now, Nick, really.'

'Oh, well, all right. If you say so.'

The town is totally asleep as we drive back. We don't talk much, and then I remember something I meant to ask him.

'Was your brother the one who was always going to take over your father's place?'

'Yes. He wanted to, of course, and I didn't. But it wouldn't have made any difference even if I had wanted to. He and my dad got on well together. I guess I never realized until this summer how much older the old man is getting. He needs more help than Jago can give him now.'

'Surely he'd never suggest that you—?'

'No,' Nick says. 'He'd never suggest that. Only—well, it's kind of difficult to see what to do, that's all. He can't cope here for ever, and he'll never give it up until he drops dead. He won't hire anyone else—he refuses completely. He says it wouldn't pay him. I don't know what he's saving his

111

money for. So he can pass it on to Julie and me, I guess. I don't know about Julie, but I don't want it. Actually, he doesn't want to pass on his money, such as it is, at all. He wants to leave his place to someone who cares about it.'

'And there isn't anyone who does, now.'

'No. I wonder if a person could make themselves care about something? I guess that wouldn't be possible. It wouldn't solve anything.'

Nick couldn't make himself care about something, if he didn't. Nor about someone, either.

SEVEN

'Hello, dear. Have a nice evening? What time is it?'

She's wide awake. I swear she doesn't take a sleeping pill on the evenings I'm out. She takes benzedrine instead.

'Very nice, thanks. It's just twelve.'

'Oh, you are a Cinderella, aren't you?' Mother cries with a carolling laugh.

This coyness, with its concealed undercoat, the tint of malice, for some reason shocks me. But when I turn on her light, I see she's frightened. Why? Her face has a blanched-almond look, whitely wrinkled, unnaturally soft.

'What's the matter? Are you all right?'

'Oh yes, dear, perfectly all right. A little restless, perhaps, that's all.'

'Too much bridge, maybe.'

'I wouldn't have thought that,' she says petulantly, 'although the girls did think it was a little odd, your going off like that, not that they actually said anything.' Then, pinchingly, like a bee sting, 'was it a party, Rachel?'

'No. Why should you think so?'

'Oh, nothing. It's just that your breath is – you know. I suppose I'm a little more sensitive to that particular smell than most people.'

'I had precisely two drinks, if you want to know. Nick took me to his house – to meet his family.'

Why did I say that? Why did I have to? She'll find out, likely, and then she'll be more upset than if I'd told her straight out. She won't find out. How could she?

Her face has gone even more wan and sunken.

'Rachel—is it serious?'

'Serious?'

'Yes—I mean—'

So that's it. I ought to have seen. She's wondering—*what will become of me?* That's what everyone goes through life wondering, probably, the one absorbing anguish. What will become of me? Me.

'No, it's not serious.'

'Well, dear, I mean to say, of course it's your own life, as I've often said—'

'It's not serious. He's just—a friend. Try to sleep now. Did you take your sleeping pill?'

'Not yet, dear,' she says. Then with a cosy smile, certain she's speaking the gospel truth, 'I forgot.'

She sinks down, relaxed now, and when I give her the pill, she's all prepared to sleep, out of sheer relief.

Is it serious, Rachel?

Sitting beside my bedroom window, in the darkness, I smoke and look at the stars, points of icy light in the hot July black of the sky. If only she wouldn't question me. If only I could stop myself from answering. Why can't she ever sleep and leave me alone? Or die.

Why can't she die and leave me alone?

And if she did, it would leave me alone, all right, completely. Would that be any better? I don't mean it, anyway. I couldn't really mean that. Of course we have our ups and downs, she and I. But as for wishing anything bad to happen—

You mean it all right, Rachel. Not every minute, not every day, even. But right now, you mean it. Mean. I am. I never knew it, not really. Is everyone? Probably, but what possible difference can that make? I do care about her. Surely I love her as much as most parents love their children. I mean, of course, as much as most children love their parents.

Nick—listen—I love you.

My forehead is on the windowsill, and then finally I'm able to look up and out. I don't know what I'm doing. The

114

curtain is drawn back so the room contains the uncertain outer light, the grey light of the evening, the leaden light of the moon. And when I turn around I can see myself in the mirror, not quite see but almost, the silver fishwhite of arms, the crane of a body, gaunt metal or gaunt bird.

I can't bear it.

Listen, my love – whatever your terms – I don't make any conditions. Nick, do you know what I love about you? I love the way your voice sounds, deep but with that scepticism I used to fear and don't fear now, and the way your skin feels, and the hair that grows blackly down to your belly and around your sex, and the muscles that lie within your thighs. It was good – wasn't it?

– They are in a warm concealed place, a room but not a room, a room nowhere, very apart, locked away, no one able to knock and enter, nothing around, only this bed. The spasm of love, and then his eyes opening, and his praising voice saying –

Relax, Rachel. And I saying *I'm sorry.* There was a Hudson Bay point blanket on the bed, scarlet with one black stripe, almost as needle-textured as the grass, and the thought shot in and out of my head, why would anyone want such a heavy blanket on their bed in the very height and heat of summer?

Why did it have to be that way? All right, God – go ahead and laugh, and I'll laugh with you, but not quite yet for a while. Rachel, stop it. You're only getting yourself worked up for nothing. It's bad for you. Why bad? I've felt a damn sight better since I stopped considering my health.

That's interesting. I *have* stopped. I didn't know. The reason is so plain. Anyone looking at it from the outside could see why, and smile. Don't they think I know?

– The car, his. He turns off the engine, and they are in the quiet, and he bends towards her, but with an unforeseen deliberation, as though he's forming words in his head and hasn't quite achieved them. She has no idea what he is going

115

to say. 'Rachel, look, honey, I'm not so marvellous at saying things –'

No. All wrong. He's quite good enough at saying anything he wants to say. And he doesn't say *honey*. He says *darling*. Somebody else must have said honey, but I can't think who it could have been, or when. Maybe it was the salesman who travelled in embalming fluid. Do that part over again.

– He makes a slightly flippant thing of it, but the reality is obvious to her, the tension of him, the sureness that hides some unsureness.

'Listen, darling, do you think life as a Grade Eleven teacher's wife would be a fate worse than –'

No. He wouldn't say it like that. I don't know how he would say it. Maybe I can't imagine it only because he never would. Why not? There's nothing wrong with me. He said he liked my shoulders. And the skin of my thighs. He said –

Nothing else. He said nothing else. He told me about his grandmother's samovar. But that was my fault.

I'm out of my mind. Mad as any Grecian woman on the demented and blood-lit hills. I'm sitting here thinking of all this, when I should be doing something. I must get up now. I must go to my dresser and take out what is there. I must walk ordinarily to the bathroom, and perform the ritual ablution.

I don't know how. I have never done it. Anyway, with a thing like that – an antique – a museum piece. Imagine the kind of museum that would harbour it. Go on – laugh. Laugh, angels. Angel-makers – that's what they used to call abortionists.

> *What is woman that you forsake her*
> *To the claws of the grey old angel-maker?*

That's all wrong, of course. It's really Kipling, about the seafarers – to go with the grey old widow-maker. *I must do something about myself right now or it will be too late.* How much time have I? I don't recall what the books said. The tadpole might swim instantly to its retreat, and burrow in, for all I know.

All right. I've got the thing in my hands, the old crimson smelling of decayed rubber and the musty sterility of anti-septics that went down the drain years ago. I never heard my mother rise, at nights, and tiptoe into the bathroom. How silently she must have gone. And he, probably, turning away so he would not need to witness her returning. Blaming himself, or her, for something or other. Wasting everything in a regret as futile as deception.

There. I've got to the bathroom and she hasn't wakened. It's all right. Quiet, Rachel. It's nothing. It doesn't matter. It's to be done and ignored. There. That wasn't so difficult, was it?

Oh God – quick – I can't help it – don't let her waken and hear. Something revolts, something revolts me and revolts in me and –

It's over. Vomiting, I'm purged, calmer. Did she hear? I go back to my bedroom but I can't sleep. I have to get up and take the equipment in my hands as though it were a dead foetus, something to be rid of for ever. I can't throw it out. It would be seen in the garbage tin. I climb on my flimsy white dressing-table chair and put it into the highest shelf above my clothes cupboard, among the old hats. A small pale straw hat tumbles out, ribboned with icing-sugar pink. I had that hat when I was twelve, and it's still here.

I'll never touch that contraption again. Never. I must do something, though. I must tell him. I can't. What would he say? What on earth would he think, that I couldn't organize myself better?

Women like me are an anachronism. We don't exist any more. And yet I look in the mirror and see I'm there. I'm a fact of sorts, a fantasy of sorts. My blood runs in actual veins, which is as much of a surprise to me as to anyone.

What would become of me? I can't believe it could happen, though. A thing like that – to grow a child inside

117

one's structure and have it born alive? Not within me. It couldn't. I couldn't really believe it could ever happen.

Nick, give it to me.

It seems four in the morning, but it's not yet one. Prowlıng, I light an unwanted cigarette, and put it out again. Then, looking from my window, I can see that the light is still on, below, in the Japonica Funeral Chapel.

These stairs were carpeted the year my father died, the stairs from our apartment leading down to the ground. Grey background, and all the red roses are scuffed now from being trodden on. I can't see a thing. I couldn't put the hall light on, in case, but I know where the trampled roses are on each step, and seem to feel them under my feet. The carpet makes the stairs silent, but not silent enough. If she wakens, I'll say I forgot to lock the downstairs door.

The door into the Funeral Chapel is much wider than ours. Hector Jonas replaced my father's plain door with a shinily varnished one, fitted with wrought-iron staves and loops and swirls, so it looks like the door of a keep or a castle prison, but false, a mock-up. Ye Olde Dungeon, as in a Disney film, where even the children know that the inmates are cartoons. And yet I hesitate to knock.

Go ahead, knock. He'll answer.

He'll think I'm off my head. What am I doing here? I should be asleep. This is no place for you, Rachel. Run along now, there's a good girl. This is no place for you.

Tick – tick – tick –

My fingers on the door sound like the beating of a clock or a heart. He won't hear. *Tick – tick –* like the heart that kept pulsing under the floor in that famous and awful story, and when we listening to it being done on radio years ago, Mother said 'Turn it off'.

Footsteps – shy, suspicious, shying away from opening the door. And then the latch released.

'What the hell's going on? Who –? Well, for Christ's sake. Pardon my French. It's you, Rachel.'

Hector squints around the edge of the door, and all I see
118

of him is an anxious green eye and a pate like a pink stone, smoothly bare and vein-mottled. Then he opens the door and stands there in dubious welcome, a short rotund man in brown wrinkled trousers and shirt sleeves and indigo braces with brass adjusters.

'Can I help you?' he says, not meaning it, only unconsciously reverting to his coffin-side manner, a blend of dignity and joviality.

He's wondering what I'm doing here, and now the notion occurs to me – maybe he thinks I've long admired him from afar and now at last have gone berserk enough to declare my burning spinster passion. I can hardly stop myself from laughing out loud. Hush, Rachel. Steady.

'It's a crazy time of night to come down, Hector, but I've been so worried lately – about Mother – and I couldn't sleep, and I saw your light was on, and –'

My voice ends, and I'm standing here, tall as a shadow, transparent, shivering. Then I don't care. Only one thing matters. *Let me come in.*

'Let me come in.'

That was my voice? That pridelessness? It doesn't matter. Suddenly it doesn't matter at all to me.

Hector Jonas looks puzzled only for an instant. Then, with some decision to accept without question, some exercise of faith, he smiles as though everything were ordinary.

'Sure. I know just what you mean. I've had insomnia myself the odd time. It's murder. Come on in. I don't believe you've seen the Chapel since I did the last renovations, have you, Rachel?'

'No. I haven't. I don't think I've been in here since – oh, for a long time.'

'Show you later,' Hector says. 'Come in here for right now. You look kind of peaky. I think you need a drink.'

The sign on the door says *Private.* The work-room. Now utterly changed since Niall Cameron's day, when the green and blue glass bottles stood hunched together, unsorted and disorderly on the long cabinet, when the dust furred the

119

corners and windowsills, and when the book stood just there, among the cluttered paraphernalia and the cosmetics of death, a drab olive leather with the scarlet letter A, but in this case meaning Accounts, like the roll of Judgement. How can I remember? I couldn't have been in here more than a couple of times in my entire life. He always said, when I hovered, 'This is no place for you'. And I imagined then that it was the efficacy of the dead he feared for me, not knowing in what way they might grasp and hold me, and I wondered how he himself could stay among them, by what power, and I feared for him, too. For a long time, whenever she said 'Your father's not feeling well', I thought that was why — because he'd caught something, a partial death, like a germ, from them.

Now the place looks like a portion of a hospital. Glassed-in cases where the neat potions rest, and cabinets with the dull clean glow of stainless steel. On one wall, a jazzy coat-rack arrangement, black metal tipped with plastic bulbs of red and yellow and blue. Two white doctor-jackets are hanging there, so that Hector can perform this aspect of his duties in a sanitary way.

'Here —' he hands me the glass of rye and water, and beckons me to a chair, the only one.

'Where'll you sit, though, Hector?'

'Oh, I'll just perch here,' he says, going to the long high table, like an operating table, which stands in the middle of the room. He hops up like a dwarf, a kick of his short legs, and then he's sitting there, his eyes owling down at me.

'What's the trouble, Rachel? Anything I can do?'

'Oh no — it's nothing, really. I suppose I've been under a kind of strain at school. And Mother's health, you know —'

'Mm,' he says, as though he disbelieves every word I've said.

'Tell me about the business, Hector. You've improved things a lot.'

He looks delighted. This is his pet topic, clearly. And yet
120

he was willing to listen to anything I had to say. He would have heard me out.

'Think so?' he says. 'It's all a question of presentation, that's what I say. Presentation is All – that's what I believe. Everybody knows a product has to be attractively packaged – it's the first rule of sales – isn't that so? Well, this is a little tricky in my line of trade, as you can well appreciate.'

'Yes. Yes, I can see your difficulty.'

'It's not so much a difficulty as a challenge,' Hector says. 'What you got to decide is – what am I selling? I mean, really, when it comes right down to it, in the final analysis – *what am I selling?*'

'Death?'

'Come, come,' he says disgustedly. 'Who wants that?'

'Well, a denial of death, then?'

'Who can deny it?' Hector says practically. 'It happens.'

'That's so. All right, I give up.'

'Basically, I'm selling two things,' Hector says, holding up two fingers. 'These are as follows. One: *Relief.* Two: *Modified Prestige.* That is where I am different from the other two funeral directors in this town. They don't know what the hell they're selling.'

'Relief? Modified Prestige?'

'You don't get it?' he says happily. 'Right. I'll explain. You take the average person, now. What's their first reaction when one of their loved ones kicks off? Can you tell me?'

'Grief? Remorse? Sorrow?'

'Sure, sure, but all that comes later. Their first reaction, take it from me, Rachel, is panic – what'll we do with the body? Just like they'd murdered the guy. Or lady, as the case may be. The prime purpose of a funeral director is not all this beautician deal which some members of the profession go in for so much. No. It's this – to take over. Reassure people. Leave it all to me. I'll handle everything, from the hospital or home removal right down to the last car away from the cemetery. The family doesn't have to worry about any of the details, see? Relief. You got to get this across to

121

them. You take Calder's Funeral Home, now, at the other end of town. He actually tells people how nice he can fix their dear ones up, and all that, and he goes through the coffin catalogues with them. Depressing, I call it. Of course it does have some appeal to the older type of person. It's the old-fashioned approach. Some people still go for it. My clientele are mostly the more modern type of person. They want to know that everything's been done properly, of course, but the less they have to do with it, the better.'

'Death's unmentionable?'

'Not exactly unmentionable, but, let's face it, most of us could get along without it.'

'I don't see how.'

I'm laughing more than seems decent here in this place and yet I know it's absurd to hold back, as though there were anything hushed or mysterious here.

'Well, sure,' Hector says, nimbly bouncing down from the gruesomely hygienic table and re-filling my glass, a lot of whisky and a little water. 'Sure, I get what you mean, but you take your average person, now. It's simply nicer not to have to think about all that stuff.'

'The skull beneath the skin?'

'Well, you might put it that way, I guess. Relief, see? You can rest assured, I tell them, that every last detail will be taken care of. You don't have to decide on a thing. I give them three price ranges, and after that, it's out of their hands. None of this unpleasant business of having to dicker between oak or pine, or will it be velvet-lined or only nylon shirring? A package deal is the answer to all that.'

'You have it all taped, Hector.'

He gives me a hurt glance, his pudgy face reproachful.

'I'm not callous,' he says. 'But when all's said and done, if you're gonna stay in business, Rachel, you got to think businesslike.'

'I know. I'm sorry. I didn't mean to imply—'

'Skip it,' Hector says, dangling his legs in their crumpled brown over the edge of the surgical table. 'It's okay.'

122

'What about modified prestige?'

How surprised I am at how easily I'm talking to him. Yet in all the years he's been here, I couldn't have carried on more than a dozen conversations with him, and those were mainly concerned with the terms of our tenancy, or repairs.

'Oh, that,' Hector says. 'Well, a death in the family puts you in the public eye, for the time being. People look at you, and notice what goes on. It doesn't continue for very long, of course – that's why *Modified*, see? But while it lasts, you got to consider it. Your average guy, now, will want his dear one to have a funeral about which people will pass some favourable comment. Everything went off well at the Dinglehoofer funeral, didn't it? Floral arrangements looked very nice, didn't you think? Stuff like that. So it's got to be good taste, see, good taste all the way, with just that little extra something to distinguish one from another – like, let's say, wreaths of all-white gladioli, in season. Just some feature which people can spot and make some remark upon. Depending on price range, too, natch.'

While Hector is talking, my eyes are searching the room, and yet this is senseless. Nothing is as it used to be, and there's nothing left from then, nothing of him, not a clue.

'Did you know my father, Hector?'

'Sure, I knew him – you know that, Rachel. Not what you'd call *well*, but I knew him.'

'He didn't know what he was selling, did he?'

Hector jumps down once more and scurries around, pouring us both more rye. I must go back upstairs. Yet I'm leaning forward, waiting for what Hector will say.

'I don't guess he ever really was selling anything,' he answers uncomfortably. 'Don't get me wrong, Rachel. He was a good guy, your dad. I thought the world of him. But not so much of a business head, was my impression. I could be wrong.'

'No, you're not wrong. Why do you think he stayed, Hector? *Did he like them?*'

My voice has gone high and attenuated with some hurt I

123

didn't know was there. The one long-tubed light burns with a harsh whiteness. Everything is the same as it was a moment ago, and yet the room looks all at once different, a room set nowhere, the stage-set of a drama that never was enacted. The steel is stainless, stained with the fingerprints of shadows, and behind a glass barrier the bottles and flasks bear legends which never could be read. I am sitting here, bound by my light wrists which touch the dark arms of this chair, bound as though by wires which may become live. And on the high altar squats a dwarf I've never seen before.

Rachel, Rachel. Get a grip on yourself. Hector is looking only mildly astounded.

'You mean – did he like the stiffs?'

I hope my face conveys my gratitude. Good for him, for me. Just what I needed, some astringency.

'Yes. The stiffs.'

'I wouldn't have said that, exactly. It was a quiet life, though, and he liked being on his own. He wasn't much of a man for company, was he, your dad?'

I set my glass firmly down on the cabinet.

'He drank because he was never happy.' I'm speaking aggressively, almost furiously. 'That is why.'

Hector's eyes are lynx eyes, cat's eyes, the green slanted cat's eyes of glass marbles. Why is he looking so?

'I don't know that I'd entirely buy that one.'

'What do you mean?'

'Oh, nothing much. I never knew him well. I couldn't really say. Look, don't get me wrong. He probably did less harm than your average guy, I know that. But I would bet he had the kind of life he wanted most.'

'What?'

'You heard me.'

'Yes.'

Hector Jonas, who has for so long plied his trade below while I tried to live above. Comic prophet, dwarf seer. *The life he wanted most.* If my father had wanted otherwise, it would have been otherwise. Not necessarily better, but at least different. Did he ever try to alter it? Did I, with mine? Was that what he needed most, after all, not ever to have to touch any living thing? Was that why she came to life after he died?

If it's true he wanted that life the most, why mourn? Why ever cease from mourning?

Hector Jonas leaps elastically down from the table like a small stout athlete from a trampoline.

'I never showed you the new Chapel. C'mon. This way. Bring your glass along.'

He grasps my hand, and I'm tugged zig-zag along a corridor, into the depths. Then a door. He opens it with a sweep and a fling, as though announcing the heaped and laden treasure of every pearled Sultan that never lived. But he's forgotten the dark, so I can't see even a gem of his riches. He gropes and swears.

'Where's that goddamn light? Excuse my French. Ah, here we are.'

And there is light. The light is blue, of all things, and faint. The chapel in the blue light is as squarely shaped and unhaunted as it would be at high noon. The pews are blonde wood, of an extreme sheen, and at the front there is a platform of the same sleek blonde, the right height for placing the burden without undue strain on the pallbearers. I am astonished that there is no handy trolley or conveyor belt, but I don't mean this meanly. I would have once, but now I'm almost gay here. On low tables at either side are set candelabra as many-branched as trees, and the wax tapers in them are violet and peppermint green. The walls are done in simulated pine, paper printed with wood knots.

'I'd hate to tell you what it costs me,' Hector puffs, leading me like a bride up the aisle and taking a swig from his glass as he goes, 'but it was worth every cent of it, if I do say so myself as shouldn't. Look at that wood. Beautiful grain. Beautiful. Real veneer.'

We reach the front, and I collapse on to the hard mourners' bench where the family is meant to sit.

'It's lovely, Hector. I never knew you'd fixed it up so.'

'Not bad, eh?' he says, gratified. 'Of course, not everyone wants the service here, but more and more do. Church funerals are going out.'

'Really? Why is that?'

'Too harrowing,' Hector says, sitting beside me. 'Tend to bring up all kinds of things – heaven, hell, stuff like that. Great strain on the nerves of the bereaved. If you believe, it's a great strain, and if you don't believe, it's even worse. However you look at it, it's a real ordeal. That's why people like this place. Tasteful, and the service is short.'

'Yes, I see.'

'I must show you,' Hector says, his voice now beaming, 'I got a really super-dooper automatic organ.'

Daftly, horrifyingly, I want to say – how splendid for you, and I hope your wife appreciates it. Once at college I heard a joke about an angel who traded his harp for an upright organ. I'd like to tell this to Hector. Naturally I won't. Rachel Cameron doesn't talk that way.

'It's there, see?'

He points, and now I see the giant out-fanned music pipes, extending in a vast screen along the front wall. Each pipe is a different height, and at the top they are painted to resemble Corinthian columns.

'It plays several things,' Hector explains. 'We got *Jesu Joy of Man's Desiring* for – well, you know –'

'The carriage trade.'

'Yeh, that's it. Some people wouldn't know Bach from the Basin Street Blues. I wouldn't, myself, matter of fact. But they think it's very dignified and serious-minded, so we get quite a run on it. I won't play that for you, though. I'll play my favourite.'

'My God, Hector, you can't play that thing at this hour of night!'

'Don't you fret, Rachel,' he says. 'It's got three tones, and when it's on *Soft*, it's really soft and I don't mean maybe.

I can positively guarantee you it won't be loud enough to wake the living, ha ha.'

With that, he's off, searching for levers to press, magical buttons to touch. He darts back, stations himself again, and slides an arm around my shoulder. I don't protest or move away. I don't care. We sit together on the glossy bench in the bleak blue light, and it's gone three in the morning. Then the music rises, slowly.

> *There is a happy land*
> *Far far away —*

'What d'you think of it, Rachel?'
'Marvellous. I think it's the most marvellous thing I've ever heard.'
'You mean it?'
'Every word. Truly.'
'My gosh,' Hector says. 'Think of that.'

> *Where saints and angels stand*
> *Bright, bright as day —*

The blue light, and the chapel purged of all spirit, all spirits except the rye, and the sombre flashiness, and the terribly moving corniness of that hymn, and the hour, and the strangeness, and the plump well-meaning arm across my shoulders, and the changes in every place that go on without our knowing, and the fact that there is nothing here for me except what is here now —

'Rachel — good Christ, are you crying?'
'It's nothing. I'm sorry. I'm — I've had a certain amount of trouble, this past while.'

Hector is patting my shoulder, and making clucking noises deep in his throat.

'There, there. Never mind. It'll be all right.'

I don't deserve such comfort. Tomorrow I'll be ashamed. But not now.

'Listen,' he is saying. 'I don't know why I should say this, but you know what happens to me? At the crucial moment,

127

my wife laughs. She says she can't help it – I look funny. Well, shit, I know she can't help it, but – '

I look into his face then, and for an instant see him living there behind his eyes.

'That's – '

'Yeh, well there it is. Who would have thought it, you and me talking away like this? You better go on upstairs now, chicadee, or you'll be a dead duck.'

'Yes.' I stand up, pull myself together, gather the fragments. 'I'm – look, I'm sorry I came down, Hector. I don't know why – I don't know what I was thinking of – '

Go on, Rachel. Apologize. Go on apologizing for ever, go on until nothing of you is left. Is that what you want the most?

'No – listen, Hector – what I mean is, thanks.'

'Don't mention it,' he says. 'The pleasure was all mine.'

The music is paling. The mechanism has almost run its course. The tune is wry in the cold chapel, gapped with silences.

There is a – far far away – where saints and –
bright, bright as –

The carpeted stairs have to be climbed one at a time, only one. If she wakens, all I have to say is hush. Hush, now, sh, it's all right, go to sleep now, never fear, it's nothing.

EIGHT

His parents have come back. They came back a week ago and now I haven't seen him for a week. I saw him almost every night while they were away. No – that's not quite true. Out of fourteen evenings, I was with him for eight. But anyway, that was more than half. And now I haven't seen him for a week. What did I say? What did I do or not do, to put him off?

I must not let myself think this way. It's not as though I ever expected anything to come of it. He was here, and there wasn't anyone else around, much, and I was here, and that's all. Of course I know that. There's never been any doubt in my mind about that.

The last time, we were sitting in the kitchen afterwards, and Jago came in. I said 'Oh heavens, look what time it is – I must be going'. I couldn't sit still and talk for half an hour with Jago there. Oh no. I had to look startled, as though there had been anything to look startled about – I mean, it wasn't Jago's business, was it, and what did he care? Jago, grey-haired, solid, did not say a word. He only looked puzzled. I thought it must be my presence that made him look that way, but now I see it was my departure. How angry Nick must have been, to have me act so. No wonder he hasn't seen me since. I could have handled the situation differently. It would have been easy. I see that now.

– They are sitting in the kitchen, the two of them, drinking coffee with rum. They don't need to talk. They are quite happy, just like this. The boots outside the back door make

129

a scuffling noise – someone wiping his feet before coming in the house. 'Jago is home early tonight. He usually goes to the beer parlour after the movie's over.' 'Never mind,' she says, 'it doesn't matter now'. He is smiling – 'No, not now.' Jago enters, makes remarks about the weather – 'Due for a thunderstorm – not a breath of air anywhere tonight'. 'Too hot for coffee?' – her voice is friendly, casual, unperturbed. Jago says he guesses not, if she'll just add a slug of rum to his as well.

For a moment it really is soothing, and I can almost believe it happened that way. But the moment evaporates, and I am left with the cold knowledge of how I actually saw it happen, myself rearing up at the door sound, rising gawkily like a tame goose trying to fly. Jago saying nothing, and Nick shrugging. How could I? If only I could say to him, so he would know – look, I didn't mean to act that way. Did he see it the same way I did, or how? If only I could explain. But I can't. I tried last night. No – I will not think of that.

My hand is still on the doorbell, and now I realize it must have been ringing for some time. I'd almost forgotten where I was.

'Rachel! This is a surprise. Come on in.'

Calla is wearing lemon-coloured denim slacks and a violet blouse. She looks about ten feet broad. The lead-coloured fringe of her hair is standing up spikily all over her forehead. Her right wrist clanks with a brace of bangles, and her feet, which are grimy, slap with the rubbery sound of her royal-blue toe-thong sandals. She puts a hand out to my shoulder, as anyone might, guiding in a visitor, but immediately she withdraws it, making us both conscious of this half-gesture which probably wasn't intended as anything at all.

'I thought I'd drop in for a minute, if you're not busy.'

'I was just taking a break,' she says. 'The pause that refleshes. Coke or iced tea for you?'

'Iced tea, please. Do you really keep it on hand?'

'I put what's left in the teapot at night into the fridge,'

130

she says, 'so as not to waste it. Then it's always there. Here –
sit down, if you can clear a space somewhere.'

Everything in her living-room seems to be piled in the
middle of the room. The turquoise chesterfield; the glass-
topped coffee table; a confusion of books and letters; two
unthriving potted pink geraniums; pictures done by her
class last year on huge sheets of newsprint with poster paints
– clumsily intricate castles and ocean liners; innumerable
unemptied ashtrays; a brown pottery bowl of coffee sugar
with a brass spoon bearing a gargoyle's leering face and the
words *The Imp of Lincoln Cathedral*; a square cushion with
a yellow fringe and an ivory satin cover painted with a
towered church and the lettering *The Turrets Twain – St
Boniface, Manitoba.*

'It's slightly a shambles,' Calla says without apology. 'I'm
painting the walls. Like them?'

They are a deep mauve-blue.

'It's an unusual colour.'

'I never knew it would turn out quite so strong a shade,'
Calla says, 'but it's still wet. Maybe it'll lighten when it
dries. How have you been, Rachel?'

'Oh, fine, thanks.'

I'm not afraid when I am with him, but when I'm not with
him, it seems to return. I didn't intend to do what I did last
night. Women shouldn't phone men. Anybody knows that.
But it had been a week, nearly. If only I hadn't phoned him.
Or if he had been out, away, not available. I had to wait
until Mother was asleep, and even then I wasn't certain, and
sat in the hall beside the phone, guarding it, guarding myself, listening towards her door. I thought (why, I don't
know) that he would be the one to answer. But he wasn't.
His mother said 'Who is speaking, please?' I wanted to say
ex-Queen Soraya or None-of-your-business, but I'm not very
composed over these things, so I said my name. He came to
the phone. He said 'Yes?' Just like that. A business reply.
Don't phone me – I'll phone you. *I adjure you, O daughters
of Jerusalem, by the roes and by the hinds of the field, that*

131

ye stir not up, nor awaken love, until it please. I had to go on and explain, didn't I? You must have thought I left rather suddenly the other evening – I'm sorry if I gave the impression – etcetera, etcetera. And then he said, laughingly, as though trying to figure out what I was talking about, 'Why no, darling, I didn't think that at all.' His voice was so present that I believed him, but now I don't know again. It might have been the easiest way of dealing with me, for him. 'I'll give you a ring, eh?' he said.

Calla is sitting opposite me, spread brawnily on to her one armchair while I insist on perching at the chesterfield's edge as though to make certain that I'm looking so temporary she won't be surprised if I take off at any moment.

'The summer's more than half over,' she is saying. 'It doesn't seem possible that it's August already. I've been terrifically busy.'

August. That's what bothers me the most. At the end of the month he will have to return to his work, and go away, and how is it that we can waste this time now? If I could be with him all the time, all the remaining time, it would be –

'Have you? That's good. What with?'

'Painting, mostly,' Calla says, holding out her blunt hands and examining them. 'I've become a real interior decorator. You wouldn't believe it. I've hardly had a moment to spare, all summer. I've thoroughly enjoyed it, though, I must say.'

I find such difficulty in focusing on what she is saying, but something of her voice's belligerence cuts through to me.

'That's good.' How can I say it convincingly enough? 'That's – I'm awfully glad.'

'Yes. We finished painting the Tabernacle a week ago. It turned out a great success.'

'Oh – fine.'

'Yes. We did the walls in eggshell. Teams of four. Any more don't get things done, you know, they just gab. Trimming and woodwork in moss-green. It's a real improvement,
132

I must say. I got so good with a roller that I'll never use brushes again for walls. Or ceilings. I did most of the ceilings, because I've got a head for heights, not that you might think it, to look at me.'

Now there is something so unassuming about her that I wish I could talk to her. But I can't talk about him to anyone.

I got the curse this week. I was – of course – relieved. Who wouldn't be? Anyone would naturally be relieved, under the circumstances. It stands to reason. You hear of women waiting for it, and worrying incessantly, and then when it comes, they're released and everything is all right again and that anxiety is over for the moment and for a while one need not think *What would I do? What would become of me?* I was terribly relieved. It was a release, a reprieve.

That is a lie, Rachel. That is really a lie, in the deepest way possible for anyone to lie.

No. Yes. Both are true. Does one have to choose between two realities? If you think you love two men, the heart-throb column in the daily paper used to say when I was still consulting it daily, then neither one is for you. If you think you contain two realities, perhaps you contain none.

If I had to choose between feelings, I know which it would be. But that would be disaster, from every point of view except the most inner one, and if you chose that side, you would really be on your own, now and for ever, and that couldn't, I think be borne, not by me.

What are we talking about, Calla and I? Where did I leave her? Painting the Tabernacle. It's all right. Only an instant has elapsed, I guess.

'I'd like to go and see it some time.'

'Would you,' she says, 'really?'

'Why, yes. Yes, of course. It sounds very nice.'

Nice. The most useful word in the language, the most evasive. Calla isn't taken in. She's brusque, sometimes, and her taste in furnishings seems so horrible to me that it creates a kind of horrible snobbishness in me and I go to the opposite extreme to admire her larkspur walls. But she's not stupid. She knows.

'You don't have to,' she is saying, quite kindly.

'No – I'd like to. I mean it.' I have to say this, now, have to go on protesting my sincerity. Yet I can't think of that place without dread. The abandoned voices, abandoned in both ways – their owners bereft and because of it needing to utter with that looseness. And the one voice which can't be forgotten. But it was a momentary thing, a lapse, an accident. It couldn't happen again. I don't think that sort of thing could ever happen again, could it?

'After it happened – I mean, at the Tabernacle that night when you were there,' Calla says, 'I didn't go again for weeks.'

'Didn't you? Why not?'

'Because of how you felt. It was contagious. No, don't say anything. I know you didn't mean it to be. But I felt the same. As though it must be awful, in some way, the place and everything there. It was then that I re-read St Paul.'

'Really?' I cannot take her earnestness earnestly. What is she talking about?

'Yes. I suppose you knew all along. That was what I kept thinking about. You'd known all along.'

'Known *what*?'

'Just exactly how much he'd warned against speaking in tongues. I'd only known bits of his sayings, here and there, the parts our preacher put into the mimeographed information sheets he passed around on the subject. Then I went and read it all. You knew all the time, eh?'

'No. I didn't, Calla. Honestly.' But she doesn't believe me. She has been worrying about this, utterly unknown to me. It has never crossed my mind. God's irony – that we should for so long believe it is only the few who speak in tongues. 'What did he say?'

Calla takes a mouthful of iced tea and leans back, deciding to masquerade nonchalance, but doing it so clumsily that all at once I know she'll painfully and unnecessarily

134

review it later when it's too late to change how it has been spoken.

'*There are, it may be, so many kinds of voices in the world, and none of them is without signification. Therefore if I know not the meaning of the voice, I shall be unto him that speaketh a barbarian, and he that speaketh shall be a barbarian unto me.*'

'Maybe he didn't mean—'

What am I doing, for heaven's sake? Apologizing for the apostle's appallingly accurate sight? I don't ever remember having heard the words before, much as I was supposed to have been reared on the black leather book. What he says isn't what should be. It's merely what is.

Calla smiles, and offers me a cigarette, her thonged feet outsplayed on the floor, her bulk now leaning forward, her spiky grey hair wavering stiffly as though her head were paradoxically covered with sprigs of dried lavender.

'Yeh, he meant it, all right, Rachel. But you have to see it in context.'

'Oh yes, I'm sure.'

The falseness of this does not escape her, and she smiles again, as though she now were protected against everything, including me, by a thousand mysteries.

'He says, as well, among a lot of other yakkity-yak, *If any man among you thinketh himself to be wise, let him become a fool, that he may be wise.* I mean, there you are. I thought to myself—Calla, you old cow, there you are.'

'Where?'

'Home-free,' she says, having apparently settled it, but still, I think, waiting for my reaction. 'So I went back to the Tabernacle, see, bold as brass and twice as loud. My old usual self, you might say. I thought, well, there's your clue, kiddo, and if the word that comes to mind is *Hallelujah*, then it's *Hallelujah*, so what can you do about it? You didn't destroy me, Rachel. Not that you meant to. But, I mean, you didn't. It's only right you should know.'

'I'm—' I don't know what on earth to say. 'I'm glad.'

135

'You're not glad,' Calla says curtly. 'How could you be? You don't know what I'm talking about. Well, pardon me all to blazes, and for heaven's sake don't put your elbow any farther back or you'll touch the wet paint. I *spoke*, by the way – that's what I set out to tell you.'

'You mean – ?'

'Yeh. Amazing, eh? It was given to me. To *me*, already. Not in the Tabernacle, I must say. Maybe just as well. I mean, who would have been able to interpret? St Paul says there should be somebody there to interpret.'

She has left me behind. I'm not following her. And yet I'm not so much frightened, not any more. It won't happen to me. I won't become eccentric, moving in some private pattern only, speaking oddities which seem quite usual to me and otherwise to others – hilarious to the cruel, terrifying to the slightly more observant. Not now. Not any more. She could be mad as any April fool and it wouldn't infect me.

Perhaps he will phone me tonight. Nick? *Listen* –

'Where did it happen, then?'

'Here,' she says. 'When I was alone.'

'Oh?'

'Yeh. It just began, and – I don't guess I could describe it, Rachel. It was peace. Like some very gentle falling of rain. Sounds funny, eh?'

'No – no, not at all.' It sounds insane.

'Well, enough of that,' Calla says, briskly clearing the glasses with the slices of lemon tea – logged and limp at the bottom. 'Listen, you never saw Jacob, eh?'

'Who?'

'My canary. He doesn't like all this painting deal, so I've put him in the bedroom for the time being.'

She leads me into the room which contains a single bed, cherry chenille-covered, and a dresser in whitewood which she has stained silver-grey, unlike any wood known to man. The cage is on the dresser, a large gilt cage, free-swinging on its stand so that the bird can rock and roll as it pleases.

136

Inside it, there is a small porcelain bath, a tray of seed and a miniature step-ladder.

'Hello, Jacob,' Calla says. Then, to me, in a quiet aside, as though the bird might hear and take offence, 'So-named because he climbs the ladder all the time. He won't sing. No ear for music. All he does is march up and down that blasted ladder.'

'I wonder why?' I have to say something.

'Search me,' she shrugs. 'Maybe the angel at the top can't be seen by me.'

She whistles and beckons the bird. It remains sitting on the lowest rung, full of disdain or simply not noticing her.

'Dead loss,' Calla says. 'I'd have done better with a budgie, like I had before.'

'Why keep it, then?'

'Well, it can't help moving about from time to time, phlegmatic though it is, and then I can hear it. I've got kind of used to it, stupidly enough.'

I want to get away. I don't want to stay here any longer. Calla listening in the early morning or in the darkness for some sound.

'Calla – Mother's expecting me home – I must go.'

'Sure,' she says. 'Okay, then. Drop in again, eh? When you've got the time.'

'Yes. Yes, I will.'

She smiles at me, lightly, politely, as though trying not to notice that I've no intention of coming again until some stereotyped conscience forces me to it.

Our tub is a very elderly one, exceptionally deep and long, mounted on claw feet taloned and grasping like a griffin's, and pebbled on the outside with years of Mother's enamelling. Despite its size, it is only just long enough for me to stretch out full length.

Once we discussed new plumbing. Mother kept saying she was sick to death of painting this dilapidated old tub and trying to make it look halfway decent, and as for the

137

toilet, it was a disgrace because who had a wooden seat any more? We got as far as deciding on colour – she favoured apricot – and then she decided it wouldn't be practical because the new tubs in the range we could afford were all short and would have been fine for her but wouldn't have done for me. I said I didn't mind paying more for a longer one, but she said no, she was certain even those wouldn't do, and we might have to have one custom-built. That's what she said. She was annoyed at me that evening over something else, I suppose. When I said she was exaggerating, she said, 'I don't see any cause to be rude to me, just because I was trying to be practical, dear.' All such words cling to the mind like burrs to hair, and I can never seem to brush them away, as I know I should do.

Yet I remember, too, the words I've picked and flung like nettles – 'How can we go to the movies this week? You know what Doctor Raven advised. You don't want to have another attack, do you?' And she looked at me with eyes as wide and shadowed with troublement as though she'd been a child told to fetch something from an unlighted cellar. Only last night I said that, when she whined a little with boredom. It wouldn't have hurt her to go out, or even if it had, better than waiting within the walls, probably. I wouldn't go out because I thought he might phone.

Listen, Nick –

I talk to him, when he is not here, and tell him everything I can think of, everything that has ever happened, and how I feel and for a while it seems to me that I am completely known to him, and then I remember I've only talked to him like that when I'm alone. He hasn't heard and doesn't know.

– The house is not large, but that is all right. They do not need a large house, both of them working and she not able to spend much time in housework. The house is not in a city – very far from that sharpness and coldness. Galloping Mountain, perhaps, with the spruce trees fantastically high

138

and closely set but when you look at night you can see through the black branches a sky warmly black and a white profusion of stars. He loves this place. He half apologizes for loving it – 'Crazy, but I've always wanted – and maybe it's a better investment, here, if the one inevitable hysterical moron yields to the seduction of knobs and dials or whatever in hell they are, and the cities are scorched to perdition. Maybe a few kids in scattered places like this will be the only ones who have ever heard of *The Tempest* or *Moby Dick*.'

Oh Rachel. He'd never say that in a million years. What is he going to say to you, then, after that touching outburst? 'Thank God you are here, darling – together we can face this wilderness and walk hand-in-hand into the etcetera.' I'm ashamed. But I don't stop. I'm addicted.

'You're an awfully long time in there, Rachel.' Mother's anxious quaver. 'Are you all right?'

I won't answer. I haven't heard. Shut up, for God's sake, can't she? No, I'm not all right. I've just drowned.

'Are you all right, Rachel?'

'Yes, I'm quite all right. Be out in a minute.'

The water is clouded with soap, and through the murkiness my flesh does have a drowned look, too pale, lethargic, drifting, as though I could nevermore rise and act. I look thin as a thighbone. Naked, I am so bone-thin and long, my legs placed maidenly together and my arms outdangling. Underwater, this cross of bones looks weird, devalued into freakishness. My pelvic bones are too narrow, too narrow for anything.

The phone.

I rise, listening, slithering on the porcelain, drenched, listening, cursing myself for not having got out before, listening.

It is. And Mother's voice is breathless, as though she can't wait to hang up the receiver.

'No, I'm sorry, she's having a bath right now.'

'Hang on – I'm coming!'

He'll have heard that, oh my God, that cry, as though I were a Saint Bernard galloping to the rescue of some stranded Alpine party.

'Hello.'

'Hello – Rachel?'

'Yes. How are you?'

'Sorry, darling, I didn't recognize your voice at first. Oh, I'm more or less fine. Are you free?'

'Tonight?'

'Yes, tonight.'

'Yes. I'm free.'

When I hang up, Mother is standing in the kitchen doorway, watching me, distaste in her face, and then I realize I haven't even got a towel around me.

'Really, Rachel, that doesn't look very nice.'

'Don't worry –' I don't know what I'm saying. 'The telephones aren't equipped with TV yet.'

Then, while her disapproval turns to concern over the worrying gaiety of my madness, I begin in relief to laugh, to laugh and laugh, and it goes on.

'I'm sorry – I'll stop in a moment –'

I close the door of the bathroom, and lock myself inside, and laugh shudderingly, light-years away from laughter.

Nick's shirt is dark brown, the sleeves rolled up and showing his forearms, brown with summer and lightly covered with fine black hair, and where his shirt is open at the neck I can see the dipping curve of his collarbone. The male smell of him, clean sweat and skin, compels me to touch him. He smiles, but abstractly, as though not really noticing, and starts the car.

'They're home tonight.' He sounds annoyed. 'Shall we just drive out somewhere?'

'All right.'

'I tried to induce them, in my tactful way, to go to the movies, but no dice. The old man and I haven't been on very good terms recently, so whatever I suggested, he was bound to do the opposite. If I'd had any sense, I would have begged him to stay home and he would've been out like a shot.'

'What's the trouble, Nick?'

'Nothing's the trouble,' he says. 'He's got such an awful temper, that's all, and I've got a pretty evil one myself.'

'You? I don't believe that.'

'You don't know me very well.'

'Enough to know about your temper.'

'No, darling,' he says. 'You don't.'

'You shouldn't run yourself down.'

'You've got it wrong,' he says. 'I'm not. You're the one who does that.'

Then I'm silenced. Is that what he thinks? Is that how I strike him? What must it be like, to be with someone who plays that drab tune repeatedly?

'I don't! Anyway, not now. I haven't recently.'

'Oh darling,' he says, and I cannot interpret his voice, something regretful in it, as though he were thinking a thing he couldn't hope to explain. 'Well, that's good, I guess.'

'Your father – has he been keeping on at you about staying?'

He has talked so much before, but now he doesn't seem to want to talk about it.

'Mostly other things,' he says reluctantly. 'Complexities all around. Goddamn spider webs. Am I the spider or the fly? Philosophical question. Never mind. Look – wild raspberries. Shall we get some?

The road is banked with bushes on either side, green stinging walls, and when we get out of the car, the smell of oil and engine fades in a moment, leaving the dusty smell of the gravel and the green dusty smell of the leaves.

'The best ones are always hidden. You have to look for them.' He scratches himself on the raspberry thorns. 'Bloody hell. My right hand seems to have forgotten its cunning.'

'Nick – he'll never ask you in so-many words to stay, but –'

141

'How could I?' His voice is aggressive, and I see I've picked the wrong time, but I have to go on.

'Well, you might teach here, I suppose.'

My voice, which was intended to be so unstudiedly casual –how has it sounded to him? He smiles, a token smile only.

'Not possible, darling,' he says. 'Let's go, eh?'

The hoarse metallic roar of the car provides some sound to overcome the lack of voices. I cannot say anything, and he will not. What possessed me, to suggest a thing like that? So openly. Haven't I any pride?

No, I have no pride. None left, not now. This realization renders me all at once calm, inexplicably, and almost free. Have I finished with façades? Whatever happens, let it happen. I won't deny it.

'It isn't so much his wanting me to stay,' Nick says suddenly. 'It's the way he goes about it.'

'How do you mean?'

'This apparently accidental way he's developed. It's what he calls me that bugs me to some extent.'

'I don't see –'

'Three times in the last week,' Nick says, 'he's called me Steve.'

'Oh Nick –'

'Yeh, well, you don't need to sound all that sorrowful on his account,' Nick says angrily. 'It's not some sad slip of the tongue or mind, with him. It's this fantastic way he has, of creating the world in his own image. He knows perfectly well what's what. He's not senile, for God's sake. It's this crazy kind of guile he has. He hasn't thought all this out. He's never thought out anything in his life, I don't suppose. It's just some instinct, maybe, that suggests to him if he can't persuade me in an indirect way, without demeaning himself to ask openly, then he may be able to shame me into doing what he wants. I'm buggered if I'll be manipulated like that. Anyway, I'm no actor, and even if I were, that rôle wouldn't suit me. I'm not going to be taken over by a –'

He breaks off, and when he goes on again his voice has become deliberately callous.

'—a dead man. That's what he is, let's face it. After all this time. Not my brother, not anybody's anything. A dead man.'

'Hasn't your father ever accepted—?'

'Maybe not,' Nick says. 'But he'll have to, or else—well, that's up to him. I can't make it all better. I couldn't then and I can't now. I've got other things to do. The hell with it. No use in talking. I'm fed up with the whole issue. C'mon, Rachel—here's the summer house.'

The summer house. The green edge of a brown river, the broken branches that clutter the shallow water, the high grass loosely webbed—a screen anyone could look through, and the road close enough for us or anyone to walk down here, no distance at all, and up from our place, within eye-shot, the sweeping half circle of fields, the barbed wire, and the grain beginning to turn the pale colour of ripeness with the autumn coming on. If only it weren't so exposed. He claims it isn't, but it seems so to me. If only we could be inside a house again, a proper house. It was better, there. I was better. Everything was all right, and it was good, and he said God darling that was marvellous, you are really—

A lie. He said *I like you, Rachel,* and once he said *That's better, darling, you're getting used to me.* I don't know how it is that I can want him, want him specifically, and yet can't lose sight of myself and still worry whether I'm doing well, and so don't. I am fine only in dreams.

On the tall couchgrass, Nick spreads a meagre dark blue car rug. It hovers for an instant, impaled on green spears, and then it sinks and he treads it down to make a room on the ground.

'I brought this along this time,' he says proudly. 'I thought it would be an improvement. For you.'

'Thanks—you're very thoughtful.' I try to make my tone like his, bantering, but mine emerges too serious.

'That's me,' he says. 'Gallant to a fault. Well, I thought—

143

you know – it's okay for me, but I assume you would just as soon not have a flank full of thistles.'

I want to yield to his laughter, to have everything happening on his terms, lightly, not as though it were the beginning of the world. But I can't. I don't know how to make it unimportant enough.

'Nick – '

'Mm? That's right, darling, right here beside me. That's comfortable. Want a cigarette?'

'Yes, please.'

'Here you are. You're getting a tan after all, Rachel, on your arms.'

'What do you mean, after all?'

'Oh, I don't know. I never thought you were out enough in the sun, to change colour. Your skin's very pale. I thought probably the sun didn't affect you well, and that you couldn't take too much of it, or something.'

'I used to be like that, I guess. I don't actually get burnt, but I suppose I still expect to. When I was a kid, my mother was always after me to wear a sun hat because fair-haired people always burned, she said. I had fair hair then. It's darkened.'

'I can't imagine you as a blonde, Rachel.'

'No – I suppose not.'

'Well, don't sound discouraged. I meant it as a compliment, as a matter of fact.'

His voice sounds vaguely irritated. I've misinterpreted something again. Now I can only try to get away, if that's possible.

'You tan quickly, Nick. In only a few weeks you've – '

'That's right, I do,' he says, peeling off his shirt. 'Look – how about that for a tan? I've got it in the past week, mainly, working with my shirt off. I say *working*, but what I actually mean is I have to get the hell out of the house so I mooch around after Jago, getting in his way, until finally he gets fed up and says to me, "Nick, how come you are so useless around here? Don't you remember nothing from when you

144

was a kid?" And I say—you know, taking some low kind of pleasure from the double negative—"That's right, Jago, I don't remember nothing." And then my mom comes out and yells *Lunch*, and that's half a day gone, praise God.'

'You hardly ever talk about her.'

'My mother? Well, it isn't necessary, I guess.'

'You're fond of her?'

'Unfashionable as it may be,' he says, slightly sourly, 'yes, I am. She's—oh, you know—solid. Physically and spiritually. She's not eccentric like my old man. Or if she is, she never lets on. And yet in some ways she is eccentric, I suppose. Or—not so much that, just completely inner-directed. You'd never think it to look at her.'

'How do you mean?'

He's lying beside me now, and I touch the skin of his shoulder. My fingers explore a little the thicket on his chest, and his nipples which seem to me so strange on a man— what evolutionary freak or chance left them there? He is talking. He wants to talk, right now. *For God's sake hold your tongue and let me love.* But it's a man who is supposed to say that.

'She believes in omens,' he is saying, 'which she interprets in any way that happens to suit her. She's got this marvellous belief in her own intuition. Not towards everything—only where her kids are concerned. Something magical, she thinks, given by heaven to mothers like her, the devout, those who are really bound up with their kids. She wouldn't give you fifty cents for these women who park their kids and go out to work. A spit in the face of God, she thinks. For herself, she *knows*. She knows what is going on without being told.'

'Is she ever right?'

'Quite often,' he says. 'Of course, like any other oracle, the times she goofs on the predictions are forgotten in the wonder of the times she happens to be right. "Julie's husband is no good," she says to me. This was years ago. "What makes you say that?" I asked her. "I feel it," she says.

145

Naturally I laughed. She hardly knew Julie's husband at all. However, as it works out, she is not so far off the beam. *No good* is a kind of easy way of putting it, and even if I say he was off his rocker, what do I know of it? That was Julie's first husband, and she pulled out. My sister has this very unreasoned but strong urge for self-preservation. At the time I thought she was just being a first-rate nut, as she sometimes is, leaving this guy who was making a good living as a long-distance driver. That was in B.C. and he was doing the long hauls, Alaska Highway and that, and I thought – if she doesn't like him so very much, hell, she only has to see him one day out of seven or whatever it was. I was all for basic security in those days. Let's worry about the subtleties after we've paid the rent, that kind of thing. I thought she was out of her mind. But she took off, nevertheless, with the one kid. Divorce, the whole jazz. She re-married and went to Montreal. Not long ago her first husband ended up in the morgue because he played chicken with his truck once too often, and this time the other guy didn't swerve and neither did Buckle Fennick, prince of the highway.'

'That's – terrible.'

'Why?' Nick says. 'He got what he wanted, didn't he? It was a good thing Julie wasn't there, that's all. I give full marks to my mom, though. She never said *I told you so.*'

'What did she say?'

'She didn't say anything,' Nick says, leaning back on an elbow. 'When something can't be said, she doesn't try to say it. Not like my dad. Or me. Steve was like her. The old man always feels Steve was like him, but he wasn't. He was like her, able to rely on faith, and not having to make everything public. My dad has to see to it that everybody knows what he's feeling. He makes a kind of theatre out of his life, and yet in the end he doesn't intend anyone to know how much of the act is real or if any of it is. Pretty corny. I understand it, though.'

'Do you?' The words have no relation to what he is saying. They're only spoken to make some sound, to draw him

146

back and away from where he's been, back to here, because I want to make love with him.

He laughs, and the past thread dwindles, and he is looking now at me.

'I like the way you do that, Rachel.'

'Do what?'

'Oh – run your fingers along my ribs.'

'It's because they're amazing.'

'Are they? Why?'

'I don't know. I can't say. Just to feel you living there under your skin.'

'Darling – be careful, eh?'

'Why should you say that to me? I thought it was the opposite I should try for.'

'That's what I thought, too,' he says, 'but now I don't know.'

'Your spine isn't quite straight. The bones jut, right here. Did you know?'

'Yes, I knew. It's from – I had polio, as a kid.'

'And you got better. That's unusual, for then.' I don't know why I say this – only out of gratitude. 'You weren't crippled.'

'Not so anyone would notice,' he says.

'Nick – take off your clothes.'

'Darling – ' he says, surprised and smiling, 'is it really you first, this time?'

'Never mind.'

'All right,' he says. 'Never mind.'

'Go into me. Now. Right now.'

'All right, darling.'

Nothing is complicated. He inhabits whatever core of me there is. I can move outward to him, knowing he wants what I am, and I can receive him, whatever he is, whatever. And then this tender cruelty, always known to him but never before to me, the unmattering of what either of us is – only important that what we are doing should go on and go on and go on –

147

'Nick – *Nick* –'

Only his name. Only, at this moment, his name. The only word.

A gap in time. Then our makeshift bed returns to my sight. And he is still here, with me.

'Rachel –'

'Yes?'

'That was good luck,' he says.

'Yes.'

He wants to sleep, to be left alone. I want to sleep, too, but not for the first thing. I want to draw away only slowly and gradually, so it will not hurt to break and be separate. And something else. If one speaks from faith, not logic, how does that turn out? I do not know, except that I am so strong in it, so assured, that it cannot possibly go wrong.

'Nick –'

'Mm?'

'If I had a child, I would like it to be yours.'

This seems so unforced that I feel he must see it the way I do. And so restrained, as well, when I might have torn at him – *Give me my children.*

His flesh, his skin, his bones, his blood – all are still connected with mine, but now suddenly not. Not a muscular withdrawal. Something different, something unsuspected.

His face turns away from mine. He puts his mouth momentarily on my shoulder. Then, still not looking at me, he brushes a hand across my forehead.

'Darling,' he says, 'I'm not God. I can't solve anything.'

Unaccountably, we are apart, maybe against both our wills. He untangles himself and begins searching, highly practical, for his cigarettes. We light two and then find we cannot bear to be together naked any longer, and so we put on our clothes, which mysteriously protect us against one another.

'What are you thinking, Rachel?'

'Thinking? Oh –'

'Look up there,' he says, as though battling for distance.

148

'Along the ridge. I never realized you could see the cemetery so well from here, did you?'

'Yes. I don't like it much, though.'

'I don't, either. I dislike graves on principle. I don't know why I went there last week.'

'Nick, why don't you ever say what you mean?'

'Don't make a major production of it, eh?' he says, defensively. 'I've said more than enough, about everything. Look – did I ever show you this?'

He pulls out his wallet and extracts a photograph. It has been in there for some while, and the edges of the paper are softened with handling. It is a picture of a boy about six years old, not set against any background, just a boy standing there. A boy whose face and eyes speak entirely of Nick.

Why is it that it should never have occurred to me, that he was married and had children?

'Yours?'

My voice is steady. When it actually comes to it, I can manage at least this much. Your son? What a nice photograph.

'Yes,' he says, taking the picture away from me. 'Mine.'

Anyone in her right mind would have known this a long time ago. He is thirty-six. If a man intends to marry, he will usually have done it by then. The pain is unspecified, as though I hurt everywhere. Any seventeen-year-old would at least have wondered, before, and asked him.

'Nick – I have to go home now.'

As always, he accepts this with no question or argument.

'Okay, darling. If you say so.'

The peach-coloured nightlight is not on in Mother's bedroom. She seems to be asleep. It's so unusual that I'm worried, and listen at her door, and then I hear her breathing, a whispered snore, and know she's all right. I can hardly believe that I'm to be spared her interested questions, her care. And yet, paradoxically, I wish she were awake. She often likes a cup of tea, late at night, if she's had trouble sleeping. I don't mind making it for her.

In my bedroom, I undress in darkness. I lie down quietly, and place my hands on my thighs, and now I don't remember and won't remember anything except how it was tonight. All I will ever remember is that he arched over me like the sun. I won't remember anything else. Nothing.

It does not make any difference, his being married. It isn't as though I ever thought it would come to anything. The idea hardly crossed my mind. Everything is just the same as it was. I still would have done the same, even if I'd known. I'm not so stupid as to imagine these chance encounters ever lead to anything permanent.

Except that all of my life seems a chance encounter, and everything that happens to me is permanent. That isn't a clever way to be.

How much the boy looks like him. I wonder if she is glad about that, whoever she is. If she has any brains at all, she ought to give thanks every day of her—but I don't suppose she does. She's like my sister, no doubt, complaining every minute how tired she is, how worn out, until you feel you would like to take a woman like that and throttle her with extreme slowness, your thumbs on her neck veins, and her eyes very gradually blurring—

Oh my God. I didn't mean it. Honestly.

I ought to be thinking of practicalities. I will have to do something, get out the antiquated equipment, sluice all traces of him out of me. Why now, when I didn't a week ago? If I had got pregnant then, I wouldn't even have told him. I'd never set that particular steel trap, never. I didn't think of it as a weapon. I swear it. I thought of it, I guess, as a gift. If he found out (which, very unobtrusively, he conveniently would have done), he'd have been delighted. 'God, darling, why didn't you tell me sooner? Were you afraid to? That was foolish of you—but everything's all right now.'

The layers of dream are so many, so many false membranes grown around the mind, that I don't even know they are there until some knifing reality cuts through, and I see the sight of my other eyes for what it has been, distorted, bizarre, grotesque, unbearably a joke if viewed from the outside.

This I cannot take. This I could argue with You (if You were there) until doomsday. How dare You? My trouble, perhaps, is that I have expected justice. Without being able to give it.

I'm evading again. Anything to put off the moment when I have to rise and do what now seems necessary. I can't. I cannot. Oh yes, you can Rachel. Repugnance is for those who can afford luxuries. You're not that wealthy now.

NINE

Why? What I can't understand is why. What purpose was there in it? What was he afraid of? I wouldn't have had the right to argue. Maybe he thought I'd splinter like a shattered mirror, create some unlucky scene, scatter sharp fragments which he could only stand and look at with embarrassment. I wouldn't have. I never would have done that. Perhaps I would have, though. I don't know any longer what I might or might not do.

I waited ten days and then I phoned. I thought – I don't care whether he is married or not. It occurred to me that he hadn't phoned because he thought I'd mind too much and wouldn't want to see him. I had to let him know. A woman's voice answered, faintly familiar to me, his mother.

'Hello.'

'Oh, hello. May I speak to Nick, please?'

'Nick's not here. He went back a week ago.'

'Oh. I see. Well – thanks very much.'

'Who is speaking, please?'

But I didn't say. I put down the receiver and walked out of the phone booth in the bus station. I had the absurd thought – at least they can't trace the call. As if they would have tried, anyway. I did not notice whether there was anyone in the bus station who knew me. People were sitting there, waiting, suitcases at their feet, but they had no faces. I had the conviction that since their faces were unfocused and hidden to me, I would be faceless to them as well.

I noticed I had quite a severe headache, and I thought it

must be due to the sun, although the day was nearly evening now. I stopped at the cigarette and candy counter and bought a small packet of aspirins. I don't know why I did that, because we had plenty of aspirins at home. I was not thinking, I guess, or perhaps I knew I wouldn't be going home for a while. I went to the *Ladies*. The machine that dispenses paper cups had run out, so I took a paper towel and folded it carefully to make a cup. My father showed me how to do that a long time ago. 'You never knew when it might come in handy,' he said, 'but you have to drink quickly or it soaks through and gets wasted.' Probably he wasn't meaning plain water by itself, now I come to think of it. I drank some water quickly and took three aspirins. I remember thinking I must get my eyes examined because maybe the headache wasn't the sun.

Maybe it wasn't the sun.

Two girls had just come in. One was in a toilet cubicle and the other was applying orange lipstick, holding her face close to the mirror as though she wanted to enter it like Alice and go through into an image world. Then I saw she was staring at me, in the mirror.

'What did you say, Helen?' The voice from the cubicle.

'I never said a thing,' the mirror girl replied.

Then they both began giggling, and it was only then that I realized it was I who had spoken aloud. I dropped the paper towel-cup on the floor, and ran. In the long wall mirror I saw myself running, the white of my dress, the featureless face, the tallness, a thin stiff white feather like a goose's feather, caught up and hurtled along by some wind no one else could feel.

I walked for some time. I thought—why shouldn't I walk in the evening by myself? There are parts of this town I've hardly seen. Then I noticed where I was, and that what I'd been doing, actually, was walking on Japonica Street and around the block and back again. This became clear to me when I saw the blue neon sign dancing outside our place and recognized that I had seen it a few minutes earlier. I saw there was no use in this parade, so I went inside. I made the supper and then we looked at the TV.

He might have had another flare-up with the old man, and left on impulse, not having considered it but simply driving away. If that was the case, he may write.

—Darling—I left in a hell of a hurry, I know, but everything became kind of chaotic and I couldn't stand it any longer. What I'm wondering is whether you'll be coming here some time, and when. What about—

No, Rachel. That has to be abandoned. Some poisons have a sweetness at the first taste, but they are willing to kill you just the same. He left because he could not bear their loving reproachful need for him to stay. He could not bear it even for the few more weeks he'd planned to be here. You did not figure at all in his going or his staying. That was not an aspect which he had to consider. He did not phone because it never entered his head to do so. It wasn't significant enough to warrant a phone call. He was busy. He packed his suitcase and went.

There. That's stating it at its most brutal possibility. Look at it, Rachel.

And yet I don't believe it. I don't believe it was completely nothing, for him. Do I deceive myself? More than likely. I don't know—that's the thing. I never knew him very well. We were not well acquainted. We talked sometimes, and I tried to hear what he was saying, but I'm not certain I did hear. I may have heard only guarded echoes of his voice. He never spoke of his real life, the one he leads away from here. Only the photograph of the boy. Nothing else. If he had wanted to say more, I would have listened, but not necessarily with comprehension. And all he knows of me is what he has guessed, whatever that may be.

August is nearly over. Next week we return to school.

Nick—listen—

They troop in, two by two, all the young animals into my Ark. And I must take an interest in them, because I'm the

154

keeper. It wouldn't be fair to them if I didn't. They trust me very little, but at least they trust me this much – whatever happens, I will take charge, they believe.

They enter sophisticatedly, because this is their second year here and not their first. They nudge and bump one another, daring to cry an astonished *Hi!* to long-lost comrades last seen yesterday, daring to stash around their persons pieces of noxiously pink bubble gum or black jawbreakers with an unidentified seed at the candied core. Maybe they are remembering, with condescension towards their ignorant earlier selves, the time when they entered mutely or shamed themselves by bawling for their mums. Now they are full of jauntiness. They swagger, make their aggressive declarations openly, and lord it over the cautious young. Most of them, that is. Here and there, I can already spot one who by nature is no joiner, and I wonder what's there, curiously, as though they were codes which I might partially decipher if there's enough time.

I did not think I could muster any interest at all, and yet I have. No – it isn't I. They've drawn it from me, being as they are – present and unaccounted for, here in the flesh, with loud voices which irk and beckon.

I wonder who will be the one or ones, as it was James last year? All at once I know there will be no one like that, not now, not any more. This unwanted revelation fills me with the sense of an ending, as though there were nothing to look forward to.

I don't know. I don't know what is the trouble. What I'm worrying about, underneath, isn't really so – it's an impossibility which frightens me so much that if I think about it I won't be able to work. I have to concentrate. It's my living.

There. And the first autumn leaves come out, paper cutouts, crimson as no leaves have ever been seen hereabouts, yellow like goldenrod, the dream leaves we concoct to teach – what? That dreams are more garishly coloured than trees, perhaps.

In the hall, at recess, I encounter James Doherty. I was looking for him, I guess, to confirm what I've always known — that I have nothing to do with him. I glimpsed him a very little, for a year, and that is that. He looks taller from the summer, but with the same quickness, in-held yet always ready to take off. The same auburn hair — hasn't it darkened, though? What business is it of mine? And now I recall Grace Doherty, and how, then, I couldn't bear to know she cared about him.

'Hello, James.'

'Hi, Miss Cameron.'

That's all. From now on, we will probably never say another word to one another. Maybe, after all, he has forgotten that I hit him once.

After school, Willard Siddley comes padding into my room in his built-up brown suède shoes. Still the same ostentatious briskness, the sloping smile that hints at wily meanings beyond his words.

'Had a nice summer, I trust, Rachel?'

'Very nice, thanks.'

I've scarcely thought about Willard at all, these past two months, and yet it seems to me now that I've been considering him without knowing it, planning how I'd be with him, how different. There never was any need to be afraid. It was only my nervousness that invited his sly cruelties. This year it will not be the same. I hope he won't stay long, though. Just this time, let him go quickly. Tomorrow I'll be able to deal with it better.

'Didn't see you around very much,' he is saying. 'We meant to ask you over, but Angela wasn't feeling up to scratch, and then we went to the lake in August. I suppose, however, you were probably fully occupied anyway.'

What a choice of words. He couldn't have meant anything by it. He could, though. He knows. He must. He could not possibly, and even if he did, so what? Yet I find myself fumbling, as I've always done, for the pencil on my desk, holding it between my fingers as though I meant to snap it.

And my eyes turn towards the window, hiding or seeking, anything for a quick getaway.

Suppose Willard was walking in the valley one evening, accompanying Angela who'd gone to catch the willows drooping paintably beside the Wachakwa, and suppose they came close to the place, and saw —

Now I am forced to look at him, to examine his face, to detect. Behind his navy-framed glasses there is nothing, nothing lurking, nothing gathering itself to pounce. Only his whitefish eyes, hoping for some slight friendliness from me, possibly, while I sit here conjuring up dragons to scare myself with. How easily I slip back into the set patterns of response.

'Yes, I was fairly busy. Did you have a good summer, Willard?'

'Oh, so-so,' he says, placing his hands on my desk, just as he always has. 'The lake was extremely crowded this year, which was certainly something of a disadvantage. We attended all the open-air sing-songs, however, and those were — oh, reasonably entertaining.'

Suddenly I wonder if what he is asking for, really, is condolence, and if he's asked for it before, and if at times he's asked for various other things I never suspected, admiration or reassurance or whatever it was he didn't own in sufficient quantity. I don't know if he is speaking differently or if I am hearing him differently.

I'm mistaken. I must be. I'm imagining things again. And yet — I wonder if he goes into all the other classrooms, after school? He couldn't. There wouldn't be time. I never thought of that before. I always believed he came in here because of the game he loved best to play, the delicate unacknowledged baiting for which I was such a damnably good subject. There *was* that. I know it. But now I'm not sure it was the only thing. Whatever the disparity in our heights, or maybe, perversely, because of it, he might —

He might, quite simply, think I am attractive, and want, in a mild way, some exchange.

157

'I suppose at least it was cooler at the lake. You're looking very fit, anyway, Willard.'

He preens with a gratitude so visible that I'm ashamed – ashamed of the trick's ease, but also that I never did it sooner, if it could ease him.

I suspect myself, though. I could be seeing the situation all askew. I so often have. And now I can think only of matronly maidens I've known, in whom solitude festered until it grew a mould as gay as a green leaf over their vision, and they would lightfoot around with a mad flittering of eyelashes, seemingly believing themselves irresistible to every male this side of the grave, and hankering after heaven so they might evolve into flirtatious angels and lure all those on the other side as well. Why did I speak? Why did I open my mouth? That's what he'll think – Rachel's going the way they sometimes go – fancies herself as a –

I must not think this way. I mustn't. I thought I might have shed that tic. But here it is.

'I was quite glad to get back,' Willard is saying. 'To tell you the honest-to-goodness truth, I'm happiest when I'm here in school. One has a certain sense of – well, I suppose you could call it a sense of accomplishment.'

'Yes.'

'I think we're going to have a good year. A rewarding year. We haven't had to change any members of the staff, and I always think that's a great asset, if one can carry on with the same team. Provided, of course, that the team is harmonious, which I think I can safely say ours here is. Oh, by the way, Rachel, you remember our little disciplinary problem just before the summer holidays?'

'Yes.' I press my palms together and find they slither with a cold wetness.

'I just want you to bear it in mind this year – if you have the slightest trouble with any of them, send them straight to me.'

'I – I'll remember.'

'Positively no need for you to worry,' he says. 'I'll deal with them.'

'Thank you.'

'Not at all,' he says courteously. 'It's a – it's no bother. That's what I'm here for. To sort out these little day-to-day problems.'

When he's gone, I walk to the window and look out at the playground, the gravel, the swings, everything the same as last year. Nothing has changed. Not anything or anyone.

Willard will never know he yearns to punish. And I will hardly ever be certain whether I am imagining it or not. Only sometimes, when I've betrayed one of them.

Then I will be afraid. As I am now.

Eleven days. Eleven – really that many? Maybe I've miscounted. No, I haven't. Eleven days. Never before. Two or three, sometimes, when I've had a cold or 'flu, or when I've been upset. But never this long overdue. Every day I've thought – *today* – and kept looking. How strange to have to keep on retreating to the only existing privacy, the only place one is permitted to be unquestionably alone, the lavatory. On a bedroom door other people can knock and force a reply, or even walk in as she sometimes does.

For the first few days, then a week, I couldn't believe it at all, couldn't take it seriously because I was so certain nothing like this could happen. God knows why I thought that. *Not to me* – always to someone else, as one naturally thinks of disaster. Not to me – *always to someone else* – as one thinks also of the most wanted.

I would like only one thing – not to have to consider anything except this, itself, by itself. When I think of it like that, away from voices and eyes, it seems more than I could ever have hoped for in my life. How I feel about it does not depend on how he might feel or might not feel. Whatever he felt, or anyone, it would be mine and I would want it to be. How could I do anything against it that would not kill me as well? Would I have felt the same if I had detested

159

him, if he'd been anyone and no one? *No.* That I couldn't have borne. I'm certain of nothing and yet I'm certain of that. I never knew before. That would be more bitter than death, to grow an alien. I never knew before how terrible that would be. If it were Willard's, say – then everything about me, my deepest inner flesh, would refuse it and expel it. That wouldn't happen by itself, though – it could grow, however coldly. I never saw before the brutal determination of seeds. But with me, with this, if I did not have to consider anything else, I could feel only warmth at being its place.

All this is irrelevent to here. I open the bathroom window and look out at the dusk hovering around our house. Then back to the white porcelain sink, the bathtub with its griffin feet, the cellophaned bath cubes stacked on the corner shelf beside the toothpaste and the never-used tins of birthday talcum, *Cactus Flower, Scarlet Lily, Young Lilac.* Our bath towels and face towels always match. This week mine are yellow and hers are rose.

What will become of me?

It can't be borne. Not by me. What am I going to do? It does not matter at all what I feel, or what the truth is. The only fact is that it cannot be allowed to be.

Imagine it. I can't. I won't. Yes. Imagine it. Go ahead, Rachel. She would be – how? – broken up, wounded, ashamed, hysterical, refusing to believe it, believing it only too readily, willing to perjure her soul or pawn her wedding ring to be rid of it, never able to trust again (she would declare), not able to hold her head up forever after on Japonica Street, outcast and also seeking exile because unable to meet the sympathetic stutterings of the world, and worst of all, perhaps, blaming herself (or claiming she was) for something unknown and unsuspected in her rearing of me. 'What, I ask myself, Rachel, could I have done, in bringing you up, that you would go and do a thing like that?' Bringing her grey hairs with sorrow to the etcetera. And underneath all the frenzy, all the gimmicks, she would

160

mourn really. As though it were a death. And no one could ever convince her otherwise.

'Rachel, where are you going?'

'I'm not going anywhere. Just out for some cigarettes.'

'Oh. Then you'll be going to the Regal?'

'Yes, or the Parthenon. Do you want anything?'

'Well, if you could get me just a bar of the plain chocolate. Not the milk, you know, the plain.'

'Yes. All right.'

'Thank you, dear,' she says. 'I don't often have a sweet tooth. Just from time to time. Somehow tonight I—'

'All right. I won't be long.'

Japonica Street is silent, only the late sparrows speaking, and on River Street the sidewalk is gritty with dust, and the first blown leaves of autumn make their small wind-compelled assaults against my ankles. The store windows have their lights turned out, mostly. Only here and there one has been left burning as an advertisement. In Simlow's Ladies' Wear, I am faced with a brown orange-speckled tweed suit for autumn, and a charcoal white-piped smock and matching skirt labelled in Ben Simlow's unlaughing printscript—*For the Lady in Waiting*.

Nick? I would just like to see you for a little while. I wouldn't mind if I couldn't touch you. I would accept that. I would just like to speak with you. That isn't asking a great deal.

— The hospital smells of disinfectants and subdued sickness, but this ward is apart and not peopled by the sick. Her hair is slightly damp with perspiration, and spread long and loose across the pillowcase. Her face is composed, owning herself. She is absorbed in her own thoughts. The nurse, white and rigidly upright as a bleached board, stands by her bed, softening momentarily. 'Someone to see you—will you?' She has no idea who it could be, but she nods yes. He comes in, frowning, sceptical of all this, not liking the surroundings, and then he sees her, one bed among six (ten? twelve?). 'Rachel.' Yes. Hello. 'You might have told me

161

before, darling.' I thought you might not want to know. 'Is that really what you thought? You've got it all wrong, darling. I saw him — you know? I've seen him already. Not bad, eh? You did pretty well, darling.' Did I? 'Rachel, you know I can't help talking about everything as though I didn't mean it — don't you know what I mean, darling?' Yes, I know, it's all right, I know, everything's all right now —

The wind, whipping dustily, circles in a cold chain around my feet. Parthenon Café. The letters are in crimson neon, daring the dark street. I don't want to go in. It will be full of teenagers, and perhaps one of them will say 'Hello, Miss Cameron', a carried-over politeness from when he or she was one of my children. The Parthenon is beside the Queen Victoria Hotel, and there is a door from the hotel lobby which leads into the café. If you sit in one of the Parthenon's front booths, you can look through and observe the oak counter, the wheezing horsehair chairs and the brass spittoons that are considerately kept there for the old men who congregate each afternoon and evening to parse the past, put it in its place and establish their place with it. The management suffers them. There aren't so many of them now. Only three tonight, I see as I open the door and slip into the nearest booth. Only three old men, quite uncommunicative, hard as iron spikes. The door into the hotel lobby is open, and I'm relieved that the old men aren't speaking. I remember once being embarrassed by hearing an old man in there singing in a creaking voice as light and brittle as mouse feet on straw —

> *Fare you well, old Joe Clark,*
> *Fare you well, I'm gone.*
> *Fare you well, old Joe Clark,*
> *Good-bye, Betsy Brown.*

What I thought in those days was — whatever you feel, don't say or sing it, because if you do it will mortify me. If I went in there now, unbidden, young to them, strange in my

162

white raincoat, and said *Forgive me*, they would think I had lost my mind.

'Yes?'

'Oh. Coffee, please.'

The kids of sixteen and seventeen are not actually dancing, but making as though to do so. They look so assured, so handsome. If only they don't look in my direction, it will be a stroke of luck for me. Am I bent over my coffee cup? No, damn it, I won't. Haven't I as much right to be here as they have? I know this, but I don't believe it.

All right. I know, I know. I know I have to do something. I can't bear it. I have to get rid of it. I guess that is the phrase which is used. Get rid of it. Like a casual itch which one could scratch and abolish. I have to get rid of it. Excess baggage. Garbage. If I could just get rid of everything, and belong to myself, and not have to consider anything else. I have to get it out of me.

It will be infinitesimal. It couldn't be seen with the human eye, it's that small, but the thing will grow. That is what will happen to it and to me. It will have a voice. It will be able to cry out. I could bear a living creature. It would be possible. Something you could touch and could see that it had the framework of bones, the bones that weren't set for all time but would lengthen and change by themselves, and that it had features, and a skull in which the convoluted maze did as it pleased, irrespective of theories, and that it had eyes. It would be possessed of the means of seeing.

'Want anything else?'

'No. No, thanks. That's all.'

The coffee is pallid and lukewarm. I have to drink it. It seems to be a peculiar medicine.

The tall and handsome children dance very restrained, now, as though the world were too terrible to be tackled outright and had to be held at arm's length instead. And I admire them.

Rachel. You must decide what to do. Do I have to? What will you do, else? I don't know. I don't know what will become of me.

'Could I – could I have another coffee, please?'

'Certainly, madam.'

Madam. Ten years ago Miklos would have said Miss. He has a built-in acclimatizer to take note of the years without having to notice.

> *Where you're goin', girl,*
> *The road ain't long.*
> *Take from your shiny purse*
> *Your two-dollar song.*

The machine music whirls around me, and I hear it and don't hear it. I don't know where to go. I know what I have to do, and what I have to have done to me. But how in hell am I going to do it? I don't know where to go.

Let us be practical, because in the last analysis that is all that matters. Could I go to Doctor Raven? What would I say? Look – I want you to recommend to me someone who is willing to perform an act that is classified as criminal and illegal? Obviously, Doctor Raven isn't quite the man for the job. So – what else? If I go to the city, any city, what difference would that make? Where do I begin? I am not accustomed to this kind of thing. Of whom, not knowing anyone, could I enquire? A taxi driver? A waitress? Pardon me, but could you tell me where I could go without fuss to find an angel-maker? I do not know where to go. I've read all the articles in magazines, saying so-many thousands are performed every year and isn't it dreadful and so on. *How do all those women find out where to go?* I would be willing to pay. But I don't have the address.

Even if I could find a hangman ready to my hand, could I have it done? Would it kill me, in one way or another, even if I went on living?

Nick – if I couldn't speak with you, all right. I would accept that. If only I could be with you and hold you. If I

164

could lie very quietly beside you, all night, and then the
pain would go away.

> *This is the highway, girl,*
> *Can't move slow —*

He called Julie's first husband prince of the highway.
I said 'That's terrible.' Meaning, to die like that, in a game.
And he said, 'Why? He got what he wanted.' Hector
Jonas said my father got the life he wanted most. I don't
know what they're talking about. As though people did get
what they wanted. They don't know what they're talking
about. Left to myself, would I destroy this only one? I can't
bear it, that's all. It isn't to be borne. I can't face it. I can't
face them.

The faces of the dancing children are hovering around
me, but I don't seem to see them clearly. Do I know them?
Do they know me? It doesn't appear so. They don't look at
me. They are looking at one another, naturally, and don't
see me. Thank God for that, anyway. I'm anonymous, as
though I weren't here. And now I feel I'm not here, and I
wouldn't mind if they looked in my direction, whatever
expression was on their faces. It would prove something.

In the lobby of the Queen Victoria, I can partially see the
three old men. They're drowsing, I think, and their eyes are
closed. That's why I can't see them properly, because their
eyes are closed.

What am I going to do? I'll have to write to him. He'll
know. He'll know where I can go to get it done. Why would
he know? There's no reason why he should. He wouldn't
know any more than I, likely. How can I write, anyway?
What would I say? I didn't do anything to stop this happening — or next to nothing — and now it's happened and it is
my fault but save me anyway. Help me. *Nick — please —*

No. He can't. No one. There isn't anyone. I'm on my own.
I never knew before what that would be like. It means no
one. Just that. Just — myself.

— *Rachel.* She looks up, startled, and he is standing there.

165

Standing here, right here in the Parthenon Café. His face shows a concealed anxiety and also relief. 'I've been looking for you – it's not going to work, all this running away, is it, darling, neither on your part or mine – we're just going to have to – '

He's a hundred miles away. I haven't even got his address. I could get it from his father.

– Nestor Kazlik is setting the white quart bottle down at the doorstep. She comes out and the old man looks up and smiles, recognizing through all the changes the child who used to catch rides on the milk sleigh in winter. 'Mr Kazlik, I've got some books I promised to send – and I seem to have lost his – '

I couldn't write to him. What if his wife saw the letter? No. That's not what troubles me. What do I care right now what she'd say or feel, or how it would affect him? But I know what he'd say, that's the thing. 'You knew better than that, darling – you must have known better than that.' There is no reply to that one.

My elbows are on the red arborite booth table, and I'm breathing the smoke-saturated air of the Parthenon, and listening to the noise, the jazz, the din, then listening for it and realizing it's not there. The bold children have gone, and even in here I'm by myself. It's late, and from the kitchen comes the clash of cutlery and cups, as Miklos cleans up for the night. I don't know how long I've been here. Mother will be worried sick. I rise, cough to call Miklos, pay, get another packet of cigarettes and remember the chocolate bar for her. I have to go home now. I must. It's the only thing to do.

What am I going to do?

'Rachel,'
'Yes. I'm sorry I was so long.'
'I was worried, dear. I really was.'
'Yes. I'm sorry. It was a – it was a lovely night, so I walked around.'

'I thought it looked like rain. The wind was chilly, I thought. I opened my bedroom window, but then I closed it again. It's very late to be walking, by yourself, Rachel. Didn't you think it might look – well, just a little peculiar?'

Not – was it peculiar? Only – did it look so?

'Well, I didn't go far. I shouldn't have been away so long. I'm sorry.'

'Oh, it doesn't matter, dear, but I can't help worrying, just a little bit, when you're – '

'I know. I'm sorry.'

'Never mind, dear. It's all right, of course. It was only that I – '

'Yes. I'm terribly sorry. I won't do it again.'

'I know you don't mean to worry me.'

'No. Well, it was thoughtless – '

'I suppose it doesn't occur to you to think how I might feel, that's all. Of course I quite understand that. It's just that I can't settle down properly until you're back, and I suppose I thought you must surely realize that, by this time.'

'I do – yes. I know. I'm sorry.'

'Oh, it's all right, dear. Never mind.'

Finally she is settled and I can go to my room. I put on my yellow nightgown and then I brush my hair as I've always done at nights. I turn out the light and open the curtains and window so I can see what's out there, if anything. The air is very cool, too cool to rain now, and the wind has gone away. In the far distances, the unreal places beyond ours, I can hear a freight train. They're diesels now and the whistle is sharp and efficient. When I was a child the trains were all steam, and you could hear the whistle blow a long way off, carrying better in this flat land than it would have done in the mountains, the sound all prairie kids grew up with, the trainvoice that said *don't stay don't stay just don't ever stay – go and keep on going, never mind where.* The mourning and mockery of that voice, like blues. The only lonelier sound I ever heard was the voices of the loons on the spruce-edged lake up at Galloping Mountain,

167

where we went once for the summer when Stacey and I were small and when my father still could muster the strength to go somewhere, not too far away, for a short time. People say *loon*, meaning mad. Crazy as a loon. They were mad, those bird voices, perfectly alone, damning and laughing out there in the black reaches of the night water where no one could get them, no one could ever get at them.

I want to see my sister.

Stacey—listen—I know it's been quite a long time since we've seen one another, and even writing to one another is something we only do after Christmas to thank for presents. But if I could talk to you, you would maybe be the only person I could talk to. Look—would you know?

Would Stacey know where I could go? If I wrote to her and said I was coming there, a brief visit, what would be so odd about that? The autumn term has started, and there aren't any holidays now. She'd think I was off my head. And even if I could say, could tell her straight away, just like that, what then? She's been married for years. She has four children, all born in hospital and in wedlock, as the saying goes. What would she know of it? Her dealings in these matters have been open and recognized. She goes to her doctor, is given diet sheets and vitamin pills, attends clinics. She has a right to be doing what she is doing.

What does she know of it? She'd be sympathetic, no doubt, from the vast distance that divides us. She'd give me good advice, maybe, not needing any herself. God damn her. What could she possibly know?

Cassie Stewart. That was the girl mother told me about. She had twins, twice as bad in Mother's eyes. If I could go into the hardware store and speak to her, that might be a good thing. But it isn't possible. Cassie is ten years younger than I, and I'm Miss Cameron to her, and if we spoke it could only ever be politely, nothing given or gambled on either side. She's kept the children. But her mother looks after them while she works. Whatever it may have been like, or however her mother regarded it, Mrs Stewart takes
168

charge of the twins while Cass works. The thing one doesn't know before is that the process doesn't end with birth. It isn't just that, to be reckoned with, explained, faced, brazened out. You're left with a creature who had to be looked after and thought about, taken into consideration for evermore. It's not one year. It's eighteen, maybe. Eighteen years is quite a long time. I would be fifty-two then. All that time, totally responsible. There would not be any space for anything else – only that one being, and earning enough to keep you both, and hoping you could find someone who could look after the child while you worked.

Mother wouldn't. That is certain. Even if she could bring herself to, which she couldn't, she wouldn't be able to. Physically, she's not up to it.

It can't be borne. I can't see any way it could be.

It can't be ended, either. I don't know where to go.

I don't exactly know when I bought this. Perhaps a week ago. I don't recall details well, these days. I put it in the top part of my cupboard. I take it down now, the known brand of whisky, and then I see I haven't a glass.

Mother is sleeping. I can tell from the way she is breathing. The bathroom glass is blue plastic. Her sleeping capsules are on the top shelf of the medicine cabinet. Quietly, quietly, Rachel. There. Everything necessary is here, gathered together in my own room.

How many? As many as possible in order not to take any chances. She's had a new lot only last week from Doctor Raven, so the bottle is nearly full. It isn't necessary to count them.

I pour the brown fluid into the blue plastic tumbler, and juggle a little while with the blue and crimson capsules, rolling them in my hands. They are incredibly small. They take up practically no room at all. And then I find I've counted them, despite myself. There are fourteen.

Enough?

One is enough for a night, so surely these will be all right, with the other. I swallow some of the whisky. I thought I

169

would hate it, straight, but I don't. It is like swallowing flame which burns for a second only and then consoles. It's all right. It's going to be all right. There is nothing to be afraid of.

Actually, it is very simple. Anyone could get down a few capsules – this shouldn't be difficult in the slightest. And this liquid – anyone can open their throat and drink, if they've decided to. *Firewater.* This makes me want to laugh. The Indians, or so we're told, used to call it firewater. How accurate they were.

Half the glass has gone down. But no capsules. That remains to be done. All right. One at a time. One. That's the first. Thirteen to go. Unlucky number, but after the next it will only be twelve. Come on, Rachel. Only a little way to go, and then everything will be all right.

Oh Christ.

Time must have stopped for a time. What have I done? And now I see that what I've done is that I've taken the bottle of my mother's barbituates and have emptied the crucial and precious capsules out of my window, zanily, on to Hector Jonas's trimmed lawn beneath. The whisky is not gone. It is still here. Something prevents my pouring out good whisky. I'm my father's child, no doubt. Niall Cameron would have dropped dead at anyone who poured out a bottle of whisky. Let us give respect unto the dead. I turn the cap on to the bottle and put it again among the other relics in the highest cupboard.

How can I have this lightness? It's temporary, a reaction. It won't last.

At that moment, when I stopped, my mind wasn't empty or paralysed. I had one clear and simple thought.

They will all go on in some how, all of them, but I will be dead as stone and it will be too late then to change my mind.

But nothing is changed now. Everything is no more possible than it was. Only one thing has changed – I'm left with it, with circumstances, whatever they may be. I can't cope,

170

and I can't opt out. What will I do? What will become of me?

The floorboards are splintered here, where the rug doesn't reach, and their roughness makes me realize what I am doing. I don't know why I should be doing this. It is both ludicrous and senseless. I do not know what to say, or to whom. Yet I am on my knees.

I am not praying—if that is what I am doing—out of belief. Only out of need. Not faith, or belief, or the feeling of deserving anything. None of that seems to be so.

Help me.

Help—if You will—me. Whoever that may be. And whoever You are, or where. I am not clever. I am not as clever as I hiddenly thought I was. And I am not as stupid as I dreaded I might be. Were my apologies all a kind of monstrous self-pity? How many sores did I refuse to let heal?

We seem to have fought for a long time, I and You.

The ones who do not have anyone else, turn to You — don't you think I know? All the nuts and oddballs turn to You. Last resort. Don't you think I know?

My God, I know how suspect You are. I know how suspect I am.

If You have spoken, I am not aware of having heard. If You have a voice, it is not comprehensible to me. No omens. No burning bush, no pillar of sand by day or pillar of flame by night.

I don't know what I've done. I've been demented, probably. I know what I am going to do, though.

Look—it's my child, mine. And so I will have it. I will have it because I want it and because I cannot do anything else.

TEN

I can't go to the doctor's. He'll ask about things that are none of his concern. 'Have you told the man, Rachel? Would he be willing to marry you?' Or else he'll say, 'It's going to be a pretty bad shock for your mother, Rachel, and with that heart of hers – '

Mother's heart. I've only just thought of that. What if my telling her did actually bring on another of her attacks? It would be my fault. If it was fatal, it would be all my fault. I can't. I can't tell her, or Doctor Raven, or anyone. I'll have to go away.

I can't go away with no explanation. That would be impossible. Anyway, where? I have to get away. Where am I going to go? Stacey's? No, not there, not ever.

I won't be able to work, at least not as a teacher, once it shows. What will I do for money? I can't see how I will be able to live.

There is only one thing to do, and that's for me to get rid of it. By myself. No one will know, then. I was out of my mind to think I could have it. There's only one thing to be done.

How? A knitting needle? That's the favoured traditional way. Nobody knits, here. I'd have to buy a set for the purpose. How odd. Or a straightened wire coat-hanger? When I think of performing it, my flesh recoils as though hurt already. And if it all goes wrong, what then? Who would be there, to do anything? I wouldn't only have killed the creature – I'd have killed myself as well. Barbiturates would have been kinder, if that's what I'm really after. What am I really after?

172

– She is in the bathroom, and the door is locked, and she cannot cry out. The pain distends her; she is swollen with it. Pain is the only existing thing. On the floor, all over, and all over herself, lying in it, and even on her hair, the blood.

No, I won't. That I cannot do. I refuse.

Maybe it wouldn't happen that way. It would, though. What do I know of my own anatomy? What I need is a good book. Do-it-yourself. How to be an angel-maker in one easy lesson. Oh Christ, it's almost funny, isn't it? Isn't it?

Steady, Rachel. There is no time for letting go. Not now. You've got to do something. If I were very careful, perhaps it would be all right. How could anyone be calculatedly careful about a thing like that? They're surprisingly difficult to kill. I've read that. No delicate probing would ever dislodge it.

Dislodge. It is lodged there now. *Lodged*, meaning it is living there. How incredible that seems. I've given it houseroom. It's growing there, by itself. It's got everything it needs, for now. I wonder if it is a girl or a son.

– She is conscious. She has refused anaesthetics because they sometimes (she has read) damage the child. She sees the boy at the moment of his birth. He has black hair, and his eyes are faintly slanted, like Nick's.

I am not going to lose it. It is mine. I have a right to it. That is the only thing I know with any certainty.

But where will I go? What will I do? The same questions, over and over, and never any answers. If only I could talk to somebody.

Nick – listen –

No. Don't do that, Rachel. Everything only hurts more than before, when you leave off talking to him and acknowledge that he hasn't heard. I have to speak aloud to someone. I have to. But I don't know anyone.

Yes, I do. Only one person. And I've avoided her, gone to see her only rarely and only out of conscience, all of which she knows. Since school began again, I've hardly spoken to her. She doesn't drop into my classroom any more, bringing potted plants or the other quirky gifts she used to place on my desk – once it was a tin tea-canister with scenes of New York, that she'd got free with detergent and thought I might like. Now she knows I don't want them, so she stays away. Yet she's the only one I can think of.

'Are you going out, Rachel?' Mother says.

'Yes. But only for an hour. To Calla's.'

'You won't be gone long, will you, dear?'

'No. Not long. I promise.'

'That's all right, then, dear.'

She sighs a little, as though relieved. She believes me because she must, I guess. If I came back late a thousand nights, I now see, and then told her I'd only be away an hour, she'd still believe me. As I leave, she looks at me trustingly, like a child.

Calla has painted the outside door of her apartment. I marvel that they allowed her to, whoever they may be. I'd never try, anticipating someone's refusal. The door is quite a mild lilac, but in this warren of cream and beige doors, it makes its presence known. She'd do it and ask afterwards. I wish I were like that.

'Rachel – well, hello. Come on in.'

I don't know what to say to her. She takes my coat, fusses me to a chair, slaps on the kettle for coffee. She is still in her teacher clothes – navy blue skirt which makes her hips and rump look like oxen's, and a green long-sleeved smock that bears dashes and smears of poster paints.

'I haven't even changed yet,' she says. 'I've just been – Rachel, what's the matter?'

'Why should you think there's anything the matter?'

'Only that you look like death warmed over, that's all. Honey, what is it?'

'I – wanted to tell you. I wanted to tell you – but now I don't believe I can.'

'Rachel, listen –' Calla is standing beside me, and her voice compels me to look at her. Her face looks as though

174

she were trying very hard to get something across, to explain in words of genuine simplicity to someone who might find everything difficult to comprehend. 'I don't know what it is, and if you don't want to say, then okay. But if you want to say, then I'll listen, whatever it is. And whatever it is, if you need to get away sometimes, you can always come here. I won't ask any questions.'

'How can you say that? Wouldn't you make any conditions?'

'You mean, what would I ask from you? I don't know. I hope I wouldn't ask anything. But I can't guarantee. I'd try – that's all.'

'Whatever it was, with me, even if it was something you hated? I could still come here?'

'I guess I can't promise. You have to gamble on where the limits are. I don't know where they are.'

'Calla –'

'Honey, it's all right. Everything's going to be all right. Okay – so go ahead and cry. It's fine. It doesn't matter. Here – have a Kleenex.'

Then, finally, I'm sufficiently restored to myself. She hands me a lighted cigarette and brings coffee.

'What if I was pregnant, Calla?'

She doesn't reply for a moment, as though she were considering carefully what to say.

'Staying in Manawaka wouldn't be a very good thing, but you might have to, until after, when you could get organized,' she says. 'If your mother couldn't take it, the only thing to do, probably, would be to find a housekeeper for her so she could stay where she is. You could move in here, if you wanted. Or if you wanted to move away entirely, beforehand – well, there isn't any particular reason why I couldn't move, if you wanted someone by you. It might be kind of a strain on your finances for a time, but I don't think you need to worry all that much. We could manage. As for the baby, well, my Lord, I've looked after many a kid before.'

She halts abruptly. When she begins again, her voice is different, subdued.

'I'm sorry,' she says. 'I shouldn't have said any of that, should I? You think you're not asking anything of someone, and then it appears you're asking everything. To take over. I didn't mean to.'

'It's all right. I know.'

'I don't know what I can say or offer to do. Nothing much, I guess. Except that I'm here, and you'll know, yourself, what you need to ask.'

'Calla—'

'Yes?'

'I don't know—I want to thank you, but—'

'Don't bother,' she interrupts. 'It's for nothing. I've got a collection of motives like a kaleidoscope—*click!* and they all look different. Would you like a drink, child? I've got some wine. It's foul, but it's better than nothing.'

She doesn't realize that she has called me *child* once more.

'No, thanks. I don't think so.'

She looks at me, trying not to appear worried.

'Are you going to be all right, Rachel?'

If I'd been asked that, yesterday, I wouldn't have known. Maybe even an hour ago I wouldn't have known.

'Yes. I'm going to be all right.'

Maybe she'll pray for me, and maybe, even, I could do with that. But she hasn't said so, and she won't, and that is an act of great tact and restraint on her part.

My mother's tricky heart will just have to take its own chances.

The waiting room is full of people, and I sit edgily, tucking my cotton dress around my knees, edging away from the stout-skirted mother bidding a spectacled five-year-old to behave himself and shush. We are waiting to be called for examination, as though this were death's immigration office and Doctor Raven some deputy angel allotted the job of the initial sorting out of sheep and goats, the happy sheep

176

permitted to colonize Heaven, the wayward goats sent to trample their cloven hoofprints all over Hell's acres. What visa and verdict will he give to me? I know the country I'm bound for, but I don't know its name unless it's limbo.

Rachel, shut up. Shut up inside your skull. Yes, I am, that's it. Oh, stop this nonsense.

Death's immigration office indeed. You have to watch against that sort of thing. Is it madness, though? That bleak celestial sortinghouse, and the immigrants' numb patience, all of us waiting with stupefied humbleness to have our fates announced to us, knowing there will never be any possibility of argument or appeal – it seems more actual than this deceptively seeable room with red leatherette chairs and a cornucopia of richly shiny magazines spilling out across the narrow table, and an aquarium of tropical fish, striped and silvered, fins fluttering like thin wet silks around the green and slowly salaaming reeds and weeds of this small sea.

'Miss Cameron – in here, please.'

'Oh. Thanks.'

And I've drawn together my tallness and loped through the waiting room, sidestepping chairs and outstretched feet, an ostrich walking with extreme care through some formal garden. Rachel, hush. Hush, child. Steady. It's all right. It's going to be all right.

I can't tell him. I can't be examined. I have to leave, right now. I'll just have to make some excuse. Say I'm not feeling well. That would be splendid, wouldn't it? To rush out of a doctor's office because you weren't feeling well.

'Hello, Rachel. It's for yourself, this time?'

We've had so many dealings, Doctor Raven and myself – mother's heart, my persistent winter headcolds, the bowels and bones of both, the inability to sleep, the migraine and dyspepsia, all the admittable woes of the flesh. This is a new one I'm bringing now.

'Yes.'

'Sit down, my dear.' He looks at me from his old eyes,

177

still competent and able to appraise. 'What's the trouble? Not the bronchitis again, I hope?'

'No. I—I've missed my period this month.'

I sit here, waiting once more, waiting for him to speak. 'It's none of my business, Rachel dear, but I've known your family for a long time, and as a doctor I have to ask—' What will I say?

'Well,' Doctor Raven is saying in his comfortable and comforting voice, 'at least we know there's no question of one thing, anyway, with a sensible girl like yourself. That at least can be ruled out, eh? Can't say the same for them all, I'm afraid.'

I can't believe he's saying it, and yet it's only too easy to believe. No words for my anger could ever be foul or wounding enough, against him, for what he's saying. I could slash gouges out of his seemly face with my nails. I could hurl at him a voice as berserk as any car crash.

I sit on the chair opposite his desk and I do not say anything. I see now that when he discovers what it is, with me, he won't be able to stop himself expressing the same feelings as my mother will. Subdued, maybe, but the same. What right has he? He's my doctor, not my father or judge. The hell with him. And yet I'm inheld so tightly now that I don't see how I can consent to any examination.

'Don't worry,' Doctor Raven says. 'I know what you're worried about.'

I strain to meet his eyes. 'You do?'

'Of course. Look, Rachel, you're an intelligent woman. I can say this to you. Half the people who come into my office are worried about a malignancy, and with most of them it's been absolutely unnecessary, all that worry. This could be due to any number of causes. But for heaven's sake don't jump to the worst possible conclusion. Wait until we've seen. I may as well examine you internally now.'

He calls the nurse. There must always be a nurse present, even though he's pressing seventy. Where one or two are gathered together. I don't know what I'm doing. Will he be
178

careful enough? If a person expects to find something life-
less, he wouldn't worry, would he, whether he was careful
or not? What if he damages the head? Would it be formed
enough, yet, to be hurt? Would it be formed enough for him
even to feel it? I have to tell him. I must. I have to warn
him.

'Doctor Raven —'

'Yes?'

'Look, before you examine me, I wanted to say —'

'It's all right, Rachel. What is it? Don't be nervous, my
dear. This is nothing.'

'I just wanted to say —'

A hesitance. A silence.

'What is it, Rachel?' he asks gently.

'Just be careful, won't you?'

'Certainly, certainly. You've had an internal before,
Rachel, I'm positive. Haven't you? Yes, of course you have.
It was when you had a little trouble with your periods a
few years back. No need to be tense, now. This won't
hurt.'

'I don't mind — it isn't that.'

'Just relax, now,' he says. 'Just relax.'

Relax, Rachel. And I said *I'm sorry*. Nick — listen. Even if
I couldn't talk about any of this, even if I couldn't tell you,
if I could just be beside you, with your arm across my
breasts, through a night. Then I would be all right. Then I
would be able to do anything that was necessary.

This coldness pierces me more than any physician could.
The intense and unearth-like coldness of this metal table
I'm lying on, like the laying-out table in the deodorized
anteroom to the chapel where the jazz hymn plays in the
blue light.

I'm frightened. And now I think for the first time that
maybe it will kill me after all, this child. Is that what I am
waiting for? Is that what is waiting for me?

'Mm, all right,' Doctor Raven is murmuring. 'You can get
down now, Rachel. There's certainly something there. Now,

you're not to get worried. My guess is that it's a small tumour, just inside the uterus.'

I cannot speak for a while, and then, gradually, I can.

'Are you sure? Are you sure that's what is there?'

'Certainly, I felt it.'

'No – I mean –'

'Yes, there's definitely a tumour of some sort there. What we don't know yet is what sort. I'm being frank with you, Rachel, because I know you can't stand me to be otherwise, and I know you can take it. There's every chance that it'll turn out to be benign. You'll have to go into hospital in the city – you need a specialist. I'll arrange it, and let you know when.'

'Are you sure it's a – tumour?'

'Oh yes, quite sure. No mistaking it. I've diagnosed this kind of thing often enough.'

He's quite sure. He could be mistaken. But how could he? His hands have a knowledge beyond his brain. A foetus doesn't feel the same to those seeing hands as the thing in me. He's diagnosed this kind of thing often enough before.

'Rachel, listen –'

Doctor Raven puts a hand on my shoulder. His face is anxious. He is anxious about me. Anxious in case I should be too concerned over the nature of the thing in me, the growth, the non-life. How can non-life be a growth? But it is. How strange. There are two kinds. One is called malignant. The other is called benign. That's what he said. Benign.

Oh my God. I didn't bargain for this. Not this.

'Rachel – please –'

It is Doctor Raven's voice, but I cannot any longer see him, or else I'm seeing him through some changing and shimmering substance utterly unlike air. I looked down once through the water at the lake, and it trembled and changed, and still I could see, far below, the thousand minute creatures spinning in a finned dance, and my father said *Fishes*,

180

only just spawned, and there were thousands of them, thousands. The waters are in front of my eyes.

'All right, my dear. Just sit down here. I know it's been a shock.'

'No. No, you don't know—'

My speaking voice, and then only that other voice, wordless and terrible, the voice of some woman mourning for her children.

How long? I don't know. What does it matter? It does not matter now that I've been sitting here, touchily attended to by one embarrassed nurse and one well-meaning physician who wants to help me pull myself together and yet can't help having an eye on the clock, the waiting room still full.

'I'm sorry. I'm all right now.'

'Take your time,' he says.

'No, I'm fine, really. It was just for a minute—'

'Of course. I know. But try not to think of it too much. Not at this stage. These things are operable, you know, even if it's what we hope it isn't.'

'Yes. Well—thanks.'

I am outside now, walking on the streets, walking somehow along in the late afternoon sun that gilds the store windows and turns everything to a dusty brightness.

Only now do I recall the long discussions with myself. *What will I do? Where will I go?* The decision, finally. It cost me something, that decision, you know? Then telling Calla. I did tell her. What if I was pregnant, I said. And she said, my Lord, I've looked after kids before.

All that. And this at the end of it. I was always afraid that I might become a fool. Yet I could almost smile with some grotesque lightheadedness at that fool of a fear, that poor fear of fools, now that I really am one.

ELEVEN

He was right. Doctor Raven was right, dead right. And now that I'm back at home, the time in hospital seems to have been anaesthetized, bled of any shade except the pallor of dreams or drugs, the colour of sleep. I hardly noticed what they were doing to me, or who they were. As though it were all being imagined in one of those late-night spook features repeated with eerie boredom on the inner TV. As though I might be able to switch it off, finally, or turn away, and come back to life and find that the child had begun perceptibly to move.

They said I was a co-operative patient, to lie so still. How did they know? They thought I was worried about having cancer.

And of course I was, as well. There is room enough in anyone's bonehouse for too much duplicity.

Nick, at first in there I talked to you all the time, on the private telephone of silence. I thought I would ignore the walls, the hollow needles filled with oblivion, the faces, the kindly prodding eyes. I thought if the old game could be coaxed and conjured up once more, it would be a way of seeing the days through by not seeing them. So I allowed that I was in a hospital, but it was always visiting hours and you were there. Sometimes you were there because everything had been done and settled in advance. *Item on City page — High School Teacher's Wife Dies In Tinned Salmon Ptomaine Case.* Or more satisfactorily, in an obscure column of small print close to the obituaries, *Notice of Divorce*, and after a decent interval of thirty seconds, printed notices to

182

friends and relations, *Mrs Niall Cameron has pleasure in announcing the forthcoming* – and so on. Sometimes you were there with nothing settled, but that didn't matter – I never held out for any precise settlement. You wanted to be there, was the thing. Naturally, you were concerned about the child. Thousands wouldn't have been, but you were. Of course. It went without saying. But even more, you were concerned about me. You kept saying 'Are you sure you're all right, Rachel?' I had to laugh a little at that, because men always think it's much worse than it really is, and as I told you, unless a woman is positively deformed there's actually nothing to get alarmed about in ninety per cent of cases, barring bad luck. Stacey's voice, her exact words, those years ago, the last time she visited here – 'As I told Mac, unless a woman is positively –'

Then the operation. Afterwards, I felt only sick. Nothing else mattered, not even you.

You weren't there, after that. Something collapsed, some edifice. No – not so much that, not a breaking, nothing so violent. A gate closed, quite quietly, and when I tried to open it again, it wouldn't. There wasn't any way around it. No way in, not there, not any more. Visa cancelled. I don't know why. The gate just shut. I once used to try to stop myself going there, but now when I tried to get in, I couldn't. I needed to and wanted to, but I couldn't.

Nick – listen –

That's what I was afraid I would say under the anaesthetic. When I came to, there was only myself in the room, and then I saw there was a very young nurse as well. I asked her, and at first she wouldn't say, although I could see she knew, because I suppose they're not supposed to tell, and I was certain I had spoken your name and God knows what else. 'Nick, what I love is the way the hair grows under your arms and down from your belly to your sex, and the way your thighs feel, and your voice's never-quite-caught mockery –'

What did I say?

I must have sounded so obsessed that finally she told me, explaining beforehand that patients said some funny things and it made no sense and so one shouldn't mind. Then she repeated what she'd heard me mumble.

I am the mother now.

The tumour turned out to be benign. The surgeon told me the next day. 'You are a lucky young woman,' he said, and I felt weak-mindedly touched by the adjective, although he was all of sixty and would have thought of me as young no matter how haggard I looked. 'You are out of danger,' he said. I laughed, I guess, and said, 'How can I be – I don't feel dead yet'. And he looked at me for the merest flick of an instant, only curiosity, and then he passed on to another bed.

The days and trays followed one another. Flowers were received, and letters. Calla sent a dozen yellow roses. Willard and Angela sent a potted begonia. How like Willard, something practical that would last. My kids sent russet asters with a card in Calla's beautiful script – *From Grade Two*, and they had all signed their names, the faint spidery printing of Eva Darley, Petula Thomas, Marion MacVey, the heavily pressed-down pencil strokes of David Torrent, Ross Gunn, George Crawley, and one who had evidently thought his surname too laborious and so put only Jim L. I felt something at the sight of that card, the first of anything I'd felt since the operation was over, and when I once started to cry went on for a long time and the nurses said delayed shock and seemed unperturbed as long as it could be readily explained.

Mother had wanted to come into the city with me. I said *No*. She was hurt. 'I won't hear of you going in there all alone, dear – why, that would be simply awful.' *No*. 'But Rachel, all on your own with no family – it's unthinkable.' *No*. Later, when it was over, I wrote to her and explained I hadn't wanted her to undergo the strain, what with her heart and everything. I suppose she knew I lied. I was sorry. I couldn't help it, but I was sorry. She sent letters every day.

184

She was worried the whole time. Yes, I know. She really was. I know.

When I was discharged – like a freed prisoner, I think, slightly dazed at the sudden concrete presence of the outside – I travelled back to Manawaka by bus. Calla came into the city to get me, to come back with me. She didn't fuss or treat me like an invalid, the way some people might have done, for ever asking after one's comfort until the burden of reassuring them that you are fine becomes unbearable. No, she simply said, 'You won't want to talk much, I expect,' and for the whole three hours we hardly said a word. I wanted to thank her for this gift, which had cost her something, but I could not seem to clarify my mind enough to decide what could be said and what could not. So I never mentioned it, and she thinks still, no doubt, that I never noticed.

I felt, those first few days back at home, brittle and thin-textured, like a dried autumn flowerstalk that might snap in the slightest wind, an empty eggshell skull that might crumble at the slightest tapping from the outside. I wanted only to take great care. Not of my flesh and bones, which were resilient enough, as I had discovered, but of the other. *Nothing must disturb me.* That's what I thought. Nothing must happen to disturb me. Everything must be exceedingly calm. We must have no difficulties. Do not let there be any arguments or anything unexpected which demands decision or response. This was all I prayed, to no one or to whoever might be listening, prayed unprayerfully, not with any violence of demand or any valiance of hope, but only sending the words out, in case. *Do you read me?* This message is being sent out to the cosmos, or into the same, by an amateur transmitter who wishes for the moment to sign off. Don't let anything happen.

I wasn't quite myself.

Mother pampered me for a week, which was appreciated, and then for a further week, which wasn't. Then she had an attack and her mouth went dark lilac and Doctor Raven came in the night and I got up and was recovered and now we are back to normal.

When she was reasonably all right again, that night, and Doctor Raven had gone, I made tea and sat beside her for a while. Just as she was beginning to go off to sleep she murmured something so fretfully that I wondered how many thousand times she'd stabbed herself with it.

Niall always thinks I am so stupid.

I looked at her – she was asleep now – the ashes of her face, the ashes of her hair. I drew the sheet and blanket up around her scrawny and nicely lace-nyloned shoulders, as people do when there is nothing they can do. Then I went back to my own room and got out my clothes, ready for the next day, knowing I would be returning to school.

That was the night I quit sending out my swaddled embryo wishes for nothing to happen. No use asking the impossible, even of God.

'Rachel, do you think you should go out this evening, dear?'

'I won't be long. I'm only going for some cigarettes.'

'Oh – do you really need them, dear?'

'Well, I've run out.'

'It's up to you, of course, dear, but I would have thought – what with getting back to school and everything – it might just be advisable for you to conserve your energy, that's all.'

'It's only a step from here to the Regal. I'm all right. Now please don't – '

'Well, I know you think I'm being silly, dear, but it's only because I – '

'I don't think you're being silly. But I feel all right. Honestly. Look, should I get you a chocolate bar, while I'm there?'

'Nothing for me, thanks, dear. I've got everything I want. Only, do take it easy, won't you? And don't be too long.'

Walk slowly but hurry back.

'Yes, I will. And I won't be long.'

I had forgotten it was Saturday night. River Street is

crowded as it always has been on this particular evening, with women in from farms to do their shopping, and teen-agers bound for the Flamingo, and men with a six-days' tiredness and yearning for voices bound for the beer parlour of the Queen Victoria.

I don't like the lights and noise, and I walk along the extreme outer edge of the sidewalk in order not to bump into anyone. Then I see them, walking towards me. Astonish-ing that I never saw them all summer, all the time he was here, and now they are directly in front of me, not ten paces away.

She is not hanging on to his arm. Nothing like that. They are walking beside one another, but disconnected, as though it were sheer chance that they happened to be on the same sidewalk at the same place. Yet when I look again I can see that she keeps glancing at him, checking his bear-ings, making sure he's there. He walks as though the rest of the world were an interesting but unlikely story he had once told himself.

Nick said she was the one who could live by faith although she didn't look it. I haven't seen her in a long time. She certainly doesn't look it. She is short and squarely solid, a low stone tower of a woman. And yet there is an ever-onwardness and thrust about her.

Nestor Kazlik is not so immense a man as I used to see him when I was a kid, but he is still large. He hulks along the sidewalk. He is a head at least taller than his wife, and he is dressed in a dark-brown suit and yellow tie, pressured into this decent garb by her, probably, for he looks as though he wouldn't notice what he happened to be wearing. He has a wide hard bony face, high-cheekboned as a Cree's, a crest of thick grey hair and a grey ferocious moustache. *What a crazy man he is*, Nick said. I'm not going to speak, or ask them. I won't.

'Hello – '

'Hello.'

'I'm – Rachel Cameron. You remember me?' I am speaking

only to him, the old man, I don't know why. His face comes back from its inner tale, focuses and recognizes.

'Sure, sure.' His voice is rasping, as though from a half century of tobacco. 'I know. I never – how is this? – I never see you for a long time. But I know. Your father, he is a good man, eh? I say to him, it is my son, and he says don't worry, Nestor, it will be done very nice. A good man. You tell him hello for me, eh?'

He smiles at me, confidently. Nick said *He's not senile or anything*. Nick could bear to feel that Nestor was difficult, eccentric, even a giant buffoon, but not diminished. Not saying *Steve* because he no longer knew. Nick could look at everything. But not at that.

'Yes, all right. I'll tell him. Thank you.'

He shrugs massively, as though it were nothing, no more than he owed, a recognition for a well-performed rite. Mrs Kazlik turns away, not wanting to see him betray himself in this way, not wanting to hear my playing along with it, my acceptance of messages for the dead. But what else could I say to him? This man whose voice no longer in the raw frosty dawns roars his princely cursing at kids and horses. Nestor the Jester.

I remember all at once that Steven Kazlik died of polio. There used to be epidemics, scares of a month of so, and kids kept out of school because of the thing that threatened like the medieval plague. My mother would bring out the syringe bottle with the squeeze-bulb top and the dark-yellow liquid within, and would command Stacey and me to spray our throats. And we would spray – *piff! piff!* – a magic potion against fate, death, hell, damnation, putrefaction. We never worried about ourselves. We were young enough to believe ourselves immortal. When we heard that someone we knew had died, we would feel queasy for a little while, then put it from mind or pretend the person had never been.

Nick's spine was slightly twisted. They both had the plague. But Steve was the one who died.

I have to draw away from the old man, and so I turn to her.

188

'How is Nick?'

'He is well.'

'How—how is his family, his wife?'

Teresa Kazlik looks at me, not with a great deal of animation, only as though looking disinterestedly at an outsider who could not be expected to know.

'Nick is not married.'

'I—how stupid of me. I thought he was.'

'No. He's never married yet.'

We speak some more words but not about Nick. I don't hear what I'm saying, the necessary phrases of departure that people used to get away from one another. Then they've gone, and I can go on, too, to wherever I'm going.

Nick is not married.

I wonder why he lied to me. Maybe he thought it was easier that way, the least complicated way of dealing with my unconcealed hankering, the embarrassment of my obvious angling. How he must have laughed at how easy it was, at how easy I was, both to pick up and to put down again. God damn him, now and for ever.

Yet—did he lie, though? He showed me the photograph of a boy, and I said *Yours?* And he said *Yes.* When I think back on it, it seems to me that the picture had the pale grey of an old snapshot. It was, of course, I see now, Nick himself as a child. Yours? Yes, mine.

But he intended me to misunderstand. He must have hoped I would. The intention of the lie was there all right. Unless he was simply trying to change the subject. It might never have occurred to him that anyone could possibly mistake a picture taken thirty years ago for one taken recently. He may have brought out the photograph only as a diversion. He'd already done what he could, to warn me. *I'm not God, darling—I can't solve anything.*

He had his own demons and webs. Mine brushed across him for an instant, and he saw them and had to draw away, knowing that what I wanted from him was too much. Was that it? Or was he merely becoming bored?

I don't know whether he meant to lie to me or not. As for what was happening with him and to him this summer, I couldn't say what it really was, nor whether it had anything to do with me or not.

TWELVE

'Now please don't be silly, Rachel. It's out of the question, dear, I'm afraid.'

'No. It's what we're going to do.'

'I realize you might like somewhere else for a change — don't think I don't realize that, dear, because I do. I know it's been tiresome for you, sometimes. I mean, with my heart and that. I fully realize all these things, Rachel. I've lived a good deal longer than you, after all. I know it's not always very entertaining for you, here. I know it's a strain for you — no, you needn't contradict me — I can see it — a strain and a *bore*, yes, a boring life for you, living here with someone who can't help the fact that she's not so lively as once, and can't keep up in the same way any more, however much she tries.'

'Yes. That's right. It is.'

'What?'

'A strain. It is sometimes a strain.'

'Oh, indeed? And I suppose you don't think it was a strain for me, bringing you and Stacey up, with your father about as much use as a sick headache, and — '

'Hush. Hush, now. I know. It wasn't easy for you. Why should you think mine must be any easier for me?'

'Your what, for mercy's sake?'

'My life. You want me to say no of course it hasn't been a strain, and of course I want to stay here, and I'm sorry I ever brought up the subject and we won't discuss it any more. But I can't. I can't do that now.'

'Rachel, you're not yourself. You're not talking a bit

191

sensibly, dear. I can hardly follow you. I just don't see what you're getting at. You're talking so disjointedly.'

'I'm sor— I mean, try. Try to listen.'

'That's terribly unfair of you, Rachel.'

'Unfair?'

'You know I always listen, dear, to everything you want to say. I have, ever since you were a small girl. I've always listened.'

'But have you heard?'

'What? Rachel, I don't know what to think, I really don't. I'm worried about you, dear, I'll tell you that.'

'Don't be. Oh, listen, I mean it. It's going to be all right. Look, you may even like things, once we get there.'

'All my friends are here, Rachel. I can't leave. I wouldn't know a single solitary soul. No one. Think of it. I've lived here all my—'

'Yes. That part of it is too bad. I know. But there's Stacey, don't forget, at the coast.'

'A strange house, or some cramped apartment, more than likely. I couldn't, Rachel. And in a strange place, a strange city.'

'Don't you want to see your grandchildren?'

'Well, of course I do. Naturally. How can you suggest that I don't want to see them?'

'I didn't mean to suggest it. I only meant—wouldn't it be nice to see them?'

'If they could come here, yes, on a visit, it would be lovely.'

'They won't, though. We haven't the room. And Stacey won't come here, anyway, not ever.'

'I don't see why not. I've been thinking of writing and suggesting to her—'

'Mother, try to realize. I've been accepted for the job in Vancouver, the one I applied for. We're moving the end of the month.'

'The furniture—whatever could we possibly do about all this furniture? I refuse to sell it, Rachel. I won't hear of it.'

192

'We'll take as much as we can. We may have to sell some of it. Or give it to a rummage sale. There's an awful lot of old junk here.'

'Rummage sale? My things? I won't. I simply will not.'

'Yes. We'll have to.'

'Oh Rachel – it's mean of you. You've turned really nasty and mean, and I can't see what I've ever done to merit it. It's not fair. *It's not fair!*'

'Hush, hush now. Sh, Sh. I know. It's not fair. You're quite right. Try not to cry. Here – here's your handkerchief. Blow your nose. Then you'll feel better. I'll get your sleeping pill now. It'll calm you.'

'I don't want to move, Rachel. Please.'

'I know. But we have to.'

'But why? Why?'

'Because it's time.'

'Time? That's no answer.'

'I know. But it's all the answer I've got.'

'Why do you keep on refusing to talk reasonably, Rachel? What have I done? Is it something I've said or done to offend you, dear?'

'No. It's not that.'

'Then what is it?'

She sees I am not going to reply. I cannot, but she does not see that. The crinkled skin of her face looks cruelly exposed, for her tears and her dabbing hands have taken away her facepowder. She looks bewildered, and is, and there is nothing I can do. Tea and a sleeping pill will be more use than any words I could ever find, no matter how I might delve and scrabble in my mind to find the ones that seemed appropriate to me. The fact that I know it's no use makes it a little easier. She's not trying wilfully not to see, as I once imagined. And for myself, I don't really know what it will cost her to leave this place where she has over the years nursed two children, a dead man, some sprightliness of chosen draperies and china, and more dank memories than I dare to dwell upon.

She turns her face away, leans back in her chair, lifts one violet-veined wrist and lets it fall, driftingly slow. Oh Lord. The lady of the camellias, dying on silver screen, *circa* 1930. Yet I feel like hell, also, at her hurt, the unfeigned part that doesn't, to her knowledge, ever show. And then, as well, some distant-early-warning system in my own territory tells me we're not finished with the argument.

'I don't want to be a nuisance, Rachel. Goodness knows I've never wanted to stand in your way. That's the last thing in the world I'd ever wish to do, believe me. But dear – oh, I don't know if I should even bring this up, but – '

'What is it?'

'Well, dear, of course I'm not blaming you for not having considered it. Why should you? I mean, you did have all sorts of other things, more interesting things, to consider. I quite see that. But it's just that – '

'Mother, for heaven's sake, what is it?'

'I very much doubt,' she says, 'that my silly old heart would stand the move.'

The silence between us seems to spread like dusk. It is up to me to speak, and I have prepared some words for this, but now I am afraid to use them. Afraid of what? Not only of damaging her. Perhaps not chiefly that. Afraid, more, of the apparent callousness her ears will hear and mine can't bear to listen to or admit. Do it, Rachel. Or else quit.

'I have considered that. I've considered it quite a lot. But – I think we will just have to take the risk.'

She turns to me. She turns on me.

'I see. That's how you are, eh? That's the kind of person *you* are.'

'Well, in the end – the end – it's in other hands.'

I've spoken so oddly and ambiguously, not knowing I was going to deliver this nineteenth-century cliché until I heard it, compelled out of some semi-malicious hope that she would be bound to be flummoxed by the phrase, and that she might not decently be quite able to deny some sovereignty, even though she still attempts to believe in her physical immortality which must be bolstered with huge doses of quiet, care, cups of tea, heart boosters and heart calmers, sleeping potions and every available brand of sorcery. And yet, what I said was also meant, unintentionally intended, and I really wonder now why I have been so ruthlessly careful of her, as though to preserve her throughout eternity, a dried flower under glass. It isn't up to me. It never was. I can take care, but only some. I'm not responsible for keeping her alive. There is, suddenly, some enormous relief in this realization.

She is looking at me, dismayed.

'Other hands? What on earth do you mean?'

'Well, just that – what happens to you, you can't necessarily do anything much about it.'

'Doctor Raven,' she says, offended, 'has specifically forbidden me under any circumstances to exert myself, Rachel. You know that as well as I do.'

'You won't have to exert yourself. All you have to do, if that's all you want to do, is to sit and let yourself be wafted towards the coast. Mild weather, practically no snow in winter, daffodils in March or is it April, and a visit with Stacey's kids every Sunday or maybe even twice a week, let's hope. I meant, really, that Doctor Raven is not able to say, entirely, either. You know?'

I catch in my own voice something of Nick's – *You know?* I didn't mean to copy. But something of him inhabits me yet. If I could see him only for half an hour. No, Rachel. You can't. Yes, I know. It will go away after a while.

'Rachel, you're talking so peculiarly. Doctor Raven has been my doctor for goodness knows how long. If he doesn't know what's what, dear, who does, may I ask?'

'I don't know. I've no idea. God, for all I know.'

Is it some partial triumph, that I can bring myself finally to say this, or is it only the last defeat?

'God?' she shrills, as though I had voiced something unspeakable. Then she simmers down, recollects herself. She used to be a member of the choir, for heaven's sake, for the

195

sake of heaven. 'Well, certainly, dear, of course, all that goes without saying. But I don't honestly see why you felt you had to bring it up. I'm not easily upset, as you know. But I can't go along with this notion of gaily talking about all these matters.'

She is clamped, rigid, protecting herself against all comers.

'I'm sorry.'

And I am. Because I didn't know, before, how frightened she is. But there's no help for it, that I can see, except to say *Hush, it will be all right – there, there.*

I am the mother now.

Willard is sitting behind his desk. He doesn't rise. He looks up, adjusts his glasses and consents to smile. He's hardly spoken to me since I gave my notice, but now he has to say something, for I won't be seeing him again.

'Ah, Rachel. The moment has finally come, eh?'

'Yes.'

'Well, I just want you to know I certainly do wish you every success in your new – and of course Angela joins me in this wish, most sincerely.'

'Thanks.'

'I must say – I know you won't take it amiss if I say this, Rachel – I must just mention that I was a little taken aback at your decision. It wasn't what I would have expected of you.'

'No.'

'I mean, of course, it's your concern, but I can't help wondering, I'd just like to ask you one thing, quite frankly.'

'What is it?'

'Weren't you happy here?' Willard asks, peering foxily. 'I always thought you got along so well here. Taught well, fitted in with the other staff very harmoniously, and as for myself, we've never had the slightest disagreement, you and I. That's so, isn't it? You must admit that it is. I always thought you were perfectly satisfied with the way our school is run. I could be quite mistaken, of course, but I always *thought* so. I trust you don't mind my asking, but naturally this is a matter of some considerable interest to me.'

He doesn't want my answer. He wants me to say 'Of course I have always been as happy as a veritable meadow-lark in this eminently well-run establishment, Willard, and I can assure you my leaving has nothing whatsoever to do with you, who have been in every conceivable way the best of principals – it is only that my old mother wishes to see her dear little grandchildren, so I am taking off, albeit with the greatest and bitterest of regrets.'

What am I to say, though? Sometimes I was happy here, and sometimes not, and often I was afraid of him, and still am, although I see now this was as unnecessary as my mother's fear of fate. What good would it do to say that? I couldn't explain, nor he accept.

'I've just lived here long enough, that's all. It's got nothing to do with the school.'

And this, like everything else, is both true and false.

The teachers' room is empty. All the gruelling good-byes have been said to the others. I told Calla I would wait here to see her. I feel nothing at leaving. There have been, lately, a few days when I feel nothing of any description, nothing at all. This may not be good, but it's restful.

'Oh – hello, Rachel. You did wait.'

'Yes. I said I would.'

'I know, but I thought you might be in a rush, what with packing and everything.'

We stand facing one another. We're stalling. We don't know what to say. Then I see she has decided.

'Rachel, maybe this is uncalled for, but I – well, I'm sorry that things weren't different for you. That it wasn't what you thought, when you came to my place that day.'

'Oh – that.' Now I'm forced back into the total pain, as one is when somebody sympathizes with a death you had begun not to think about every moment. Why couldn't she

197

have kept quiet about it? But I see she couldn't, not now, this once.

'Yes,' she says. 'I only wanted to let you know—'

'You must have thought—' My voice rises like a speeded-up record, 'you must have thought I was a fool. As, of course, I was.'

'Yes, I suppose so. But heavens, child, that's the least of your worries.'

This really is so. It's the least of my worries. What is so terrible about fools? I should be honoured to be of that company.

'Calla—' Now, at last, it had to be expressed and offered, some acknowledgement, because the truth is that she loves me.

'What is it?'

'I'm sorry things weren't different for you. I mean, that I wasn't different.'

'Oh—that,' she says.

She glances away, then looks again at me, meets my eyes. Calla, pillar of tabernacles, speaker in tongues, mother of canaries and budgerigars.

'Not to worry,' Calla says. 'I'll survive.'

That last time I was in the Japonica Funeral Chapel was that night I came down here late and talked to Hector. Everything looks just the same, but now it does not seem to matter much that my father's presence has been gone from here for a long time. I can't know what he was like. He isn't here to say, and even if he were, he wouldn't say, any more than Mother does. Whatever it was that happened with either of them, their mysteries remain theirs. I don't need to know. It isn't necessary. I have my own.

'I'm glad you dropped in, Rachel,' Hector says. 'Can I press you to a drink? One for the road, you might say.'

Rachel Cameron, taking to the road. I have to laugh at this.

'All right. It'll be a good omen, maybe.'

198

Hector dashes from cupboard to sink with bottle and glasses.

'You wouldn't prefer sherry, Rachel?'

'No, thanks. Rye and water is fine.'

'I always keep a small supply of sherry on hand,' he confides, 'although I wouldn't touch the filthy stuff myself. Too sweet for me – I'm sweet enough already, ha ha. But sometimes one of the bereaved needs a little shot to steady them. Ladies often feel it wouldn't be very nice to drink rye at such a time, but a snort of sherry is usually acceptable.'

'I see. I think you're very considerate, Hector.'

'Really? Well, it's music to my ears to hear you say so. Actually, I only do it for business.'

'Remember when I came down here that night?'

'Yes, certainly. I should say so.'

'I thought afterwards about what you said.'

'Don't cast it up at me, that's all I ask. What did I say?'

'About my father.'

'Oh yeh, that. Well, I could've been wrong, Rachel. I hope you never took it to heart too much.'

'No, I don't think you were wrong. He probably did do what he wanted most, even though he might not have known it. But maybe what came of it was something he hadn't bargained for. That's always a possibility, with anyone.'

'Are you sure,' Hector enquires, 'that you're talking about your father?'

'No, I guess not. Or not only.'

'You were kind of upset that night, Rachel, and I couldn't help wondering, although it was none of my business. But then the bad luck you had, having to have an operation and that. Well, I mean to say, I only wanted to say – '

He draws himself up like an unweaponed flagbearer entering battle, summoning courage.

'I only wanted to say, Rachel, that whatever any blabbermouth in this town may or may not be dreaming up, I never uttered so much as one syllable about you, and what's more,

199

speaking personally, I do not give one damn what kind of operation it may or may not have been.'

At first I don't get his meaning. Then it comes across. So that is what is being said. 'You can imagine why she went into the city – that's why she has to leave, now, afraid it'll get to be known – No, it wasn't that way at all – she didn't go into the city for that – I heard she went into hospital there because she'd tried to do it herself and it went wrong. Who could he have been, though? Who can say, but I've never thought Willard Siddley seemed very happy with his wife, have you?'

I do not know whether to laugh or storm, but find I can do neither. The ironies go on.

'Thank you, Hector. It is very handsome of you to say that. I appreciate it.'

'It's meant,' he says earnestly, tapping his stomach, 'from the bottom of my heart.'

'I know. Thank you.'

For an instant I'm tempted to deny the rumours, to explain, to say to Hector, so he can pass on the message, let them ask Doctor Raven if they don't believe me. But no. I like it better this way. It's more fitting.

'Hell's bells, I nearly forgot to show you!' Hector cries. 'My new sign. Can you spare another second before you go? It's right in here. I'm going to have it put up next week. I thought it would be easier to wait until you and your mother have moved out. You wouldn't want a lot of ladders crashing around your windows. Look – not bad, eh?'

The new neon sign is vast, with tall sleek lettering. *Japonica Chapel.*

'Everybody knows perfectly well it's a funeral establishment,' Hector explains, 'so why say so? Lots of people aren't keen on that word. It's going to be in crimson, the light. I thought that would show up better than the blue. What do you think?'

'I think it's – well, I hardly know what to say. It's impressive.'

'Yeh, but what about the change in wording? You think that's okay, Rachel?'

'It's a change, Hector. It's – evolution.'

I do not know how many bones need be broken before I can walk. And I do not know, either, how many need not have been broken at all.

Make me to hear –

How does it go? What are the words? I can't have forgotten all the words, surely, the words of the songs, the psalms.

Make me to hear joy and gladness, that the bones which Thou hast broken may rejoice.

We watched until the lights of the town could not be seen any longer. Now only the farm kitchens and the stars are out there to signpost the night. The bus flies along, smooth and confident as a great owl through the darkness, and all the passengers are quiet, some of them sleeping. Beside me sleeps my elderly child.

Where I'm going, anything may happen. Nothing may happen. Maybe I will marry a middle-aged widower, or a longshoreman, or a cattle-hoof-trimmer, or a barrister or a thief. And have my children in time. Or maybe not. Most of the chances are against it. But not, I think, quite all. What will happen? What will happen. It may be that my children will always be temporary, never to be held. But so are everyone's.

I may become, in time, slightly more eccentric all the time. I may begin to wear outlandish hats, feathered and sequinned and rosetted, and dangling necklaces made from coy and tiny seashells which I've gathered myself along the beach and painted coral-pink with nailpolish. And all the kids will laugh, and I'll laugh, too, in time. I will be light and straight as any feather. The wind will bear me, and I will drift and settle, and drift and settle. Anything may happen, where I'm going.

I will be different. I will remain the same. I will still go parchment-faced with embarrassment, and clench my pencil

201

between fingers like pencils. I will quite frequently push the doors marked *Pull* and pull the ones marked *Push*. I will be lonely, almost certainly. I will get annoyed at my sister. Her children will call me Aunt Rachel, and I will resent it and find then that I've grown attached to them after all. I will walk by myself on the shore of the sea and look at the freegulls flying. I will grow too orderly, plumping up the chesterfield cushions just-so before I go to bed. I will rage in my insomnia like a prophetess. I will take care to remember a vitamin pill each morning with my breakfast. I will be afraid. Sometimes I will feel light-hearted, sometimes light-headed. I may sing aloud, even in the dark. I will ask myself if I am going mad, but if I do, I won't know it.

God's mercy on reluctant jesters. God's grace on fools. God's pity on God.

AFTERWORD

To be introducing Margaret Laurence's Manawaka novels to non-Canadian readers in 1987 looks in many ways like the kind of ironical joke that Margaret Laurence herself so much appreciates. These novels have all been published before in Britain and the United States, during the 1960s and 70s when they were first published in Canada, and in 1968 *A Jest of God* was made into a film directed by Paul Newman and starring Joanne Woodward. However, its title was changed to *Rachel, Rachel* and its locale from the Canadian prairies to the American midwest; the novels have long since gone out of print in Britain, and in the States Margaret Laurence is read as a prairie writer along with Willa Cather and Carl Sandburg. Such invisibility has been the fate of Canadian novels abroad until quite recently, mainly because accidents of history and geography have made them look so similar to British and American fictions that their subtle differences have been overlooked. It is to Margaret Laurence's credit that by writing about the Manitoba community of Manawaka she has managed to show how its history and geography shape life and fiction in ways that are distinctively Canadian. At the same time these novels, all told by female narrators, engage with the question central to women's writing of how female protagonists find the appropriate language and narrative forms to write about themselves and their own experiences. The Manawaka cycle, therefore, offers a variety of models for women's stories. The themes they treat are in no way culturally or gender specific, though through local details of weather or landscape and through certain turns of phrase they are identifiably western Canadian and unmistakably written in the feminine gender. Morag Gunn in *The Diviners* speaks for Margaret Laurence and all her protagonists when in answer to her husband's challenge that none of her themes are original, she replies, 'Well, it is important that I, as a woman, say them.'

In Canada Margaret Laurence is regarded as one of its most authoritative writers and her novels have assumed a pioneer status within contemporary Canadian women's fiction written in English. She was born in Manitoba in 1926, of Scots-Irish parents whose families had arrived as immigrants in the 1870s. She grew up in the same prairie town to which her paternal grandfather had come as a lawyer in 1881. As a writer within the tradition of Canadian prairie fiction, she is a regional and historical novelist who is peculiarly conscious of a personal need for history and for its imaginative revision. As she says in an essay entitled 'A Place to Stand On',

My writing has been my own attempt to come to terms with the past. I see this process as the gradual one of freeing oneself from the stultifying aspect of the past, while at the same time beginning to see its true value – which in the case of my own people (by which I mean the total community, not just my particular family), was a determination to survive against whatever odds.

Given her strong feelings about herself as a small-town prairie person, it may seem ironical that Margaret Laurence did not start writing about her own place or her own history until she had been away from Manitoba for over fifteen years. She left her hometown at the age of eighteen to go to university in Winnipeg, then at twenty-one she married a Canadian civil engineer. They went first to England, then to Africa in 1950 where they lived for seven years in Somaliland, now Somalia, and on the Gold Coast, now Ghana. During that time their two children were born and Margaret Laurence began writing, not about Canada but about Africa. Her first book, *A Tree for Poverty*, was a translation of Somali poetry and folk tales which were gathered together under all manner of living conditions – in a resthouse near Djibouti or by firelight while the Laurences were living in tents and mud huts out on the desert plains of the Haud. Her book, which was the first collection of Somali poetry to appear in English, was finally published in 1954 in Nairobi under the auspices of the British Protectorate in Somaliland. Over the next nine years out of her African experiences Margaret Laurence wrote a collection of short stories, *The Tomorrow-Tamer* (1963), a novel, *This Side Jordan* (1960) and a travel book, *The Prophet's Camel Bell* (1963), while in 1968 *Long Drums and Cannons*, her study of new West African literature in English appeared. Margaret Laurence has since suggested that it was only through her years in Africa that she became aware of herself as a Canadian writer and a Commonwealth writer, for she shared with the emergent African nations the same sense of resistance to colonialism while at the same time she always felt like a stranger in a strange land. Separated from the Africans by linguistic and cultural differences so that she was forever 'viewing the whole of life through different eyes', she became gradually aware of a need to go home to Canada: 'People always want to get out, and yet profoundly want to return.'

Though the Laurences did return to Vancouver in 1957, Margaret Laurence left Canada again in 1962 with her two children to live in England. She stayed till 1973 and during that time she wrote her Manawaka fiction. Indeed, *A Jest of God* was written in Buckinghamshire in 1964 and 65. As she remarked in 1970

Whether or not I ever lived in the prairies again was really unimportant. The return is not necessarily in the physical sense, but it really is a coming back in the mind, a coming to some kind of terms with your roots and your ancestors and, if you like, with your gods.

In fact she has not lived in the prairies again, but when she returned to Canada in 1973 she settled in a small town near Peterborough, Ontario. Like James Joyce's Dublin or William Faulkner's Yoknapatawpha County, her prairie town of Manawaka, presented with such detail in the series of linked novels and stories of the Manawaka cycle, is really a remembered place that has been reinvented in fiction. In 'A Place to Stand On' Margaret Laurence said,

The name Manawaka is an invented one. Manawaka is not my hometown of Neepawa – it has elements of Neepawa, especially in some of the descriptions of places, such as the cemetery on the hill or the Wachakwa valley through which ran the small brown river of my childhood. In almost every way, however, Manawaka is not so much any one prairie town as an amalgam of many prairie towns. Most of all, I like to think, it is simply itself, a town of the mind, my own private world ... which one hopes will ultimately relate to the outer world which we all share.

Margaret Laurence's spiritual return to the prairies in her fiction makes her a regional novelist in the same way that Charlotte Brontë, Thomas Hardy and D. H. Lawrence are regional novelists. For all of them writing is set firmly, as Margaret Laurence puts it, 'in some soil, some place, some outer and inner territory which might be described in anthropological terms as cultural background', where the sense of local identity becomes an
206

imaginative strength as fact is transformed into fiction.

Manawaka is structured through the stories the characters tell, and though their realism makes it possible to construct from them a map of the town and a detailed account of its history from settlement in the 1880s through the Depression and droughts of the 1930s up until the 70s, what strikes the reader is the multiplicity of viewpoints presented. There are as many different Manawakas as there are narrators, for Manawaka is successively reinvented by every teller in her own idiom out of her own experiences, from ninety-two year old Hagar Shipley in *The Stone Angel* through Rachel Cameron in *A Jest of God*, her sister Stacey MacAindra in *The Fire-Dwellers*, Vanessa MacLeod in the story sequence *A Bird in the House*, to Morag Gunn in *The Diviners*. All these women are engaged in coming to terms with the past, frequently by recalling the childhood place from which like Margaret Laurence they have moved away, revising their stories about themselves in order to create acceptable fictions within which to assume their own separate identities as they face the future somewhere else. Rachel's coming to terms with the past gives her the necessary strength to leave Manawaka as the others have already done. What they all need to recognise is that everybody is an inheritor: Margaret Laurence's fiction investigates how far the individual exists separately while also being part of a wider historical continuum that goes beyond an individual life-span, back into the past and forward into the future. The Canadian multicultural inheritance is focussed through the history and population of Manawaka, where as Rachel says, 'Half the town is Scots descent, and the other half is Ukrainian ... The Ukrainians knew how to be the better grain farmers, but the Scots knew how to be almightier than anyone but God.' Because *A Jest of God* is told by Rachel, who speaks out of her own genteel Scots background, Manawaka's history and social geography is more lightly sketched here than in any of the other novels. There is no mention at all, for example, of the Tonnerres who figure so importantly in *The Diviners* as the last remaining family of the indigenous Métis population, whose colonial inheritance of dispossession is the other side of the history of prairie settlement. However, Rachel knows nothing of them for she rarely goes beyond the boundaries of town – except with Nick Kazlik, when they go down to the 'neutral territory' beside the Manawaka River to make love. This is Rachel's wilderness experience which is so emblematic a feature of Canadian fiction. *A Jest of God* is no less obsessed with the past than the other Manawaka novels, but in Rachel's narrative it is all driven underground, for this is a novel about interiors rather than a looking outward at the community.

Rachel Cameron is not an immediately attractive protagonist for a novel any more than Jane Austen's Fanny Price in *Mansfield Park*. It is all the more difficult for readers of a novel set in the 1960s to find that Rachel shares Fanny's feminine insecurities while lacking her youth or moral certainty, and then goes without the conventional reward of marriage at the end. Yet oddly Rachel does find a strength to resist the social pressures upon her, a strength commensurate with Fanny's, through which she gains both a moral victory at the end and the promise of a future for herself. In many ways Rachel's career moves in the opposite direction from Fanny's, for this is not a homecoming but a homeleaving. Rachel's story of resistance is a late twentieth-century woman's narrative which struggles to unwrite the old inherited romantic fantasies in a way that is at odds with cultural conventions, just as it is at odds with plot closures. As she boards the bus for Vancouver with her mother (for she cannot leave her past entirely behind her) Rachel commits herself to the unknown.
208

She has walked out of the culturally conditioned tale of her upbringing and faces a new uncertain future where 'Anything may happen. Nothing may happen . . . What will happen? What will happen.' There is no return to Mansfield Park here but instead a slipping away from inheritance into a new openness for the future, as Rachel approaching middle-age recognises the necessity for her change of life.

What makes Rachel's story compelling is her own narrative voice, for the novel is told mainly in the present tense through her interior monologue. In one of her rare essays on the craft of fiction Margaret Laurence said, 'I am concerned mainly I think with finding a form through which the characters can breathe', emphasising the importance of the subject, and what being the subject of one's own story means. Defining the self, or rather creating images of the self through a continuous process of revision as traditional stories break down, is one of the recurrent themes in contemporary women's writing. It may well be that women's experience highlights the unstable nature of human subjectivity and that this perception affects the way women write about themselves in narratives that emphasise discontinuity, disruption and self division. It is certainly true of Rachel that though she appears to be confined and defined by the social mores of Manawaka, she insistently contradicts her own self image – as a school teacher, as a dutiful daughter, and as a decorous unmarried woman of thirty-four. Her silent monologue questions and criticises inherited codes of thinking and feeling, while at the same time it registers her fears and fantasies and her gradual evolution into a limited kind of freedom by the end, 'I will be different. I will remain the same.'

We would misread the novel however if we overlooked the fact that Rachel's dissenting voice is not always repressed into silence.

The most dramatic moments are when she speaks out unin-
hibitedly: once unwittingly in the tabernacle, once in full
confidence during what turns out to be her last conversation with
her lover Nick Kazlik, and once under anaesthetic. These are the
times when Rachel's deepest feelings surface, and in every case
they are the expression of her frustrated maternal feelings as a
childless woman. Like her words in the tabernacle, and like the
tumour inside her womb, they relate to the mysteries of life and
death which are at the centre of the novel. Rachel is always aware
of the coexistence of her familiar world and of forbidden secret
worlds beneath the surfaces of everyday life, symbolised for her by
a 'crypt' and suggesting the mortal fears which she carries within
herself. There is a strong undertow towards death in Rachel's
psyche which is surely a feature of her inheritance (for she is the
daughter of Manawaka's late undertaker), and also a feature of her
environment (for she and her mother continue to live above the
Japonica Funeral Chapel). Realism of action should not blind us
to either the biblical or the mythic echoes of Rachel's story, which
is a gradual coming to terms with her death instinct as much as
with her maternal instinct. What is Rachel's midnight visit to the
funeral chapel but a descent into the place of the dead and a being
freed from her father's ghost? And what is Dr Raven (of ominous
name) but a secularised version of the priest who effects Rachel's
exorcism by his medical diagnosis of the tumour which is growing
inside her? Her operation is a kind of delivery – not indeed what
she had bargained for when she thought she might be pregnant,
but a delivery all the same – from her unacknowledged obsession
with death. This is surely the Jest of God with its multiple ironies
signalled in the title: not a child but a tumour, yet what looks like a
brutal joke is also a life-giving joke for it releases Rachel from fear
into new hope. After her midsummer love affair and her autumn
210

operation (for both events are in their ambiguous ways beneficial) she finds that she can leave Manawaka, taking her mother away from the funeral chapel to a new place, transformed into her 'elderly child'.

Though the novel ends quietly with Rachel sitting in the bus and her mother asleep beside her, this is not a story about silences. It is more like the Tower of Babel for it is filled with voices crying out in confusion – the voices of Rachel, her mother, Nick, Calla, Willard Siddeley – 'no one hearing anyone else, no one able to know what anyone else was saying'. No doubt living in Africa heightened Margaret Laurence's awareness of the dimensions of non-communication between people, and in *A Jest of God* she explores limits of comprehension among the inhabitants of a prairie town. The speaking in tongues at the Manawaka Tabernacle of the Risen and Reborn is only an extreme manifestation of the commonest human dilemma, for as it appears to Rachel this is one of God's jests, 'God's irony – that we should for so long believe it is only the few who speak in tongues'. As Calla reminds her, 'St Paul says there should be somebody there to interpret', and in this novel there never is anyone to do so. Yet perhaps there is again a merciful twist to God's jest. Just as the gap between language and meaning is emphasised by the nonsense words spoken by Rachel in the tabernacle where 'the forbidden is transformed cryptically to nonsense', so too is the truth that the words conceal. Alice Munro remarked in one of her stories that 'translation is difficult, dangerous as well', as Rachel discovers to her cost in her one attempt at partial translation of her feelings to Nick, 'If I had a child, I would like it to be yours.' Confronted with her statement of need Nick, like Jacob in the Old Testament story of Rachel begging for children, protests that he is not God. Rachel's words have brought them to the limits of mutual

211

incomprehension – and Nick leaves her and Manawaka. Out of this human failure Rachel has only God to turn to, yet the voice of God is even further beyond her powers of comprehension than Nick's words were: 'If You have spoken, I am not aware of having heard. If You have a voice, it is not comprehensible to me. No omens. No burning bush.' Rachel refuses to believe in revelation or divine possession even after the episode of speaking in tongues so that to her, God is never anything more than antithesis, a concept that scarcely transcends her own self contradictions. Yet she invokes God and thereby unconsciously affirms the creative power of language; words may not be easily translatable but still it is only through words that Rachel can invent a God to pray to in her own desperate need. Religion and humanism, mystery and scepticism, incomprehension and insight are closely interwoven in the language of this novel, which is not about redemption or dramatic self transformation but about the acknowledgement of human limits and undreamed-of human capacities.

A Jest of God might be seen as a feminised version of Auden's misanthropic 'Miss Gee. A Ballad', told from the childless woman's point of view. Yet its resonances are wider than simply gynaecological, for it is also the story of a woman's ambivalent relation to the cultural traditions which she has inherited and about her power to revise these in her own life. At a more abstract level, it might be seen as a novel about the untranslatability of human desire or as Margaret Laurence so optimistically put it, 'a coming to some kind of terms with your gods'. Rachel's departure from Manawaka confirms her in her role of reluctant jester as she privately celebrates another irony, 'I like it better that way. It's more fitting.' The ironies go on being generated both inside and outside *A Jest of God* as the Manawaka cycle is republished twenty years later in the country where much of it was originally written.

Coral Ann Howells, Béléac, 1986

Subsequent to the writing of this afterword, I must record with great regret the death of Margaret Laurence in January 1987.

VIRAGO MODERN CLASSICS

The first Virago Modern Classic, *Frost in May* by Antonia White, was published in 1978. It launched a list dedicated to the celebration of women writers and to the rediscovery and reprinting of their works. Its aim was, and is, to demonstrate the existence of a female tradition in fiction which is both enriching and enjoyable. The Leavisite notion of the 'Great Tradition', and the narrow, academic definition of a 'classic', has meant the neglect of a large number of interesting secondary works of fiction. In calling the series 'Modern Classics' we do not necessarily mean 'great' — although this is often the case. Published with new critical and biographical introductions, books are chosen for many reasons: sometimes for their importance in literary history; sometimes because they illuminate particular aspects of womens' lives, both personal and public. They may be classics of comedy or storytelling; their interest can be historical, feminist, political or literary.

Initially the Virago Modern Classics concentrated on English novels and short stories published in the early decades of this century. As the series has grown it has broadened to include works of fiction from different centuries, different countries, cultures and literary traditions. In 1984 the Victorian Classics were launched; there are separate lists of Irish, Scottish, European, American, Australian and other English speaking countries; there are books written by Black women, by Catholic and Jewish women, and a few relevant novels by men. There is, too, a companion series of Non-Fiction Classics constituting biography, autobiography, travel, journalism, essays, poetry, letters and diaries.

By the end of 1986 over 250 titles will have been published in these two series, many of which have been suggested by our readers.

Other works by Margaret Laurence

THE STONE ANGEL

In this beautifully crafted novel, first published in 1964, Margaret Laurence explores the life of one woman, the irascible, fiercely proud Hagar Shipley. Now over ninety and approaching death, she retreats from the bitter squabbling of her son and his wife to reflect on her past— her marriage to tough-talking Bram Shipley ('we'd each married for those qualities we later found we couldn't bear'), her two sons, her failures, and the failure of others. Her thoughts evoke not only the rich pattern of her past experience but also the meaning of what it is to grow old and to come to terms with mortality.

Forthcoming Novels in the Manawaka Series

The Fire-Dwellers
The Diviners

Margaret Atwood

THE HANDMAID'S TALE

Offred is a national resource. In the Republic of Gilead her viable ovaries make her a precious commodity, and the state allows her only one function: to breed. As a Handmaid she carries no name except her Master's, for whose barren wife she must act as a surrogate. But Offred cannot help remembering subversive details of her former life: her mother, her lover, her child, her real name, women having jobs and being allowed to read, fun, 'freedom'. Dissenters are supposed to end up either at the Wall, where they are hanged, or in the Colonies, to die a lingering death from radiation sickness. But the irrepressible Moira shows Offred that it is possible to cheat the system . . .

'An unrepeatable and starkly individual performance'— London Review of Books
Shortlisted for the Booker Prize for Fiction, 1986

Other Novels by Margaret Atwood

Bodily Harm
Dancing Girls
The Edible Woman
Lady Oracle
Life Before Man
Surfacing

AMERICAN MODERN CLASSICS

D